THE BLOODLETTING

THE BLOODLETTING

An American Tale of Revenge

— Book I —

By
Michael R. Seymour

Copyright © 2005 by Michael R. Seymour.
Printed in the United States. All rights reserved.

ISBN 1-58597-322-X

Library of Congress Control Number: 2005921854

LEATHERS
PUBLISHING

A division of Squire Publishers, Inc.
4500 College Blvd.
Leawood, KS 66211
1/888/888-7696
www.leatherspublishing.com

To those who, without question,
understand and love me —

Marsha, Mike, Heather, Mattea, Nathan,
Brenden and Josh and
Jim and Jeanie,
Mom and Dad.
(Thank you, Brian!)

Blood'let'ting, *n.* *Med.* Act or process of letting blood or bleeding …phlebotomy….

Phle-bot'o-my ———— 2. The drawing of blood; bloodshed; **rough or violent method of remedying;** bleeding.

— *Webster's NEW INTERNATIONAL Dictionary 1922*

1

THE GENERAL STOOD in the doorway; there was a slight grin on his face as he watched the technicians do their work. He was a large man with graying hair, perhaps 55 years old. The room was located in the basement of a warehouse building near the air base.

The room was large with a low ceiling and brightly lit by many bare light bulbs in open fixtures at the ceiling. The walls were painted a drab green color, and the floor was covered with well-worn green tile. There were three desks in one corner of the room; each had a chair and filing cabinet. The rest of the room was bare except for one single chair; that is where the General's gaze rested.

Seated in the chair was a young girl, perhaps 23. She had been stripped of her uniform; it lay on the floor, the stripes on the sleeve indicating the rank of NCO3. She had been strapped to the chair and her face was covered with dried streams of blood that had come from several gashes on her cheeks and forehead. The blood was mostly dried except where recently shed tears had moistened it.

The two technicians busied themselves at a table that was near the chair. The small box on the table was an electric generator plugged into a wall outlet. Two wires left the box where they were connected by clips to the nipples of the girl's small white breasts.

The air in the room had a foul odor, but the technicians did not seem to mind as they adjusted the box. The older of the two technicians spoke to the girl. "You know we enjoy this, surely you do; we can just go on forever. You might as well make it easy on yourself and tell us where you got the cigarettes."

The General looked down at his own left hand — he was smoking an American Marlboro. He thought how ironic it was that this girl was being punished for doing no more than this. He had acquired a taste for American cigarettes when he had visited the States. He was especially fond of Marlboros. He considered it to be a privilege of rank, and this girl had no rank.

The younger technician slapped the girl hard on the face to get her attention. "Who gave you those cigarettes?" he spoke in a commanding voice. She looked up at him with a look of hate in her eyes. She knew she was stronger than he.

The older man stepped to the console and flipped a switch. The machine hummed and the clips at the girl's nipples sizzled. The air was filled with the smell of burning flesh and she screamed.

Fresh tears made new paths down her cheeks, and she voided on the chair. This would account for the foul smell in the room. The older technician allowed the current to flow for ten seconds; the girl's body slumped into the chair thankfully unconscious.

The older man walked past the girl and past the General and into the hallway. "This girl is tough," he said. "She won't give up the answer."

"That's all right," said the General. "Play with her another hour or so if you like, then let her go, just don't kill her."

"Don't worry," said the doctor, "you have used my skills many times before."

The General left the building and walked to his office two blocks away. The sidewalk that led to his office passed beside the large runway. He looked out upon the expanse of concrete to the 10 large planes parked in a row. Workmen on lift trucks were removing the large red painted stars from the tail sections.

The base was designed to resemble an American airbase, American cars, American clothing, American billboards, and only English was spoken here. The thing most lacking was shrubs or trees. They would not grow in this harsh climate. It was not necessary to waste the extra time or expense for decorations.

As he neared his office, he passed a young lieutenant who saluted. "Good afternoon, General," said the young man.

"Your English is improving, Chen-Yo," complimented the General.

"It should, General," said the young man, "I have been watching American television. I am especially fond of the show 'Friends.' "

"I wouldn't know," answered the General, "I can never seem to find time to enjoy the American pastimes, but perhaps there will come a time when I can."

He entered the side door of a large three-story red brick building. As he entered the door, an NCO3 who had been nearly napping snapped to immediate attention and saluted. The General walked past the man without returning the salute.

He walked briskly across the tiled floor and up the three steps to his office. He had to pass through a large room that was filled with desks behind which were seated men and women in uniform. They were all reading American newspapers and listening to a country western radio station that was being broadcast in real time from Lubbock, Texas.

The station was playing a Charley Daniels song. Each side of the long room had windows all along the side, and the atmosphere was bright and airy. It was in stark contrast to the room he had just left.

He walked quickly to his office without saying a word to anyone. His door was locked; he produced a key to unlock it and closed the door behind him.

The office was large and well lit as befitted a man of his rank and years. In one corner was a desk with a large leather chair. This was one of the few luxuries that he allowed himself in an otherwise Spartan existence. Along one wall were three chairs, straight-backed and uncomfortable. This was to discourage guests from overstaying their welcome. He had no friends.

The walls were painted yellow and were bare except for two pictures. There were two large windows with no shades behind his desk; he opened one, sat in the leather chair and placed his shiny black boots on the edge of the desk. He leaned back in the chair and looked at the pictures on the wall. The one picture had been taken from this very window; it was of the parade ground filled with marching soldiers. That view was the reason he had chosen this office.

He opened the lower drawer of his desk and produced an ashtray. He stood up from the chair and opened the other window, lit a cigarette and took a long deep drag. That was the best part of the cigarette, that first hit.

He stepped over to the other picture on the wall. This one was an aerial photo of an Iowa farm, the picture including several hundred acres, with a large two-story white house, a detached garage, a large red silo and large red barn. He removed a magnifying glass from the top left desk drawer and used it to look more closely at the picture. Two tractors were sitting outside the barn, one pulling a large trailer filled with large bales of hay. Below the picture was a plaque. The plaque read: "George Taylor Farm, Timberlake, Iowa."

As he stood before the picture, his mind wandered.

He had visited this farm three years before when he had gone on vacation to the states. He had acquired a travel visa, using another name, through his connections in the government. This had been his second trip to America, and he had grown fond of the country. He had traveled to Des Moines airport, rented a car and driven himself to Timberlake. Previous intelligence had taught him that the Taylor family were Baptists, and that every Sunday morning at precisely nine o'clock a.m. the entire family went to church. Mom and Pop, who were approaching retirement age, would load up the girl and boy and drive into town and pick up her aged mother and take her to church. After church they would always eat lunch at the Bonanza Restaurant.

His plane had landed at 6:30 a.m., which had given him time to drive to the farm before church. As he neared the farm, he had passed the Taylor van on their way to church. He drove past the farm and parked his rental car at the mile intersection past the farm and waited half an hour to assure that the Taylors had not forgotten anything.

When he was convinced that they were not coming back, he drove into the farmyard and was greeted by two black Labrador Retrievers and several lesser dogs, all barking. He was not afraid of the dogs and would only hurt them if they appeared dangerous. Once he had gotten out of the car, the dogs appeared to be friendly and only wanted to be petted. This he didn't mind doing.

He walked briskly to the back porch of the home. The back door was unlocked, and it opened onto a porch with an upright freezer and coats and overalls and boots lining one wall. He walked through the spotless kitchen and into the dining room, admiring the tall oak cupboard with the rounded glass front that held the fine china. This was an old house and the floors were made of shiny wood. He walked back into the kitchen; beside the sink were two coffee cups, recently used and well rinsed. The coffeemaker beside the sink was unplugged but held a half pot of warm coffee. He took one of the cups and poured himself a cup of coffee.

He made sure that his feet were clean as he walked up the stairs and down the hallway looking into each room, making a memory. He took his time, knowing that he had several hours. He slowly walked down the stairs and into the front room. Like most farmhouses, this one had a front door that led to a front porch that was seldom used.

He walked to the mantelpiece and looked at each picture in its turn. There were many pictures of relatives, living and dead, young and old. The only picture that caught his eye was an aerial photo of this very farm, in an oak frame. That very picture was now hanging on his wall thousands of miles away. He would never know if the Taylor family missed the picture, and he had no way of finding out.

In his heart he knew that this farm, the Taylor Farm of Timberlake, Iowa, would be his, but only after he had eliminated the Taylor family.

The General shook his head to release the memory and thought again about the girl. She had been a pleasant diversion, low-ranking but pleasant. She had undergone torture for nearly three days and had never told that she had gotten the contraband cigarettes from the General himself. Of course, he could have stopped the torture with a word, but this way he knew that she could be relied upon. She was loyal, and had proven it. The scars would be a badge of honor for her. Within a few weeks he would be able to promote her. She might even bear his children to help him work his new farm. He would tell her later.

2

TOM BROWN HAD always been proud of his name, a simple name for a simple man. He was a large man and was well-respected in the community. He was one of the facilities managers for the local power co-op. It was a Saturday morning and he had had one too many beers the night before. It was nearly five in the morning, and he should have been able to sleep. He reached his arm across the king-size bed and it was empty; no wonder he had been unable to sleep. He never slept well when Mary was away from home.

His wife of 20-plus years had used a rare opportunity to visit her sister in St. Louis. Her sister, Ashlee, was in the middle of a minor family crisis due in large part to her inability to stop drinking. Mary had felt it her duty to go to help solve this problem.

She had left on Wednesday and had taken her car, a Buick. She was expected to be home sometime Sunday afternoon, but this didn't help Tom. He tried to go back to sleep but just as he was trying the phone in the kitchen began ringing. His oldest son, Albert, was awake at this early hour; he had probably planned a fishing trip or something and had answered the phone after three rings.

Tom was proud of all his children, and he loved them all equally.

"Dad," Albert called up the stairs, "are you awake?"

"Yes," Tom replied in a voice weak from lack of sleep.

"Come to the phone, please, it's Mom."

"Is she all right?" Tom asked as he set his bare feet on the bare wood floor. The wood felt good.

"She's fine, Dad," said Albert.

Tom walked down the stairs and took the phone from Albert. "Thank you, son," he said.

"Hello, dear, and how are you this fine morning?" he lied.

"We didn't want to call and worry you last night, but I think we're having trouble with the car."

"Let's see," groaned Tom, "three years old, 80,000 miles, about time for it to break down. What are the symptoms?"

"There is a big puddle of oil on the driveway, I'm afraid to drive it home," she said in a worried tone of voice.

"Did you notice the oil pressure light come on last time you drove it, or does it have an oil gauge?" he asked.

"Bob had to catch a flight to Dallas last evening. He slipped in the oil and nearly fell in it. He told me about it and we checked the oil, and it was over two quarts low."

"So you parked the car and then it lost two quarts of oil?" he asked in a relieved tone of voice.

"Must have, we parked the car and brought our bags in the house and haven't moved it since."

"Thank goodness," said Tom. "If it was parked up a hill, there is a chance that the rear main seal in the engine went out."

"Is it serious?" she sounded worried.

"Just more money," he said. "Don't drive it — I guess it would be safe to move it out of the driveway and into the street. Put a big piece of cardboard or something under it though, and we'll see where the leaks coming from. Is there any reason that you couldn't stay there another day?"

"No, we could if we had to, but it would really foul up our vacation plans. Ashlee would love to have us for a few more days; we talked about it last night."

"Well, I guess the good Lord works in mysterious ways. I was thinking about rebuilding that engine anyway. Jim Riley called me last week, and he has a new short block that would fit right in. He got a good deal on it, and I just about bought the dang thing just to have it around. I'll call him later this morning and make sure he still has it. If you can stay there another day or two, I'll load up the trailer and run down there real quick and pick up the car. It may take a little bit to get it all together, but don't drive that car except to get it in the street and I'll let you know."

"Could it have been something I did?" Mary asked.

Part of what he liked about Mary was that she was always ready to take the blame when things went wrong.

"It's nothing you did, dear. It's a design deficiency built right into the car when it was built that will guarantee a few hours' work for a mechanic, or that will cause you to break right down and buy another one."

"How is the daughter doing?" asked Tom.

Their youngest and only daughter was 13 years

old this year. A bright child who took after her mother and was always on the honor roll.

"She is behaving herself, no thanks to my sister who thinks she needs a boyfriend," said an exasperated Mary.

The Browns had four children, three boys and a girl; Albert was the oldest, followed by Marshall and Edward, then came the girl. They had named her Mary Elizabeth, which turned out to be a big mistake. The boys had over the years begun to call her Mary II which was shortened to Mary Two, and that had stuck. Sometimes they called her Junior. As a further downside to this, the two younger boys had begun to refer to themselves as simply Two and Three, and those two names had stuck as well.

"So how are the boys doing?" Mary asked. She had taken little Mary with her and had taken her out of the last week of school. Everyone involved had approved her absence; therefore, little Mary got an extra week of vacation.

"The boys are fine, I think," he had to think about it for a minute. "Albert was up early; either he just got in or he was going fishing early — you know how he is. And I assume that the two younger ones are sleeping soundly in their beds, but I have no idea. I doubt someone came in and stole them in the middle of the night."

Mary jumped in, "Don't even think things like that; don't even say things like that."

"Okay, I'm sure they're fine, stand by." Sometimes Mary worried too much, Tom thought.

"Hey, Al," he hollered, "go see if your brothers are okay for me, would you please?"

Al hurried down the hallway and looked into the bedrooms. "They are snoring like logs, Dad," he called back.

"They're fine, Mary. Everything is fine on the home front. The house is still in one piece. I did, however, drink one too many beers last night."

"One too many, hah, I bet you drank just one too many, maybe one case," Mary said in a scolding tone of voice.

"We had a little poker game last night. I came out ahead about $30. I sure thought it was going to go the other way until the final two hands."

"Well, that's good," she said. "You need a rest, you've been working too hard lately. Did you get that hay moved out of the south field?"

"Got about half of it until I broke a belt on the tractor. It knocked a big piece out of the radiator, but I got that fixed and we're back in the farming business. Tell you what; if I can persuade Al to change the oil in Old Blue and hook up the trailer, I might get out of here late morning. If it gets too late, I'll just wait 'til tomorrow. I'll let you know either way. Have you got plenty of money?"

"We're fine," she said. "My money's no good around her, you know how that goes. We thought we might go to the zoo. If Al gives you any trouble about helping you, remind him that tuition is coming up and I gave him a lot of money he hasn't earned yet."

"Don't you worry about the car; we can get it fixed. Love you, and give my love to Mary Two."

"Love you, too," she said and hung up.

Tom set the phone down on the counter and let out a deep sigh. Al came across the room and set a large cup of black coffee in front of him.

"Son," said Tom, "I'm proud of you. How did you know that I needed this?"

"You were up kind of late last night, and I just thought you could use it," said Albert with a smile.

"By the way," asked Tom, "what are your plans?"

"I was planning on going fishing, but it sounds like I'll be changing the oil in Old Blue first."

"Thanks, son, help me get the trailer loaded and I can get out of here before noon. I would like to get that hay moved before it rains, and then I can go get your mother and sister."

"What do you suppose is wrong with the car, Dad?" asked Albert.

"It's probably a rear main seal went out of it; the darn thing's only got 86,000 miles on it. It should have made that trip with no problem whatsoever. They build them to fail, that's what they do. If this country could have redirected all of the energy that has been wasted because of the auto industry, we could have cured cancer."

"It's called planned obsolescence, Dad, designed to fail. The auto industry learned they could make more money selling parts and labor than they could selling cars. That is one of the few things we learned in school."

"Here is your classic situation; I could have spent the next two days being productive around here, but instead I will have to spend two whole days and count-less thousands of dollars to correct a problem that was designed into the car. There are so many things that mechanics know are going to break I'm surprised there hasn't been a class action lawsuit filed against some automaker. This is not dangerous stuff, it is just aggravating stuff, like the Kevlar that was designed for tires, but have you ever seen a tire with Kevlar?"

"I'll bet if she took that car into a garage in St. Louis we would be looking at $1,500 to $2,000 to fix it. By the time they got done finding the odd problem, the broken ramus and framus, we would have to mortgage the house to get it out of there. We can drop a rebuilt engine in her and get another 50,000 trouble-free miles out of it."

"Tell you what, Al, when you're down in there changing the oil, double-check all the belts and hoses and stuff and look for any odd broken thing that might cause us to have a breakdown. Check all the fluid levels, check the air in the tires, and give the tires a once-over to see if you can see any screws or whatnot. Check the lights and turn signals, please."

"You bet, Dad, I'll get her ready for you," Al said as he hurried out the door.

That's a really good boy, Tom thought. *Mary must have really shelled out the bucks to get this kind of service.*

Al stuck his head back in the door, "You don't expect me to go with you, do you?" he asked in a worried tone of voice.

"No," Tom said, "I think you guys will be fine. That is, unless you want to go."

"I gotta pass on this one," said Al. He was obviously relieved.

"There will be no big parties while we are gone," Tom said gruffly.

Al looked surprised. "You know, now that you mention it, we had been planning to have a big fish fry here. The channel cats are supposed to be biting, and we sort of expect to catch our share."

"A fish fry sounds like a pretty good idea to me," said Tom. "Keep the fire outside and the oil off the deck. And no beer."

"You know me, Dad. Tried it, didn't like it."

"If those fish are really biting, save some for when your mom gets back. You know how she likes fried fish."

"We expect to catch plenty; we'll cook just enough for us and the girls and see if we can find some girls to make some salads and stuff."

"Let's see, I'll be gone for a few days at least. What should we do about adult supervision during that time?" asked Tom.

"Well, Dad, let's see — how about Carl? Carl could be some real adult supervision."

"That won't work," said Tom thoughtfully. "I was going to see if he wanted to come with me. He's got a little relation down there in St. Louis. It would give him a little bit of excuse to get out of the house, and it would give me some pleasant company during the drive, and he could help a little with the driving."

"What about the neighbor, Taylor?" asked Al. "I'll bet he would love to come over and have some fish with us. He's always said if we need anything to just ask him. Why don't we check with him? He could come over from time to time; it would make you guys feel better and I kind of like the old guy."

"You know, that's a good idea. I'll give him a call after bit and see what he says."

Tom picked up his cup of coffee and walked across the polished wood floor to one of the two sliding glass doors that faced the east. The sun was shining brightly through the windows, and it lit the room with a bright light. He stepped out onto the deck and into the cool morning air.

It was a perfect morning, the sun was shining, the wind not blowing, and it felt like a morning in the hills of Arkansas. The birds were chirping, almost too loudly, and except for this nagging headache, life at this second seemed perfect.

As he looked to the east toward the rising sun, the trees were such a dark green that they looked almost black. Beyond the trees were cows grazing; animals always seemed to be eating. It didn't seem to matter what animal — cow, horse, chicken or duck — animals always seemed to be eating.

Life was good, except for the fact that he now knew he had to drive a thousand miles through heavy traffic. It could not be Mary's fault; stuff just happens.

He walked back into the room. It was a very large room, or rather several rooms with a common high ceiling. There was the large family room with the fireplace and large TV, and then there was the dining area and kitchen area all under the same high ceiling. The sliding door by the kitchen led to a large deck on the other side of the house. He walked across the large rooms and set his empty coffee cup on the table as he walked out the other set of sliding doors.

He sat in a chair on the rear deck and looked across the large driveway covered with white rocks and past the large red barn to the hills beyond. The trees cast long shadows as the sun was rising; there was a slight mist in the air, like a fine fog that covered the landscape with occasional spots of moisture that were the beginnings of the fog. The fog lay heavy over the small water pools in the field.

He had built this house on the side of this hill on purpose. It offered a view in several directions, gently rolling terrain, trees scattered throughout. To the northeast was the Taylor farm. They owned several hundred acres and had planted much of it in fruit and nut trees.

The Taylors had been the best neighbors; the two families had been there for each other whenever a need arose. After the big windstorm of '96, their barn had been a mess. By the time the neighbors had finished pitching in, the barn was back like it had never been down. Farm folks stuck together. The insurance company had threatened to drop their coverage if they filed a claim, so the neighbors had saved the day. Funny thing how insurance companies were able to get away with stuff like that.

This was the kind of community where no one locked their doors; they left the keys in their cars and trucks, it was safe.

In two years he and Mary would own this property. Truth be told, they could pay off the property now if they chose to. Then they could quit working and sit back and enjoy their grandchildren, if their children would ever cooperate and have children. This is all that Tom had ever wanted, a quiet place in the country, a chance to sit back and enjoy the peaceful things in life.

Tom's solitude was interrupted by a noise that startled him. He heard footsteps on the patio and heard a pleasant greeting. "Howdy, neighbor, got any coffee?" Tom didn't even turn around.

"Not so loud, I'll thank you," he said in an overly gruff voice.

He recognized the voice of his best friend in the world. "Come on over and sit down," he said more cheerfully. "Glad you're here."

Carl Stoneman walked up to behind where Tom was seated on the deck and placed two large hands on his shoulders and gave him a friendly neck rub.

"I'll give you a half hour to quit," said Tom.

Carl Stoneman was an imposing figure. Six foot five and very strong, he was of African descent, and he was dressed in loose overalls with patches on the knees and well-worn work boots. He wore a red-checkered shirt and a hat that looked like it was 100 years old and had never been washed. One would never guess that this man had a Ph.D. in Psychology and had been one of the best law enforcement people in the city of L.A. He had retired early, invested well, was a frugal spender, and was probably one of the richest landowners in this part of the country. You could not tell it by looking at him.

"I suppose if you have a headache it would be because you drank too much last night, and I sure wouldn't want to make any noise." Saying that, Carl stomped loudly across the deck and came close to Tom's ear and said, "You know what would really sound good for breakfast? A greasy pork chop."

"Oh, my God," said Tom. "With friends like you, who needs friends?"

The sliding glass door opened, and out walked Al with two piping hot cups of coffee. "Holy Smokes," laughed Carl, "you have this boy trained."

"He wants something," said Tom. "We'll find out

pretty quick."

"Thank you, Al," they both said in unison.

"So what's the plan today?" asked Carl. "What do we do after we get that hay in?"

These two men were about as close as any two humans could be, since Tom had moved out here in the country. He knew about farming and ranching and shared his knowledge with Carl. Carl was a very pleasant companion, probably smarter than Tom, but he never let on or spoke of his superior wealth or education. Carl referred to himself as just another field hand; he just loved physical work. Years of dealing with people had burned him out. At the end of a hard day's work a man could go to sleep fast and deep. Carl felt that the harder you worked, the longer you lived. He often expressed the satisfaction that he felt from looking out at the fields he had planted and the cows that he raised.

"Well, Bubba," Tom started to explain, "Mary called a few minutes ago. I thought I was going to have a pleasant day in the fields. You remember that she was in St. Louis visiting her sister? The car broke down. I think it's the rear main seal, and so instead of working in the fields it looks like I get to take Old Blue to the city and pick up the car."

"Bet you wish you'd have bought that short block old Riley had for sale last week, don't you?" asked Carl.

"I knew I should have bought that thing last week. You ever get that feeling?" Tom asked.

"I did get that feeling, just last week, about that same engine — Riley sold it, to me," said Carl with a smile on his face. "I haven't paid him yet; he's still got it over at his shop. Let's run over and get it right now. Hey, you need some company, that's a long old drive."

"I hoped you'd ask," said Tom, relief in his voice. "I wanted to get out of here by noon."

"I see the boy is out servicing Old Blue, " said Carl as he stepped to the railing and looked toward the barn.

"Well, I'm your man," said Carl. "Let me call over to the ranch and check in. How long do you figure this will take?"

"I need to get that hay moved, then we'll leave. It'll probably take at least two, maybe three days."

"There's that big old steak house on the way. They've got that 64-ounce sirloin steak meal, free if you can eat it all. I never could get past the first 32-ounce steak," said Carl with a gleam in his eye.

"I haven't had breakfast yet, and you're talking about a 64-ounce steak dinner, makes my mouth water."

"Need any help with the hay?" asked Carl.

"We got the tractor fixed yesterday. Couple of hours should do it"

"I'll just finish my coffee, then run back to the house and get my shit packed. That reminds me of a joke, never mind," Carl said with a smile on his face.

"What truck we taking, Old Blue?" asked Carl.

"Thought we'd take Old Blue, it's running good, and that big old diesel will pull that trailer and get 23 miles per gallon."

"You sure you don't want to take one of mine?" asked Carl in a hurt sort of voice. "I just got that new little Chevy that isn't even broke in yet."

"I appreciate it, old buddy, but I've got tools in Old Blue that I might need and a Pronto Welder under the hood and don't really want to screw with changing trucks. That Pronto Welder can charge a dead battery in about eight minutes."

"You know," continued Carl, "If you weren't such a tight son-of-a-bitch you would buy your wife a new car. I know you could afford it."

"We've talked about it several times, and she feels the same way I do. If they'd ever build one that was designed to last, we'd be glad to buy one. This one only has eighty-some thousand miles on it and should have made this trip without a problem. Don't forget, we have plans to retire in a few years, and we'll need that money to pay off the tractor and the truck and this piece of real estate. Besides, the way the prices are going up, by the time I retire it will cost 20 dollars for a candy bar."

"There's that pessimism again," Carl shook his head. "The greatest problem with America, besides the fact that we've been scared to death, is that people can't think positively. We'll spend some time working on that."

Carl stood up, finished his coffee in two gulps and placed the cup down on the table.

"How in the world can you do that?" exclaimed Tom. "That hot coffee would burn clear down past my stomach."

"I just don't know, I can do it with hot soup, too. Hot stuff never seemed to bother me. It might have been the lions," explained Carl.

"The lions?" asked Tom.

"You know, Darwin's theory of evolution, survival of the fittest. Somewhere back on the plains of Africa, one of my long dead ancestors was being chased by a lion and his ability to drink boiling hot food kept him alive to procreate. Or it could be one of those traits that just naturally makes me a superior human being." Carl stood back with a smile on his face.

"Better git," Carl said, as he stepped off the porch. "I've got some packing to do."

Tom finished his coffee and stood up, picked up the coffee cups and carried them into the sink, rinsed them and set them on the counter.

He walked into the bedroom and changed into a pair of work jeans and boots. He looked into the mirror and saw a man in his 50s, lean and fit, beginning to gray, but needing a haircut and a shave. If his coworkers were to see him like this, it would cost him his job as director of facilities for Iowa Power and Light.

As he walked out the back door, he paused for just a moment on the rear deck to look around. The house was separated from the outbuildings by a very wide driveway made of well-packed white AB3 rock. This driveway extended from the far east wheat field to the farthest west pasture. To the right were three large grain bins, one filled with milo, one with corn, and one with winter wheat. Ahead of him and to the north was a large silo with a winding staircase and a landing in the middle. Beside the silo were two barns with a white picket fence enclosing the space between them. To the left of the house was the white gravel driveway that led to the county gravel road.

Tom walked across the driveway to the first and smaller of the two barns.

A large green tractor was backed into the barn, and the loader part had a six-foot-long steel spike with two smaller spikes at the sides.

As he was climbing into the tractor, a thought came to him that something was wrong. He thought for a moment and concluded that the generator was running in the generator building. The generator building was the size of a large storage shed. It was located across the road from the house and across the road from the barns. Two large diesel tanks sat beside it. An earthen dam that was large enough to contain the diesel fuel in the event of a leak surrounded these tanks. He had triple-insulated the walls of the little building and installed two mufflers on the engine because Mary hated the noise.

He was concerned because normally when the power went out the plant called him. Maybe it was because they knew he was taking a few days off.

It was probably just a blown fuse somewhere. He started the tractor, drove it to the other barn, and stopped it by the large door and let the engine idle down.

"Hey, Al," he yelled, "how long has the generator been running?"

Al slid out from under the truck and said, "Well, it was like clock work. I noticed the lights flicker and the generator came on at precisely eight o'clock. You were in the back of the house. I was watching the weather channel and the TV station went off at the same time. I just thought it was a normal power problem."

"What's the weather supposed to do?" asked Tom.

Al thought for a minute, "Highs in the 50s, with no chance for rain."

"Thanks, Al," Tom said, as he jumped back in the seat of the tractor and drove it eastward. He wondered why the satellite signal and the power would go out at the same time. If it were a serious problem, they would have called him.

He drove into the field, and using the large steel point attached to the front of the tractor, he soon had moved all the big round hay bales.

He put the tractor away, and as he walked back to the house, he noticed that the generator was still running. He didn't know for sure, but it must have been running for at least two hours. The small tank that fed the generator was only good for 16 hours; before it went dry he would have to transfer fuel from the big tank. He always kept several thousand gallons of diesel fuel in the big tank, especially during planting season.

He walked all the way to the house and called for Al, but there was no answer. He turned around and retraced his steps past the small barn and into the large barn. Al must have just finished the oil change because he was just closing the hood. Standing beside Al was his best friend, Juan Delgado.

"Buenos dias, Juan," said Tom.

"Hello, Mr. Brown," said Juan. Part of the reason that Tom liked Juan was because his parents had brought him up to respect his elders. He was always polite and respectful.

"How are your parents doing?" asked Tom.

"Just fine, sir, except Mom says Dad is working too hard."

"He is," said Tom in a matter-of-fact way.

"How is that algebra class coming?" Juan had come to Mary for a little help in his algebra class.

"Oh, shucks, Mr. Brown, I think I'll pass, but I hate algebra. I can't imagine what it's good for."

"You know, you never can tell, son. We use algebra in our daily lives all the time. Farmers use algebra often, not every day, mind you, but from time to time. Even if you don't use the math right now, it is more the idea that you are building your brain. The brain is a muscle and the exercising of it is just like lifting weights. Algebra is just a bar bell for your brain."

"Don't believe him, Juan," laughed Al. "This man is a total lunatic; he is an embarrassment to his family, his friends, and all who dwell on this planet."

Tom turned around and walked to the door and screamed at the top of his lungs, "Hey, world, I am this boy's father!"

Both boys began to laugh.

Tom returned and became serious, "How was the truck, Al?"

Al responded in a serious voice, "Seems fine, Dad, the belts were a little loose but in good shape. The oil was black as pitch, but it's a diesel. Checked the tires, no nails that I could find and no leaks. This baby should be good to go for another 8000 miles."

"Thanks, boys," said Tom with pride in his voice. "Seen Carl yet?"

They shook their heads.

"Have you boys noticed if the power has tried to come back on in the last hour or so?" asked Tom with a note of worry in his voice.

"I think we would have heard those big fans in the grain bin come back on, Dad. They're not on the generator and we've had them running pretty much full bore for the last couple of days," answered Al.

"Damn," said Tom, "excuse my French. I wonder if I should call out there and see what the heck?"

"If you do, Dad, you know you'll end up going out there, and then you'll be late and it won't have mattered if you do go. Isn't Charlie on board today?"

"Last I heard," said Tom.

"Well, there you go, Dad," said Al, speaking to Tom like a mother. "You may be good, but Charlie's been there longer than you have, and even though you're his boss he's plenty able to handle whatever it is, just like before you got there. Besides, you need to go get Mom and Mary Two, and the sooner you leave the sooner we can start planning that party that's not going to happen tonight."

"Thanks, son, you have a way of putting things in perspective." Tom was grateful sometimes. "Let's get that generator turned off for a while, and fill that small tank up, please. While you're at it, fill Old Blue and fill those jerry cans that will give us an extra 10 gallons just in case."

"If I didn't ask already," Tom hated to ask, "would you please hook up the trailer and make sure the extra chains and come-alongs are in the toolbox so we can get the car?"

"We're on it," said Al.

Tom ran back to the house, took off his work boots by the back door and walked stocking-footed back to the back bedroom where he undressed and jumped into the shower.

While in the shower, his mind went to the plant. Charlie was there and should be able to handle any situation, and Louise was working today. She would never hesitate to call Tom, night or day.

What Tom did not know was that Louise had gone by the post office on her way to work that morning.

She had picked up the magazines and letters and one manila envelope addressed to the "Director of Facilities." It was not addressed to Tom by name, so she opened it as she had done countless times before. It contained a set of revised maintenance instructions for a newly purchased variable speed drive. The papers were in a sealed plastic wrapper that was marked "VERY URGENT." She felt that it might be important and that she should take the letter to Charlie to look at before she called Tom. She had hurried down to see Charlie.

Charlie was a short, gray-haired man who had been trying desperately to lose that 30 extra pounds for 10 years. He would be 63 next year, and he planned to retire and move in with his son in Las Vegas where it was warm. He had been the head of maintenance since the plant opened and had been resentful of Tom when Tom took over. It wasn't long before they became fast friends. Very few problems had come up that Charlie couldn't handle.

When Louise brought the papers to Charlie's shop in the basement, he was a little puzzled. He did not remember a variable speed drive being purchased lately. He felt that if he opened the envelope it might give him a clue as to where the drive had been installed. He unfolded the four-inch Buck knife that he had carried for 24 years and opened the sealed packet. As he thumbed through the paperwork, he became light-headed, and suddenly the room went black. Louise had handed the envelope to Charlie and stood idly by as he opened the sealed package. As he began to read the documents, she had looked away for a moment. When she turned back, Charlie had collapsed on the floor. She hurried to him, thinking that perhaps he had had a heart attack or something. As she bent down to help him, she suddenly couldn't catch her breath, and her dead body fell to the floor beside that of Charlie's.

In all, 2,467 such packages were shipped in various ways — UPS, U.S. Postal, Fed Ex, DHL, etc. The packages were all different and were sent to police stations, hospitals, clinics, power plants and seats of government. Some contained fast-acting chemicals; some would take many hours to show effect.

* * * * *

Tom stepped out of the shower, shaved and packed quickly. He always felt that if he got into a bind all he really needed was a little cash and he could buy whatever he would need. He picked up the packed bag, took three shirts out of the closet on hangers and walked down the hallway.

He set the bag beside the back door and stuck his head out the door. "Hey, Al," he yelled.

"Yeah, Dad," answered Al.

"How are you set for cash?"

"I've got about 50 bucks left," said Al.

Tom turned back into the house and walked into the living room and moved a chair away from the wall. He grabbed the side of a large picture frame that was hanging on the wall behind the chair, and it swung out on a set of hinges.

Behind the picture was a wall safe. He used the combination to open it and took out $2,000 in 20s. He closed the safe and folded the money and put it into his pocket. He then walked out the back door, taking his shirts and bag as he went.

He carried the bag and shirts to the truck, hung the shirts in the back and threw the bag onto the back seat. He then walked back into the house to the cupboard above the refrigerator and took down a nickel-plated Smith and Wesson 357 magnum revolver in a shoulder holster. He took the gun out of the holster, opened the loading door and spun the cylinder to make sure that it was loaded. He reached back into the cupboard to get two boxes of ammunition. He carried these out to the truck and placed them under the back seat.

He stepped back for a short time to look at the truck. Not much to look at, several dents and scratches, he could tell you where almost every one had come from. New tires, new engine, new transmission, bearings and U-joints replaced every 50,000 miles. This truck was old, but Tom never hesitated to spend the extra money on the better parts. He was the epitome of the guy that Detroit hated. When people would drive up in their new trucks and ask for an opinion, Tom would tell them that he would be impressed with a new truck when it would go a million miles, get 50 miles per gallon and be built of aircraft aluminum and never rust. He felt that a person should buy a car when they turned 16 and be buried in it 80 years later.

He called his truck Old Blue, and had had extra-sized fuel tanks installed so he could easily make it to St. Louis and back without a pit stop. He had a Pronto Welder under the hood, a fifth-wheel hitch for the trailer, a cutting torch and other tools. It got fairly good gas mileage and drove good down the road. If there was a downside to this truck, it was that it drove like a truck, sort of stiff, but that was the price you paid.

Tom had installed a special compartment behind the rear seat that was only accessible through the cab and that would only open with a special release. The boys used this truck more than he did, so he approached Albert to ask what they had left in it.

"What have we got in the box, Al?" he asked.

"Last time we used this we were deer hunting and had that Remington 30-06, with about three boxes of 150-grain shells. We cleaned it and just left it there. I just added that special little 12-gauge shotgun you like to travel with, the pump with the barrel sawed off just a half-inch over legal. There is a box of buckshot and a box of birdshot for the shotgun. If you feel like you need a handgun, there is that Smith and Wesson in the kitchen."

"Got it and thanks," said Tom.

Tom had lived in the country all his life, where there was never anyone to take care of you or your family. He realized that this country was only a couple of generations removed from George Custer. He felt strongly that every American should be armed just like Switzerland, and that this was the key to a free America. He felt that marksmanship and gun safety should be taught in grade school and that marksmanship should be a part of the county fairs. He had seen to it that all of his children could use a firearm and that they knew how to be safe with one.

"Did you top off the tanks, son?" he asked.

"You bet, Dad. I put five gallons of unleaded in the back jerry can marked unleaded, just in case Mom needs it. I also put two gallons of drinking water in the tool box," answered Al.

"Here," he said, and gave Al $100. "If you need

more, it's in the safe."

"Thanks, Dad," said Al with a grin on his face.

"Looks like we're all packed and ready to roll, just waiting for Carl." He turned to face the road and yelled, "Carl, where are you?" at the top of his lungs.

No sooner than the words were out of his mouth, than down the driveway came a big black Mercedes at a high rate of speed. Carl parked the car beside the rear deck and jumped out. He was wearing coveralls, a red-checkered shirt and work boots, all new. He had opened the trunk from inside, and he walked to the rear of the car. He pulled two bags from the trunk and carried them to the back seat of the truck. He returned to the trunk where he removed a smaller stainless steel case. He closed the trunk and put the case in the front passenger seat of the truck.

"We ready?" he asked, he was short of breath from the recent exertion.

"You bet," said Tom as he climbed into the driver's seat of Old Blue.

Carl tossed a set of keys to Al. "Take good care of my car while we're gone, just treat it like you own it. Oh, and try not to get it shot full of holes," he laughed like a crazy man as he climbed into the truck.

"You don't mind if the boys use the car, do you? They might get some pussy with it," Carl said in a joking manner to Tom.

"Isn't that about $60,000?" asked Tom in a worried manner.

"Full coverage, I get cheap insurance through the military. I want a new one anyway. I hope they wreck it without injuries, of course. Wish I had a kid just like Al," he smiled.

31

"Wagons ho," said Tom.

"Wait just one second," said Al as he hurried back into the house. He returned in a moment with a large sack in his hand. "Figured you could use some snacks for the road."

Tom took the sack through the window and passed it to Carl. Al held out his hand to Tom. Tom took Al's hand and shook it.

Tom looked Al in the eyes and said, "Thank you, son, I'm proud of you."

"Be careful, Dad. I love you," said Al.

" I love you too, son," said Tom.

They drove down the lane to the main gravel road and turned to the left. They drove along the center of the gravel road, in the two ruts made by farm traffic, piles of reddish-colored rocks along the side of the road waiting for the occasional road grader to scrape them back onto the road. There were five-strand barbed-wire fences on both sides of the road, and this fence was separated from the road by a continuous drainage ditch that filled with water during rain-storms. About a mile and a half up the road the two men could see a spot where trees were growing in a long line to the right and to the left. This was the spot where Simmons creek crossed the road. There was a low place in the road that was made of concrete that had large tubes in it through which the creek passed in times of low water.

Carl turned to Tom and said, "I guess you don't have to think very hard about how this got the name low-water bridge. When the water is low, there is a bridge; when the water is high, no bridge."

Tom replied, "People tell me that back in '51 there

was a pretty good flood in these parts. A farmer by the name of Jenkins had his wife and boy and dog in an old '39 Ford pickup and tried to beat the flood waters. Guess the waters were only a couple of feet deep and he didn't want to drive all the way back to town to cross at the big bridge. Anyway, he got a running start and tried to drive through the water and the truck stalled. The water washed the truck about a half-mile downstream and got stuck in a tree. The boy and the dog made it out, but the old boy and his wife drowned. They recovered the bodies when the water went down, and the pickup is still down there half buried in the bank of the creek. Rumor has it that the kid bounced around from foster home to foster home and ended up a Baptist minister up north somewhere."

They drove to the other side of the low-water bridge; two boys were fishing in the deep water on the downstream side of the low water bridge. The two men pulled the truck and trailer to the side of the road, left the engine running and got out of the truck.

"Catchin' anything?" asked Tom in a cheerful tone of voice.

The younger of the two set his pole down and walked to the edge of the water and raised up a stringer half full of fish. He could not hold it in one hand and had to use both hands.

These two boys could spend their whole lives on the creek bank, thought Tom. He wondered if that would ever change.

"How big are they?" asked Tom.

The older boy answered, "The biggest is about

five pounds. There's a couple there that should go three or four, and the smallest is about two. We're only keeping the catfish; we caught a couple of bass, but threw them back."

Tom turned to Carl, "Water came up last week with that big rain we had; these fish swim upstream with the high water and got as far as the low-water bridge. Then when the water goes down here they sit in the hole. Maybe we could figure out a way to just fish for a little while and then go."

"Better not," said Carl in an exasperated tone. "We'd smell like fish all the way to the city."

"You're right, as usual," said Tom. He surely wanted to fish for just a minute.

"You boys be careful," said Tom in a fatherly manner. "We're going to run up to St. Louis real quick and get your mom and sister. The car broke down and we're going to haul it back home."

"Rear main seal, right?" asked the older boy.

"How did you know?" asked Tom. He was somewhat surprised.

"Shop class," said the boy. "Mr. Martin has a list of stuff that always goes wrong with certain cars at certain mileages."

"Why didn't you tell me about this?" asked Tom.

"We told Mom and she said she would talk it over with you. She didn't want to worry you," said the boy.

There it was, thought Tom. So many times in life you get that one shot at the big old buck, that one little noise that tells you the water pump is going out, just one shot.

"Al will be in charge while we're gone, as always. You be careful and do what he says, you hear?" Tom spoke sternly. It was always best to have someone in charge.

"We've got two cell phones with us; your mother has hers as well. I left a list of numbers by the phone in the kitchen. You need any money?" asked Tom.

"No thanks, Dad, we're fine. We're just going to slaughter these fish and then con somebody into cooking them for us and probably come back here and do it all over again tomorrow."

"Come here," he said to the boys, and gave each one of them a big hug. "Love you, Dad," they said.

"Love you both," he said. "You be careful now and we'll see you in a few days."

Tom thought of what a wonderful thing it was to have your kids be old enough to fend for themselves, to go out and catch fish and bring them home. Life was sweet.

Tom jumped back into the truck and headed east. Carl leaned back in the seat.

Tom thought a minute and then spoke. "I can't think of any reason not to take the shortest, most direct route. Head east to Des Moines, take I80 to Iowa City, head on down to Davenport, pick up 74 and go south, go through Peoria, Springfield and end up in the south part of St. Louis. There is a quicker way, 218 out of Iowa City, but there was some road construction that would slow us down, Mary said. Even though it's 30 or 40 miles to go from Galesburg to Peoria, probably be quicker taking 74 south."

"You're driving," said Carl, "head down the road."

3

DAVID LOWE FACED south looking through the double windows on his fourth floor office. It was a large office with thick green carpet, and the wallpaper was heavily embossed with gold designs. The patterns were of pretty oriental flowers, and the heavy woodwork was stained a deep reddish color. The ceilings were of stamped metal and painted a golden color. The room was large enough that the lighting was two large chandeliers whose lights were dimmed somewhat. He had chosen this office because of its close proximity to the stairwell so that he would not be dependent upon the elevator. He looked down upon the morning traffic. It was perhaps 6:30 in the morning. He liked to start the morning early; he liked to watch the commuters come to their offices. The secretaries dressed in their business suits and wearing tennis shoes, carrying their dress shoes in a shopping bag, and carrying their lunch buckets and their thermos jugs. In the front of the building was First Street, a one-way street heading east; on the east side of the building was Douglas, a one-way street heading south. He watched a late model red car pull to the left side of the street, and two young men got out of the car, one out of the passenger side front and one out of the passenger side rear. The first was dressed in blue jeans and a tan sweater, the other wearing tan slacks with a short-sleeved polo shirt with a dark pattern, and they were nearly the same age. He was only mildly surprised when the two young men embraced and kissed each other on the lips. The first man got back into the front seat, and the driver opened the trunk. The second man reached into the trunk and removed a briefcase and a 12-pack of Coke and a 12-pack of Pepsi cans. He walked to the curb and waited for the traffic to abate and then scampered across the street to an office building.

He would never really be comfortable with sights such as this, but such was life in the city. There was an awning below his window that spanned the length of the building. It was covered with black tar and white chat. Around the fringe were ornately sculptured concrete pineapple-like things every four feet. This puzzled him — who in the world would have built a canopy thing with pineapple things around it? Oh, well, he preferred gargoyles or grotesques. This was his last day. He had spent 20 years here and this was his last day. He had come to the States from China to complete his MBA from Yale and had graduated with honors. He had been set up in business and financed, his responsibility was to set up a corporation of telemarketing buildings — 40,000-square-foot buildings all identical, all filled with computers, and every one had a central computer in the center that fed the remote computers. He had named the corporation the Syracuse Corporation. The name had come to him as he passed through Syracuse, New York on a train. It was a good old American name.

Besides the central computer, each building contained an emergency generator capable of producing three times the power needed for the building and which had a reserve of 30 days' supply of diesel fuel, a 5,000-gallon tank. Each of these generators was exercised once a week. Each building was fed with a fiber-optic cable that came from two different locations, along with a 1,000-pair copper cable to ensure that there would be no interruption of the phone service. Aside from the central computer location, there was a full kitchen capable of feeding many hungry people.

The buildings were split into two. Each half was the mirror image of the other. Each half was connected to the central computer and the central kitchen. Each half was completely filled with office cubicles. Five-foot-high partition walls that formed squares, eight foot to a side, created these cubicles. Each cubicle contained a computer, keyboard and chair. Each half contained just over 200 cubicles. They were manned 24 hours a day seven days a week by technicians trained to troubleshoot computer problems for various computer companies. The Syracuse Company had also contracted to man several 800 numbers to satisfy such customers as Microtrend and ShopAtHome TV network.

Each building was designed with a loading dock, to accept a 52-foot semi-trailer. The buildings were fully sprinkled in case of fire and had a fire alarm system designed to shut down all power in the event of a fire. The main computer room possessed a dry system, a preaction system that was only charged in the event that one detector detected fire.

The real purpose of the Syracuse Company was to construct these buildings under the guise of creating a telemarketing network. The seed money allowed the first 20 buildings to be constructed for two million apiece. After the first 20, the company went public, and with the public capital was able to construct the remainder of the buildings. The Syracuse Company had become quite successful, and the profits had allowed the construction of over 100 buildings.

The way that it worked was that David would approach a number of Chambers of Commerce and tell them that they would create several hundred new high-paid, high-tech local jobs that would stimulate the local economy. They would tell the prospective Chamber of Commerce that they intended to build two buildings and that if they were able to train enough help that they would build the second building and create 400 more jobs. That would be 800 new high-paying jobs.

The plan always required enough land for two buildings; they would take bids from several local communities. The land must be located near an airport that was capable of landing a 747.

As a rule, these communities would fall all over themselves trying to give them a good deal. There were the few odd holdouts, but most of the communities would cave in and give up the land to Syracuse. These high-paying, high-tech jobs were highly sought after by many college towns. They would then hire anyone who had the slightest inclination to become computer literate. Since all of these computer terminals were centrally fed from the central computer, it was fairly easy to generate a program that would create a subliminal directive that would cause these applicants to behave in a particular manner.

Only certain select employees were aware of this subliminal training. If it were determined that an employee was not susceptible to any kind of training or proved to be an otherwise troublemaker, they were gotten rid of. Some highly susceptible ones were kept for further training and development. Mind control had long been on the minds of leaders, but the personal computer took it to a whole new level.

David had done an admirable job; he had created approximately two of these facilities in each state with more in some of the more populous states. Each facility had at least 400 employees. He was somewhat saddened this morning knowing that his work was done. He was also anxious to get on with his future. It was going to be a bright future because his work had been a great success. He would be rewarded.

He looked across the street to the parking lot beyond. It was an attended parking lot that cost him $10 a day, but it was well worth it. He looked at his new blue Suburban that was loaded with his clothes, his money, food, and other survival stuff and his guns. He knew he had to leave soon; he wanted to be out of the city by eight o'clock. It would be a 20-minute ride down the interstate assuming no problems.

He turned to look at his briefcase that contained the three hard drives from the three computers in the office. He had gone through the drawers and had gathered all the floppy discs and CDs. He looked around the office to make sure that every bit of data was removed, not that it would make any difference in just a few short hours. People would have a lot of other problems on their minds.

He took a last drink from the bottle of water on his desk, closed the lid extra tightly and placed the water bottle into his briefcase next to the hard drives.

As he walked out the door, he reached for the light switch and turned it off. He stood for a second and thought and instead turned the switch back on, along with two other switches. He turned and locked the door and walked into the hallway. There were three elevators, and to the right of them was the door to the stair well. He looked at the elevators, looked at his watch, and chose the stairs. He walked swiftly to the stairway door and took the stairs down two at a time. The walls were in desperate need of paint, and the old yellow paint was pealing to reveal an earlier ancient coat of green paint. There was old writing on the walls put there by some hand probably long dead.

What in the world were those things he thought as he passed a landing? Why would someone put yellow traffic cones on a stair landing? Probably some janitor had put them there to cordon off some floor that had just been mopped.

He reached the lowest stair level and came to the door at the main lobby. He opened the door, passed through the lobby and hurried past the elevators to the entry. There was a large revolving door in the center, and on either side were two man doors. He ignored the rotating door and chose the door on the right. He nearly ran into a man and a woman at the entry smoking cigarettes. And he noticed the man had a badge that had a funny little gold ball attached to the bottom of the badge. How unusual, he thought, and he wondered which one of these companies this man worked for.

He looked to the left and there was no traffic. He looked to the right even though it was a one-way street; he began to hurry across the street, half expecting to hear a policeman yell at him. He hurried to the parking lot and gave the attendant a $5 tip for watching his car. He walked to his car, started it and headed south to the interstate to go west out of town. The rear tank was full, but the front tank was only half full. He thought he had better stop and top off the tanks; gas would be a little hard to get pretty quick. It was 7:15.

4

THE GENERAL'S THOUGHTS went back to the last meeting he had had with his superiors. There was a faction of the government that was not fully behind his mission. It seemed like the powers in control of the other plan were gaining strength. His primary sponsor, Commissioner Wang, was getting up there in years, had, in fact, been a close friend with the General's father who had been dead for 15 years.

He had pushed this plan ahead by two months knowing that once the operation was underway it would be difficult for the government to not support him.

The General looked out of his window onto the parade ground where his troops were forming. The several divisions had full backpacks with loaded weapons, and each man carried rations for two days. Two thousand men here on one parade ground were his to command. All was in place except one platoon. He would have to make a note of this and punish the NCO4 as an example.

He turned and looked back into the office that had been his home for the last two long years. He walked to the pictures on the walls, removed the frames from the walls and removed the pictures from the back of the frames. He rolled them up and secured them with two rubber bands that he produced from his top desk drawer.

He walked out of the door and left the lights on. He was met at the door by a soldier with a backpack and two rifles. He turned to look back in the office that for the last two years had been filled with people and computers. It was just the two men now. He looked at the soldier and then glanced toward the floor where a backpack was resting against the wall. He merely pointed at it, and the sergeant, without a word, hastened to pick it off the floor. The General turned his back to the man, and the man raised the backpack onto the General's waiting arms. As the General was securing the straps, the soldier reached over and picked up the rifle that was leaned against the wall and handed it to the General.

This was still the people's army; it was good for morale to let the men see that their General could carry his own weight.

He checked the action of the rifle to assure that it was fully loaded. He gave his first order of the day, "Please see to it that the group commanders are aware that mine is to be the only loaded weapon until we land."

"Yes, sir, General," replied the soldier.

He turned quickly, and leaving the door open walked briskly out the door and down the stairs to the busy parade ground.

As soon as he made his entrance, 2,000 voices broke into a cheer. It was a good thing that morale was high. They would need it for the coming event.

He walked onto the parade ground and was surprised at the weight of the pack; a man of his years should not be expected to shoulder a fully loaded pack. It was too late now; he strode with his head high and a straight back to the end of the parade ground where a small stage had been erected of new lumber. On the stage was a microphone, and he walked to it.

He tapped the microphone to assure that it would work, and after the cheering had died down he addressed the crowd. "Comrades, we are gathered here for an important event. It will go down in the history books. You are the spearhead and the first wave. You will be the first wave of a global assault that will result in total world domination. You have been hand-picked and specially trained. I am proud of each and every one of you, and I know that you will do your duty."

The troops cheered as he walked down from the podium.

Along the side of the parade route was a long line of green buses. He walked to the first one and removed his backpack and rifle. The interior of the bus had been specially made for this event. There were two seats on the left side of the aisle, and on the right side of the bus was a metal cage arrangement designed to hold weapons and backpacks. The General placed his backpack in the first space, hung his weapon on the hook provided and sat down in the first seat behind the driver next to the window. He was followed by a line of soldiers who followed his example. Soon the bus was filled. As soon as the bus was filled, the driver started it and drove down the road, past the gate and into open country.

All of this had been timed so there would be no spy satellites to see this. As the buses left the gates, each went in a different direction, some headed to the same location but by different routes.

A great deal of planning had gone into this adventure. One worry had been how to get a great number of planes to take off at the same time without arousing suspicion. This had been accomplished in a rather cruel manner when a fully loaded plane, an older Boeing 747, had crashed, killing many civilians and one high-ranking official. This official had been martyred for the cause and would receive the order of Mao, albeit posthumously. He had killed two birds with one stone with this crash. Two days later another plane had crashed for no reason. The government had ordered an immediate grounding of all aircraft, and all planes were scheduled to come to one of four airports for a thorough inspection.

These planes, instead of being checked, were really equipped with rocket launchers and extra fuel tanks. He had wanted to have them loaded with a few suitcase-size thermonuclear weapons, but he lacked the political stroke at this time. That would have created one of the most powerful forces ever assembled at one staging area.

The government had announced that they had isolated the cause of the crashes, that it had been an imported fuel-sensing device that, when overheated, caused the fuel tanks to rupture. And now all planes had been released. The government, with great fanfare and great grief, had announced the resumption of flights.

The General would enter a fully loaded aircraft that could reach the center of the U.S. without refueling. His plane would reach a strip just east of Des

Moines, Iowa. The other planes would be spread out to various other airports that were adjacent to a Syracuse Corporation facility.

The buses drove to the various airports, passed through sliding gates opened and closed again by guards, and parked on the runway next to the big planes. The troops dismounted; each man gathered up his weapon and his backpack and walked to the plane. They placed the backpack and the weapon in specially designed racks similar to those on the bus. The explanation for the sudden exodus from the mainland was that now that the planes would fly again there was a backlog of tourists who wanted to get back home. The tourists were being detained in holding cells. These cells had no phones, and the walls had been specially equipped to prevent cell phone transmissions. Many in the government were still unaware that this event was taking place; it was a gamble.

5

JOHN SANCHEZ HAD graduated from Ohio State Medical School five years ago. He drove down the streets of St. Louis toward the new office complex. His thoughts were more on golf than on his patients. He had a very successful practice and was planning on a comfortable retirement in 10 years. The red Mercedes he was driving was a testimony to his investment plan. This car was an investment; even though he had spent $53,000 for it, he would probably get most of his money back. He had no family and was happy that way. He had come from a big family and was enjoying his single life.

He drove into the parking lot of the office complex, it was nine o'clock; he looked at his building, a fortress. The front of the building was built of gleaming white slabs of concrete with slits for windows. It looked like a World War II pillbox. The sign on the front said Sanchez Medical Complex. It housed 10 doctors with various skills, mostly internal medicine. Most of his money had come from his father's oil business.

The other sides of the building were made of glass and overlooked a scenic valley below. There was an ornate garden in the back of the building that was a pleasant place for the patients and doctors alike.

He greeted the receptionist. "Good morning, Theresa. Qué pasa this fine morning? You are looking very lovely this morning."

"Thank you, Doctor," she said

"How is our patient load the rest of this week?"

"We've had a number of calls, referrals from throughout the city, some kind of an epidemic or something. Your first appointment is at nine-thirty."

Well, he thought, this would be good for business, but he didn't say it.

"Is my nurse here yet?" he asked. Nurses were in short supply; quality nurses were gems.

"Yes, Doctor, she has been here for a half hour," said the receptionist as she answered a ringing phone. "Dr. Sanchez' office, how can I help you?"

He walked down the hallway to his office and took note of the spring in the carpet. It was worth that little extra for quality padding.

He raised his eyes from the carpet and looked down the hall at his nurse coming out of his office with a chart in her hand. He didn't know what he would do without her. Marsha was a very good nurse.

He walked over to her as she stood next to a filing cabinet. She was nearly two inches taller than he and had the most beautiful long black hair. Her hair was in contrast with her uniform, which was always white even though he had never set a dress code.

"Good morning, Doctor, how are you doing?" She always spoke in a cheerful voice.

"Well, thank you. Sounds like we're having a busy day."

"Sounds like some sort of epidemic. Several people have been referred to us from throughout the city." She became serious.

"What are the symptoms?" he asked.

"They are having stomach pains, diarrhea, chills and fever. Sort of like the flu last year, only it doesn't respond to medicine. Sometimes there is rash and bruising."

His office was down the hall three doors, and he walked into it and hung his coat on an oak coat rack and put on a white coat with a stethoscope in the pocket. His office was small and unimpressive. He had the smallest office of all the doctors, small for this building.

On his desk was the morning edition of the *USA Today*. He sat in his chair and opened to the money section of the paper and opened it to the stock section. After reading for a few minutes, he closed the paper with a smile and threw it toward the wastebasket on the floor.

He hadn't been keeping up with the news because he had been golfing and recreating on a three-day cruise in the Caribbean, a business trip.

Marsha said from the other room, "Your first patient is here."

"All right," he said as he walked to waiting room one.

A 35-year-old woman with red hair sat uncomfortably in the chair in the first waiting room. She looked pale and weak.

"Ah, Mrs. Jonson," he said. "I've seen you before, is that correct?"

"Why, yes, Doctor. About three years ago I had an ulcer."

"How did that work out for you?"

"Just fine, Doctor."

"Is that why you're here, about that ulcer?" he asked.

"No, Doc, I'm not sure what is wrong," she said in a worried manner. "The nurse came in earlier to take pulse readings, and my temperature was 102.2," she said worriedly

"How long have you had this fever?" he asked.

"About three weeks," she answered. "I went to my family doctor, and he didn't have a clue, said he had several patients with the same symptoms, so he sent me here. I specifically asked for you. About two weeks ago I had diarrhea and had a slight fever for two weeks and a rash. I tried aspirin and Tylenol and Advil, and nothing helped."

"How do you feel otherwise?" he asked.

"Fine, except I'm tired all the time and getting weaker," she said.

"Had plenty of liquids?" he asked.

"Three or four glasses of water a day," she answered. "My doctor said to keep drinking fluids."

"Coffee?"

"No, I drink hot tea."

He looked at the chart and saw that she had good insurance.

The doctor's Mercedes was a 300d.

"Well," he said, "we better get you in for some tests."

"We'll schedule for a colonoscopy and see if you have another ulcer."

"Is there anything you can do for me now, Doctor?" she pleaded.

"We'll get you some medicine to help," he said.

51

"I've lost 10 pounds, and I'm worried," she said fearfully.

"Any other people in your family with symptoms?" he asked.

"My husband, he works at the bulk mail facility. He had this before I did, but he got better except for that rash."

"We'll do some blood work and get you on some vitamins. Maybe put you on a clear liquid diet for a week and get you back in here in a week or so. We'll get this under control." He knew that many times the symptoms of the virus would just go away.

"I'll have the nurse come in, and she can help you get to the receptionist and set that appointment," he told her.

"Thank you, Doctor," she said. "Do you have any idea what this might be?"

"Could be a number of things. I don't think you have a lot to worry about," he told her as he walked back to his office.

Good insurance, he thought, might get another two visits out of this one. If the problem resolved itself, which was sometimes the case, he would get the credit.

"You have a patient in exam room two, Doctor," said the nurse.

"Very well," he said. He walked to the lavatory and washed his hands, then walked out the door and into exam room two.

The patient was an elderly gentleman, perhaps 66 years old.

He remembered Mr. Thompson; he had come in about a year ago with a parasite he had picked up in

Arkansas deer hunting. After the tube down the throat and the tube up his butt and three office visits, he had been cured with a short dose of quinine.

Good insurance.

Good patient.

"What seems to be the problem, Mr. Thompson? I see from your chart that you have lost a little weight."

"Yeah, Doc, can't seem to keep anything down. Headache, stomach ache, diarrhea, fever."

"Have you been to see your family doctor?"

"No, Doc, I came to see you first. After old Doc Meeks died last year, I just haven't found someone I get along with. That young girl took over old Doc's practice, and I just try not to go there."

Mr. Thompson lived on the west side of St. Louis, and the last lady lived on the east side.

"How long has this been going on?"

"Well, Doc, about two weeks. I've tried Imodium and Tylenol, and none of it seemed to help. I even tried a liquid diet and I've still got the drizzling shits, and look at these funny bruises and rash on my arms."

"Okay, Mr. Thompson, get comfortable and I'll send the nurse back to get a little blood."

He walked out of the exam room and down the hall to where beautiful nurse Marsha was talking with another nurse.

"Marsha, please contact the CDC and see if they have heard of anything going on around here. We've got two people with the same rash. Maybe we've got a case of food poisoning going on here."

"Right away, Doctor." She walked back to her office and picked up the phone.

He returned to Mr. Thompson.

"We'll schedule a colonoscopy for next week and get to the bottom of this. Do you need any pain medicine?"

"No, Doc."

"We'll get you in here next Tuesday, and we'll do the procedure in the office upstairs. You know the drill, clear liquids the day before and that laxative and nothing to eat or drink after midnight. Marsha will give you all the instructions."

"Sure, Doc, no problem."

"I'll have the nurse set you up. See you next week, and drink plenty of liquids in the meantime."

He returned to his office.

The entire day went this way with several more patients with the same tell-tale rash. Many complaints were the same that day — diarrhea, stomach ache, fever, rash.

Marsha had brought a CDC report. Many people throughout the U.S. were having this same complaint, and it had all started about two weeks before.

Well, he thought, perhaps it's a virus and it will just work itself out.

The following day was the same as the day before. Ten patients with the same complaint: stomach ache, fever, weakness. Except the fevers were inching upward, and everyone seemed to have come down with it at about the same time.

The symptoms were getting worse.

He called his colleagues in the same field, and they too were reporting some sort of outbreak.

This stuff seemed to be contagious, as one family member would get it and another family member would come down with it.

The CDC was clueless; they had been swamped with calls from Internal Medicine doctors. There had been two deaths so far, one a three-year-old child and one a 72-year-old man.

His patients weren't getting better. He found himself washing his hands more and more. He had always been meticulous about washing his hands. Now he found that his hands were becoming chapped and raw from washing and he was using a hand crème.

He had always hated sick people.

* * * * *

Bob Wilson weighed 345 pounds. He loved the King Buffet, crab rangoon and scheszwan beef, and General's chicken and sweet and sour pork. He couldn't believe that they let him in the door. He had been asked to leave several restaurants in his career. But there were a lot of buffets and he was way ahead. Lo mein was his favorite. He had quit smoking two years ago and had gained a lot of weight.

Today there was some taste in this food that had an unusual flavor, sort of like the curry that pervaded Indian cooking. Usually he had had no trouble with two plates, but today he couldn't finish one.

He pushed his plate away and left a meager tip.

He decided he wouldn't come back here.

As he was leaving, he asked the manager. "Are you guys using some new kind of spice in this food?"

"As a matter of fact, we are using a new spice," said the manager.

"Well, you need to stop it," said Bob.

As he walked out the door, the manager smiled.

He had failed to notice that the food servers were wearing white gloves and coats and cough masks like were seen in operating rooms.

Had he noticed, it would have seemed odd to him.

Had he looked in the kitchen he would have seen that it looked like an operating room.

As he drove home, his left arm began to itch. He didn't make it from the car to the house before the diarrhea struck.

6

ERIC FISHER HAD been a coroner for the state of New York for 25 years. He was not looking forward to retirement; after this excitement he was afraid he might die of boredom.

He couldn't remember a case such as this. Six dead people in a pawnshop. The complaint was made when a passerby looked in the window. There was a man slumped over the counter, an elderly female customer lay on the floor as if she had just walked in the door and she was dead. The police had no idea what had gone on.

Apparently, the passerby had called the police and the dispatcher had sent a squad car with Officer Peterson and Sergeant Sanchez. These two officers had entered the shop and died immediately. Their bodies were lying just inside the door.

Now the police were afraid to enter the building. The coroner's office was called because it was the logical choice. They had also called the CDC who were supposed to meet him there.

The police had cordoned off the area in front of the shop. There were probably 100 people milling about near the tape, trying to get a better look.

Eric Fisher had driven up in his little white Ford Escort with the City of New York sticker on the side.

"Who's in charge?" he demanded.

"That would be me," said a tall young man in a new police uniform. "I am Officer Tidwell. And who might you be?"

Eric turned around, and on the back of the black jacket that he was wearing were the words "Coroner" in bold yellow letters.

"I'll say one thing, young man. You had best get this crowd to go away. We have no idea what we are dealing with, but we do know that it is very deadly. All these people are at risk, so please get us more room."

The young officer spoke with two other police officers, and they began to move the caution tape further from the scene.

"They won't move back," said a burly-looking policeman of perhaps 40.

"Let me help," said Officer Tidwell. He walked up to the caution tape and to the crowd and addressed the largest male. "You know, mister, what we've got here is about five dead people who died from some unknown gas or something. Now I can't stop you all from standing there just so long as you know that whatever it was might be contagious."

The crowd began to leave rapidly.

Eric smiled with amusement, what a refreshing thought — tell people the truth and they help you.

He addressed Officer Tidwell in a lower voice. "Officer, it might be wise to evacuate this street, at least until we can find out what we're up against."

Fifteen minutes later a white van pulled up to the tape. Two very different men stepped out of the van.

"Who's in charge?" the oldest one of them asked.

"That would be this officer here, Officer Tidwell," said Eric.

"Say, man, would you like get these people out of here?" the long-haired one asked.

"Yeah," said the one with glasses, "the farther the better."

"Are you Fisher?" asked the taller of the two.

"That's me," said Fisher.

The tall hippie stepped up and shook hands with Fisher. "Good to meet you. I'm Mutt, Tim Jackson, that is, and this is my young partner, Jeff, also known as Elliot Rubenstein. He's from Berkeley, but we try not to hold it against him."

The smaller man nodded his head in the direction of Fisher and walked toward the back of the van.

"Let me get this straight," said Jackson, "we've got a few bodies in that pawn shop. Has anyone else tried to go in there?"

"Just the two officers that drove up in that patrol car," Fisher said, and pointed to a black sedan with the lights still flashing. "You can just make out their bodies just there inside the door," he said as he moved his pointing finger in an arching motion.

"How much time has elapsed since they fell?"

"One hour and 57 minutes," he said as he glanced at his watch. "No, make that 59 minutes."

Jackson turned without another word and walked to the back of the van. The two men emerged a short time later fully dressed in white protective suits with oxygen bottles and full head protection.

The door was still propped open with the feet of the last customer, and they had to clamber over the bodies of the two officers.

The taller one removed a sample jar from a side pocket and opened it and waved it around in the air and put the lid back on. They did this at three different locations.

The older one pointed to the air conditioning ducts and said through the microphone, "Let's get someone to kill the power to this building." As they turned to leave, one of the men dragged the body away from the door so that it would close. They walked back to the van, and 30 minutes later they emerged from the van still dressed in white clothes.

"It's a foreign agent, it's airborne, it's deadly. We need to get these back to the lab," the red-haired man said as he walked toward Officer Tidwell. "Please see that no one enters or leaves the building."

"But we have to get the bodies out of there," said the officer.

"In due time, Captain. We need to know what we're dealing with and we should know in an hour or so. Luckily, home is only three blocks from here. Please have someone shut off the electricity to the building. We'll be right back."

The skinny one turned to Eric and said, "In this case no news is bad news. Whatever it is doesn't match with any of a dozen or so common bugs that could cause this. We'll let you know; we need to fight our way through the crowd."

This was a hell of a note, he thought to himself; he had five bodies that he couldn't get to. He gave his card to Officer Tidwell and said, "My cell number is on the card. Call me as soon as you can. Please fill your captain in on this so far." He got back in his car and drove back to his office.

The white van drove off through the crowd.

* * * * *

Eric just stepped into his office when the phone rang. A husky male voice on the line said, "This is Bob Carmichael from the CDC. We've studied this little bug of yours and don't have a clue what it is. It's a fast-acting airborne, waterborne something that is obviously extremely toxic."

"What are you saying, that we have some new bug loose that's killing people?"

"We just know that anyone around that building is subject to being killed. It is like an anthrax that is more virulent than we've seen."

"Is there any way to kill it?"

"If we could find the source, perhaps we could burn it out."

"You say this was a coin dealer?"

"It was a pawn shop that deals in everything — coins, guns, antiques, a coin dealer."

"Perhaps a customer brought in something and opened it up and it killed them all. "Perhaps it's in a box or jar or urn and we could contain it."

"I'd like to send in two people in suits, and we'll try to find the source. We need to make sure that the whole block is contained. We have no idea how far this could spread, whatever it is."

Eric called the policeman in charge and told him what he'd been told and reinforced the idea that the whole block must be isolated.

Mutt and Jeff arrived back at the pawnshop. The police were pushing back the tape where a small group of people had gathered.

They stopped their van in the middle of the street near the yellow tape and a few moments later emerged wearing oxygen suits. As they approached the pawnshop, they discovered that the policeman who had been standing outside the door was now sitting on the sidewalk leaning against the wall, apparently asleep. They assumed that whatever it was had crept out of the building and claimed another victim.

This was seven victims. In one spot at one time.

They pulled the dead policeman's body away from the door and entered the place of death. They crawled across the elderly lady, across the two police victims, and to the spot where the owner was slumped dead across the counter.

They confirmed that the dead owner had nothing in his hands. They worked around the counter to see if they had missed something.

Behind the counter was an old oak roll-top desk that was covered with an assortment of papers and coin books. There were numerous cubbyholes in the desk, filled with coins and papers. The top of the desk was covered with felt, faded green in color. They could smell nothing, but they imagined that it smelled musty. In front of the desk was an old oak swivel chair. Mutt pulled the chair out of the way.

On the desk was a magnifying glass attached to a swivel arm, and there was a round fluorescent lamp around the glass. Under the glass was a coin about the size of a silver dollar. It had an imprint in the likeness of the Statue of Liberty and looked to be stamped of pure silver. He picked up a pencil out of a coffee cup and flipped the coin over. The other side of the coin had an American eagle and the words "God Bless America." So this seemed to be the kind of a coin that someone would buy as a souvenir from the Statue of Liberty.

There was another coin identical to the first, lying next to the green counter. There had been a cup of coffee that had spilled, and the edge of the coin was laying in a puddle of coffee as if it had been laid aside in order to look at the other coin and had accidentally had coffee spilled on it. In the center of the coin there was a space about the size of a dime that appeared to be discolored. He moved the second coin under the magnifying glass and could see that the center of the coin was filled with a blue jelly much like a tootsie roll, like a jelly donut.

The first one said to the second one there, "I have no idea what this is, but I bet this is our source. What do you suppose this is?"

The blond man admitted that he also had no idea.

Jeff picked up the wet coin with the tweezers that were lying beside the glass and placed it in a small zip-lock bag he had extracted from his tool belt. He then placed the bag in a small jar that also came from the tool belt. He then did the same with the other coin, and then laid them on the counter next to the dead shop owner.

After ten minutes they found nothing else suspicious and concluded that this was their best bet. They stumbled back over the dead bodies and out the door carrying the glass jars and carried the samples to their van.

The street was quiet, the police held a line a block away.

They drove rapidly back to their laboratory.

* * * * *

In the laboratory under a fume hood they were able to look at the coin in greater detail. The director of the laboratory, Dr. Brice Adams, was heavily involved in this investigation. As they entered the van, they had placed the jars in a sealed box and had inserted the box into the fume hood. They turned on the hood and used remote hands to open the box and to extract the jars and their content. They used a syringe to take a sample of the blue gel to the slides of a microscope. Ten minutes later the computer spit out a response.

"Good lord, Doctor, I've never seen such a concentration in my life," said the man with the limp. "Let's get another sample."

"This coin is hollowed out. We have the center filled with this gelatinous substance, and the metal is impervious to the gel but appears to dissolve in water. It looks to be metal, but is a water-soluble paste very like those little silver balls that one decorates cakes with."

"This coin was designed to kill a lot of people. It was made specifically to be placed in a building, and the center would dissolve and this substance would be released in the air. It could be used in a building or in a water supply."

"Where did it come from?

"One of these customers must have brought these coins in not knowing what they were."

"Let's go back to the building and see if the air is still contaminated," said Jeff.

"Now that we know what we are dealing with,

there is a filter that we can use to clear the air out of the building and to exchange it with good air, but it will take some time.

* * * * *

Three days later the air had been cleared. It was determined that the bodies should be cremated in place.

The police lifted the wallets of the victims; prints and pictures had been taken. Pictures and ID had been compared.

Elf Rimsdale, an 18-year-old punk, was one of the victims. He had a long rap sheet and had probably pick-pocketed the coins and had brought them in to fence them.

The other two victims were no help. A mystery, 63-year-old Gladys Jenkins, a retired school teacher who lived alone up the street who may have stopped in on her way home.

The man, 27-year-old Scott Frye, lived with his mother. She told the police that he had a girlfriend who worked as a customs inspector at LaGuardia airport.

The police considered this to be a murder investigation. They put out an APB for Anne Caruthers who was working at the airport. They considered her to be armed and dangerous.

Two uniforms entered the airport; she was working at the metal detector counter at LaGuardia at gate 52, where she always worked.

The officers approached the girl and asked, "Would you please come with us?"

"What is this about, officers?" she asked, fear entering her voice.

"Just please come with us."

One officer had his hand on his gun and the other had his hand on his baton.

"Let me get my purse."

"No, let me get it for you. Where is it?" said the officer.

"Under the counter."

He reached under the counter and got the purse.

The officer carried the purse as they led the girl out of the airport. They helped her into the back of the squad car. The officer with the purse got into the passenger's seat front, and the car drove off with squealing tires.

They parked the car in the street in front of the precinct building and helped the girl from the back seat of the car and led her, handcuffed, one on each side up the stairs, past the desk sergeant and up the stairs to the third floor.

The one partner began to cough. "Get him cigarette," said the second. "I thought you were going to quit."

The other partner tried to answer, but was struck by a fit of coughing.

They brought the girl into the office

"This is Lieutenant Willerson."

The Lieutenant looked at the girl. "Are you Anne Corruthers?"

"Yes, I am," she said.

"Sit down, please."

She sat in the chair in front of the desk

"What is this all about?" she asked.

He threw a picture in front of her, "Have you ever seen one of these?" he asked.

She immediately started to cry.

"I only did it once," she cried. "Oh, please, don't tell my boss, I'll lose my job. I didn't think she would miss them. She was dressed so well. I'll give them back. No, wait. I might not be able to; I'll pay for them somehow. I've got one I can give back," she said as she reached for her purse.

"Wait!" he screamed, "you've got one in your purse?"

"Yes, right here," she said, as her hand went to her purse.

"Stop, don't touch a thing!" said Willerson in a shaking voice. "Just sit still. Don't move."

He went to the phone and called the CDC office. "We seem to have one more of these coins.

"Don't touch it, and you should clear the building," came the voice over the phone.

"That's a ten-four."

He walked out of his office, looked back at the girl and said, "Please come with me. Leave the purse. Sergeant, would you please keep an eye on this girl? Captain, please see that this building is evacuated. Tell them we have a bomb scare."

The room was now filled with prostitutes and screaming people; he had said bomb threat too loudly.

Chaos reigned.

His whole life had meant following orders. The sergeant led all the people out the door. One young prisoner tried to use this as a means of escape; he bolted out the door and down the hallway with two officers following him.

One prisoner, a well-dressed man in his thirties, grabbed a gun and turned and fired two shots into the woman beside him.

"There, you bitch," he said. "I bet you're sorry now." The man dropped the gun and danced around the body of the fallen woman. Two uniforms wrestled him to the ground.

"Call an ambulance. Somebody please call an ambulance," one of the officers screamed.

Anne screamed at the top of her lungs.

The sergeant took her into an adjoining room and locked the door. "Look, you stay here, okay? You're not in any real trouble. Okay, those coins can't be worth more than a couple of dollars each. But they have some sort of virus on them," he said, trying to be her friend.

An ambulance finally arrived, and two attendants brought a gurney up and covered the body with a sheet.

As they carried the body out the door, the husband, now in handcuffs, spat on the body.

"Are you happy now, you bitch?" he said. "Glad you called the cops on me now?"

"Get this man in some leg irons, Sergeant," the Lieutenant said, "and I want statements from everybody in this room."

"Okay, Lieutenant."

Two men entered the room wearing white suits with air tanks.

"Where's the Lieutenant?" asked one of the men.

"I'm back in here." The lieutenant had raised his voice to be heard above the crowd noise.

"Where is the coin?" asked the other man in the white suit.

"It's in that room on a chair in a purse." The lieutenant pointed in the direction of the room.

They took the purse, coin and all, and put them all in a big zip-lock bag, and this they placed in a large plastic container and snapped the lid tightly. They had a little vacuum hose that put a slight vacuum on the container.

"This is just in case we have a small leak," said the one.

"Thank God that's over," said the Lieutenant as he watched the two men leave.

"What was all the fuss about?" asked the girl. "It was just a coin."

"I'll explain in a minute."

"How'd you find out about me? Did Scott tell? Have you arrested that SOB again? Where is he, that low-life piece of shit?"

"I'm not at liberty to tell at this time," said the Lieutenant. "Just answer my questions."

"I want a lawyer," the girl said in a startling display of courage.

"This will be a lot easier if you would just answer the questions. Look, you're not in any real trouble. We think you lifted a couple of cheap coins, but it's not you we want. Let me just ask you a couple of simple questions, and if you still feel you need a lawyer then we'll get you one, okay?" the Lieutenant said in a pleading voice.

"Okay," the girl relented. "Where did the coins come from? You know, I've seen several of them for the last two days. Well, maybe for the last week I've seen quite a few of these come through the metal detectors. They were shiny and new and came from the Statue of Liberty. People would come through the metal detectors, and it would beep and they would put the coins and keys and stuff in the tray. My aunt had come to visit me and didn't get to see the Statue of Liberty because it was raining that day, and I thought what a perfect present. Well, I tried several places to buy one, and I even went to the Statue and they didn't know what I was talking about, so when this lady came through with ten of them I figured she wouldn't miss a couple. So I palmed three of them, and when she put her things back in her pockets she didn't say a word and just walked out real fast. Oriental man and his wife, mid-50s. Typical tourists. I just took three of them."

"Didn't she miss them?" asked the man.

"He was having trouble with his wife at the time. She was screaming about her camera, and she just grabbed her stuff and went on through."

"So you say you've seen quite a few of these?"

"Probably 30 or so in the last week."

"They all had the Statue?"

"And an eagle."

"Scott said he was sure we could get a hundred dollars apiece out of them. I kept one for Aunt Gracie and gave the others to Scott. We really need to pay the electric bill. They said they were going to turn off my electricity. I really can't lose my job. I'll pay anything you want; I'll pay anything. Just please don't make me lose my job; I need the health insurance."

"That's out of my hands." The man showed no pity. He spoke loudly, "Sergeant Groves, bring Truman and Filmore in with you right away."

"What time of day did this happen?"

"'Let's see, it was right before lunch and I take my lunch at one, so it would have been around 12:45 two days ago. I remember I was really hungry."

The man spoke to the sergeant. "Okay, Sergeant, go to the head of security and get the video tapes from around 12:30 to 12:45 two days ago.

What was the gate number, honey?"

"Twelve," she said.

"Gate 12, Sergeant. Get the films from gate 12."

"Yes, sir."

"Filmore, please take this young lady to a detention cell."

"I thought you said I wasn't under arrest?" she protested.

"You're not, I just need you to watch these films. Okay?"

"Do it now, Sergeant."

"Yes, sir," as he led the girl away.

"Get her something to drink, please, Sergeant"

"Yes, sir."

"What about Scott?" she asked. "Where is Scott?"

"I'll explain everything. But not right now."

He walked back to his desk and dialed a number. "Judy, hi, could you please get me the FBI on the phone? Thank you."

In less than a minute the phone rang.

"They have an agent in the building; they can send them right up," the lady's voice said.

"Very well, send them up," he said.

Ten minutes later there was a knock on the door. "Come in," said the Lieutenant.

Two men entered the room. One was Hawaiian, with an Hawaiian shirt; the other was small and Oriental. "I'm Agent Smith, and this is Agent Jones," said the Hawaiian.

"Great," said the Lieutenant. "Smith, could you stay here and, Jones, could you wait outside?" he asked.

"We're a team, sir."

"Very well." He walked to the intercom.

"Sergeant, could you come in here for a minute?" he spoke in the intercom.

The Sergeant entered.

"This is Agent Smith and Agent Jones. Could you please take one of them to see the girl?"

The Sergeant and Agent Jones left the room together.

"Now, Smith, please shut the door and sit down. I hope you can appreciate the gravity of our problem. We have six dead people. It is a poisoning; I think it is caused by Chinese terrorists."

When he was done, Smith said, "My gosh, this has been going on for two weeks?"

"I hope you can appreciate that I want to keep this on a need-to-know basis, and the fewer people who know about this, the better we will all be," said the Lieutenant in a grave voice.

"Lieutenant, I think you're right. I'll get my superiors on this." He walked out the door. He walked down the hall to where the girl was and opened the door. "Come on, Jones, we have work to do."

They walked out of the station and down the street.

"What's the deal?" asked Jones.

"Remember Rudy's pawn shop?" asked Smith.

"Oh, shit," said Jones.

They walked to their blue sedan parked in the

street, and Smith began to drive.

"So what did the Lieutenant say?" asked Jones.

In a rapid manner Smith gave Jones a brief run-down of what the Lieutenant had said.

"So it's up to us to pass the word?" asked Jones.

"I told him we would get right on it," said Smith.

Jones pointed to the left. "Look down that alley, Smith. Wasn't that Tommy Fenwick? Isn't this his neighborhood?"

"Yes, it is," said Smith. "We've looked for that punk for three weeks. Let's get him."

"We shouldn't take the time."

"Three weeks."

They parked the car and Jones said, "I think he ran behind that dumpster."

They both drew their guns and walked carefully to the dumpster. Smith kicked a can by mistake, and it awakened a wino who had been curled up in news-papers behind the dumpster.

Jones slowed down to let Smith get ahead of him and said, "You know that Lieutenant?"

"Yeah, what about him?" asked Smith.

"You know, he was right to not trust me." As he said this, he shot Smith three times in the back.

Smith's eyes opened wide and he fell to the ground

Jones turned to the wino and shot him twice. He rolled Smith over and took the wallet out of his jacket pocket and his gun. He dragged the body to the dumpster and forced the body inside.

He left the transient where he lay. He dusted off his overcoat and walked quickly back to the car and got behind the wheel. He began to beat both fists against the steering wheel, as he screamed, "Shit, shit,

shit." Each time he screamed, he hit the steering wheel. He opened the door, got out of the car and slammed the door. He walked back into the alleyway and back to the dumpster. He dragged a barrel away from the building so that he could climb up high enough to see into the dumpster. He had to rummage around in Smith's pockets, but he finally found the keys and walked back to the car, started it and drove off.

As he got back into traffic, he took out his cell phone and dialed a number. "This is Jones."

"Good morning."

"Call mother and tell her to come over for dinner tonight."

"Not tomorrow?"

"It has to be tonight."

"Very well."

7

THIS BEGAN A series of events that had been planned for several years. The accident at the coin shop created a threat that the surprise would be lost.

Jones had been a deep cover agent, and to begin the process a day early would not really hurt. Jones made three identical phone calls to three different numbers. Each time he said merely, "Mother is coming to dinner tonight."

"Mother is coming to dinner tonight, that's tonight."

All of the old couples were in place. They had been slowly heading toward their destinations for a week now. Fifty couples had come to America each with ten discs. Enough to sicken or kill most of America. Their job was to poison the water supply of the U.S.

Each couple had been given $8,000 and a primary destination. They were to take public transportation to their target city, rent a car if possible, and to the greatest extent possible remain inconspicuous.

There was a predetermined signal that would cause them to go into action, at which time they would jump into the rental cars, drive to the target water supplies and simply drop a coin in the water. The gelatin in the discs had been developed over the years. One drop could destroy a large water supply and turn it into a toxic brew.

As a rule, Americans were unaware of how important water was to their very survival. Like so many other things, Americans took their water for granted; they turned on the tap and out flowed gallons and gallons of clean drinking water. Much of the world only dreamed of this. The threat posed by the contamination of the drinking water could have been made far less great had Americans merely thought about it and kept a few gallons of clean water on the shelf, and looked for sources other than the tap.

* * * * *

The agents were to watch the national news and read *USA Today* every day and wait for the signal. Just the front page, they would know when it was time. Three phone calls for mother to come to dinner released three operatives who had been waiting for six months, and they knew where to go.

Brent Hume was one of these who had made a circuitous journey from Mexico across the border with a suitcase that was now sitting near the door of the motel room. When the call was received, he immediately abandoned everything in the room, made one last stop in the restroom, washed his hands and face, combed his hair, looked in the mirror and smiled and walked out the door with the suitcase.

It was a large suitcase and took both hands to drag it out the door. The suitcase contained three heat-seeking missiles with launchers. He dragged the suitcase across the small parking lot and set it behind the rental car. He walked around to the driver's door, opened it and reached in and released the trunk. He walked back to the rear of the car, and with great effort lifted the heavy bag into the trunk. He gently shut the trunk, walked back around to the driver's door, got in and started the car. He then drove like an old man to his destination, an old abandoned warehouse just south of the airport in St. Louis. Large windows on the second floor faced the airport and gave him a good view of planes as they lifted off the runway.

A computer in his room was tuned into the Internet and had given him the flight data for the airport for the day, and he had determined the largest plane with the destination of Tel-Aviv. He had called the airport, and all flights were on time. What cities would this plane have landed in on the way here? How many passengers would be on board? How many children? he wondered.

* * * * *

The world would see this as just another act of terrorism. Just another Palestinian attack against the Jews. His job was to get this one plane and perhaps another. It would be the headline newsmaker. There were three men just like him; this would be a day to remember.

The letter had been written already claiming responsibility. A new terrorist group called the "Sons of Palestine."

The targeting of the Israeli airplanes was a stroke of genius. He parked in front of the warehouse and removed the bag from the trunk. He dragged it to the door and fumbled for the key. He pulled the bag into the building and up the stairs. The second floor was empty except for a folding chair sitting in front of the large window with a tripod standing beside it and a small table and chair.

He hurried back to the car and removed a small bag of tools. He took the tools upstairs and began to remove the large window from its frame When he was done, he had created an opening that was four feet wide and six feet tall.

While he was removing the window, several planes had taken off from the airport half a mile away. With the window removed, the noise level was quite intense.

He walked to the small table and chair near the window and opened the cover of a laptop computer, pressed a button, and while he waited for it to boot up, he brought his feet up to the desk top, placed his hands behind his head and leaning back closed his eyes. In a few short moments his computer made a loud dinging sound, and he quickly brought his feet down to the floor and pressed a few keys and watched the screen intently as he picked up a signal from the Internet.

He typed in a few letters and soon was rewarded with a screen that showed the status of the flights leaving the airport. He checked his watch, walked to the window, took a pair of binoculars from the bag and watched out of the window. Shortly he heard a plane taking off; he watched it for a few minutes through the binoculars and returned to the table with a smile on his face.

He double-checked the status of United flight 412 on the computer, walked to the large suitcase and began to load the rocket tube with one of the three missiles. He attached the rocket tube to the tripod, checked the wiring at the rear of the tube and practiced by aiming at the next airliner that took off.

"Bull's eye," he said out loud.

He had selected this flight because there were two large planes in a row, and they were usually fully loaded.

Flight 412 was a Boeing 747, to be followed by a

Boeing 767 bound for Cincinnati.

He checked his watch one last time and was rewarded with a loud noise at the appropriate time of departure. The large plane came into view, straining toward the heavens. He aimed the weapon, counted to ten slowly and squeezed the trigger. The room was filled with a loud noise and smoke as the small missile streaked out of the window. He had waited long enough that the second plane would be committed to the takeoff. The missile exploded nearly three-quarters of a mile away in the right rear engine of the doomed plane.

As the missile streaked toward the first plane, he quickly reloaded the tube and fired a second missile at the smaller plane that had followed flight 412, TWA flight 615. The missile struck the unfortunate plane in the left wing engine, and this followed the other to the ground in a ball of flames. Two planes loaded with fuel would cause a great lot of damage, and this same thing was happening right now at two other airports.

The big news of the day was that an Arab terrorist group had taken credit for the downing of five airliners.

This closed the airports.

* * * * *

The General woke from a deep sleep; heavy turbulence had shaken the big plane. He looked around the fuselage and saw only sleeping soldiers. The lights had been turned down low, and this created a restful atmosphere, except for the steady drone of the engines.

He was unaware that his plan had been pushed forward a day. At this final stage he would not have allowed it, but some things were out of his control.

His mind began to contemplate the stages of his plan. It was to begin with the insertion of sleeper agents whose duty was to perform various tasks that would weaken America's defenses.

The several planes would be shot down, and panic would ensue that would cause the trains to be overloaded; this would also stop air travel. It put everyone on full alert. This would stop the departure of any troops from the Middle East and would keep them safely away from home.

The American army had spread itself so thin by playing policeman throughout the world that there were not enough troops to guard the home fronts. Everyone in America had become complacent, cocksure of themselves; they had failed to remember that Custer's last stand was only two generations before.

It had been discovered years before in the '50s that the candidate who spent the most money would win most elections. It was a simple matter then to wait patiently for the proper candidate and then pour the money in. Once a candidate was elected, the laws had been manipulated that it was nearly impossible to unseat him.

Millions had been spent lining the pockets of the various special interest lobbies and the various political parties. It had been easy to convince the well-paid congress that we must police the globe, to weaken the home front.

Hundreds of agents had been trained and sent into this country.

The agents in the country knew that these planes would be targeted. It was the signal they had been waiting for. Very much like a rocket shot into the night sky. Word of these disasters would be front-page news in every newspaper in the land and the topic of conversation at every table and on every TV show.

As soon as the news became public, the sleepers sprang into action. There were a few major cities that used aquifers as their water supply. Some cities used lakes, and some supplies were guarded; most were not, the public was allowed ready access to boat and swim on these waters at will.

At thousands of locations throughout the U.S., a harmless-looking couple would walk to the water's edge and drop a lucky coin in the water. They would then get back into their rental car and drive to the next location until the discs were all gone. Or until some mistake exposed them to the agent and they perished like the pawnshop victims.

These coins were designed not so much to kill as to sicken the population and fill the hospitals and create a state of panic and confusion. The population of the U.S. had grown to be fat and content and lazy and spoiled. Their grandparents knew hardship, but the Nintendo generation was ill-equipped to deal with a crisis.

The second phase of the attack was now to begin, an attack on the soft underbelly of the U.S., the weakest link, the electrical grid.

Thirty agents, specially trained and crafty had been infiltrating this country for the past 12 months. They had purchased small houses and had begun to live a normal American life. The location of these select houses was to coincide with the location of weak spots in the great American electrical grid.

The General had been in Chicago during a short

blackout years before. Like most Americans, he had never given electricity much thought, just like the water supply; it was always there. He and 35 other delegates had waited out the blackout in a seminar room that had become well-lit when they had opened the blinds. The presenter had some knowledge of electricity in the U.S. and had explained the situation. The General had taken notes. He remembered that there is a great electrical grid that is a series of poles and wires and transformers and substations that connect most of the high and medium voltage electricity in the United States and Canada. Its failure has been the cause of what is known as blackouts. It crisscrosses various places in the U.S., and various power plants are connected together. It is necessary to have large magnets that wires pass through to create electricity. Those magnets must be created by electricity. Therefore it takes electricity to make electricity. It's like a big house of cards waiting to topple.

The presenter had explained that power plants contain one-of-a-kind components. If these transformers and relays are destroyed, it could take months to rebuild them. He explained that Americans should be made aware that the electrical grid in this country is weak, exposed and overloaded, and that every American should take whatever steps necessary to prepare to survive without electricity for several months at a time.

The General knew this would be part of his plan. What a fatal weakness!

* * * * *

The crews were composed of six men each, four soldiers with automatic weapons, grenade launchers

82

and hand grenades. Their job was to protect the two engineers. The engineers' job was to wreck the grid.

Millions of dollars in cash and weapons were easily smuggled into the country through the port in California that was controlled by the Chinese government. Custom officials had either been easily bribed or destroyed. Money was the key; spread enough around and it was possible to get the right man in the right job, and through transfers and intimidation it was possible to get anything done. Specially built SUVs had been shipped and unloaded.

The voltage at the power plants was high enough that all that needed to be destroyed was the transformer that raised the initial voltage at the plant. These transformers sat beside the plants and were surrounded by chain link fences.

Word came that the aircraft had been destroyed. Team number four knew that it was their turn to go.

Target — the Exeter Power Plant, 276-Megawatt Coal Fired.

They left the house where they had been living. It was the middle of the morning; the sun was shining. A five-mile drive down a country road led them to within a quarter-mile of the power plant. It was a simple matter to take the large caliber rifle and to place one armor-piercing bullet through the transformer housing. The transformer burst into flames and the oil began to burn.

There was not another transformer like this one in existence; they were built to order. And it would take a good six months to build a replacement. That was six months if there was electricity. With the electrical grid in the country down, it could be a very long time before that plant came back on line.

The fault currents within the transformer easily destroyed the windings, and the fire burned the insulation. Humpty Dumpty.

When the transformer went, the plant went offline, forever.

This crew was trained to not only shut down this power plant, but to see to it that it did not come back on line. With ruthless efficiency they set about their work. They easily overcame the guards and proceeded to efficiently kill everyone associated with the plant. They had taken control of the single road that came to the plant, and they shot everyone trying to enter. They had even gone so far as to learn the names and home addresses of the people who kept the plant going, and two of the crew went from house to house murdering the workers and their families and their pets.

No one in America was prepared for this ruthless assault.

When the big red bucket truck pulled into the driveway and the workers walked across the lawn with tool pouches on, no one suspected that within that tool pouch there was an automatic pistol with silencer.

Once they gained access to the control room, they used charges that were designed to create a great amount of heat and fire that would destroy all of the electronic circuitry in the computers and make the control room a mass of burned wiring. Their next stop was 50 miles away at the Lock Lear plant where the same thing happened.

They destroyed the transformers and the crew. They placed booby traps at the entrance to the units that would stop the replacements.

The crews had developed small rockets attached to conductive thread. These were fired over the high voltage lines after the plants were shut down. If the plants were to come back on line, these threads would cause a phase-to-phase fault that would cause the plant to shut back down.

The crews also had chain saws that they used to fell certain select poles. They knew that the effects of the power grid failure on the U.S. would be enormous.

Americans had no idea that electricity powered everything. No electricity, no computers, no phones, no lights, no heat, no water. People sat at their desks with nothing to do. Most commerce came to a stand-still, cash registers would not work, sales people had no idea how much to charge, and consumers had no way to pay. The banks were closed, just like the great depression. People couldn't get to their money, but the bills just kept coming.

Most service stations shut down.

The street lights quit working.

The grocery stores shut down.

All the fast food stores shut down.

People were stuck in their homes with no food, water, or TV.

The giant pumps that fed the water treatment plants and the sewage treatment plants quit. This caused the sewers to back up into the basements of many homes.

The General had determined that it would take three days for the U.S. to destroy itself. The people would break down the doors of stores and steal food.

Everywhere there would be panic and confusion.

The cities would be especially affected.

City dwellers would try to leave the cities; the bridges would be full of stalled cars, busses and trucks, the entire super highway system clogged with now useless shells of cars. The highway system, designed by Eisenhower to facilitate troop movement, would be useless.

Gangs from the cities would descend upon the country and kill for food.

The natural gas that fed the U.S. came from great wells. The pumps that pumped the natural gas used natural gas to drive them. From time to time these natural gas lines rose above ground; here they were vulnerable.

The food would be gone, the water contaminated. Into this mess would come an armada of planes filled with specially trained ruthless soldiers. The planes came in low and fast and landed at the airports next to the Syracuse buildings.

Most of the airports would be taken over without a fight.

The Syracuse buildings were used as a staging area for the drops. The key to success was the ruthlessness of the troops.

The planes would land and the troops would scour the countryside for SUVs, big four-wheel drive vehicles designed to hold several men. Perfect for an army.

The General never could understand the common man's fascination with big gas-guzzlers, but they sure fit well in his plan.

8

MARY BROWN HUNG up the phone after having spoken with Tom. She put the phone back in the cradle of its wall holder; she was standing in a kitchen with a gleaming white counter top and a stainless steel sink, the air fragrant with the smell of coffee brewing. She should have had her coffee before she talked to Tom, but she wanted to talk to him before he got out of the house and into the field.

She walked to the window and looked out on the immaculate city dweller lawn and thought about Tom. She really did love him. She knew exactly what he would say about this lawn. Why in the world would someone fertilize grass and pollute the ground water just so you would have to mow it?

She thought back to how they had met. All the trouble she had put him through.

Her thoughts were interrupted by the sound of bare feet running across the clean wooden floor. It was her 13-year-old daughter, small and athletic, with long brown hair done up into a ponytail. She wore summer clothes, shorts and a tank top.

"What's for breakfast, Mom?"

"Whatever it is that you want to cook me would be just fine."

"Waffles!" the little girl said. "I feel just like a waffle. Not just any old waffle, but a Belgian waffle with pecans, real maple syrup and blueberries."

"Let's see if your aunt's got some waffle mix here. I expect she could make it from scratch."

She opened the refrigerator door and perused the contents. There was fresh cream and milk and eggs. Looks like you can take the girl out of the country but can't take the country out of the girl, she thought to herself. But the bottom shelf was filled with beer; this was her sister's problem. This is one of the reasons she had come. They had grown apart over the years, and last night Mary had had more than her share of beer. The two sisters had talked into the wee hours of the morning. Her head felt stuffy. She was on vacation.

She went through the cupboards looking for waffle mix. She found the waffle iron; it was on the second shelf to the left of the sink. It was inserted in a plastic bag with a wire tie around it. That was Ashlee all over. She set it on the counter.

"Let's see, waffles with pecans and blueberries?" Just the thought made Mary sick to her stomach after last night's binge.

"Let's look for blueberries; strawberries we have, blueberries we have not; peaches we have, blueberries we have not. Look, the store's just two blocks away; I can easily walk that far, and the morning air will do me good. Let me take a quick shower, change into some decent clothes and we'll walk down to the store."

"I'll even buy some blueberries and pecans. In the meantime, why don't you run in and wake your aunt up and tell her we're going to the store. See if she needs anything and remind her she promised to take us to the zoo today." If Ashlee felt as rough as Mary, let someone else face the wrath.

"Okay, Mama," the young girl said, as she turned and ran down the hallway.

Mary walked into the guest bedroom and shut the door, tossed her robe on the bed, kicked off her slippers, pulled her nightgown over her head, pitched it onto the bed and walked toward the bathroom. As she passed the full-length mirror, she stopped to look at herself.

Not bad for an old lady, she thought. She pulled in her stomach just a bit, squared her shoulders and turned sideways. Not bad for three kids. She cupped her breasts in her hands and raised them slightly, then released them. She stepped one step closer to the mirror and looked into her own blue eyes, fluffed her long light brown hair and placed her two index fingers at the corners of her eyes and pulled the skin of her face tight. "Not bad at all," she said as she walked into the bathroom, "not bad for 42."

She emerged from the bathroom 15 minutes later with her hair wrapped in a towel. She rummaged in the suitcase for underwear and bra and put these on. She walked to the closet and selected a white cotton shirt with a button front and a blue plaid skirt. She sat on the edge of the bed and slipped on a pair of sandals. She walked into the kitchen area, and her sister was sitting at the counter on a barstool with her head lying on her folded arms on the counter.

The daughter was filling a cup with coffee. *Children are wonderful,* she thought.

The young girl brought a cup of coffee to her sister, Ashlee.

"How do we feel this morning, little sister?" Mary asked in a voice too loud.

"Oh, man," said the girl, "drinking too much is its own punishment."

"You have to get chipper. We have to see the zoo this morning. I called Tom and he said to push the car down into the street and put a piece of cardboard or plywood or something under it to catch the leak. He's going to bring the trailer down and pick up us and the car. He wasn't very happy about this, I can tell you."

"Oh, good, so Tom will be down in a couple of days?"

"The way he talked, he'd be able to get down here later today or tomorrow. We'll still have time for that zoo trip."

"Are you absolutely sure I couldn't have slept another couple of hours?"

"No, because my lovely daughter here, your niece, decided she wanted waffles with pecans and blueberries for breakfast, and they sounded pretty good to me, so I'm off to the store. Is there anything you need while I'm out?"

"Where are you going?"

"Just down the store to the Hy-Vee."

"The keys are in my car in the garage."

"No, thanks. I think I'll walk. The fresh air will do me good. Sort of clear up the cobwebs."

"There is one thing I need, but you'll need to take the car. I need an aspirin this big," she said as she held her hands in front of her as though she were holding a very large beach ball.

Mary laughed.

Mary walked across the room to her purse and brought forth, after some digging, a bottle. She walked across the room and set the bottle on the counter next to Ashlee.

"Here," she said. "Brand new and never been used. Help yourself. I'll get another bottle at the store. You know we used to be able to buy about a million of these for a dollar; now the plain old aspirin has gotten hard to come by. They've got coated aspirin and children's aspirin and aspirin for old people and aspirin in capsules. I used to stick with Bayer until Tom went on one of his buy-American kicks. I try to take one a day since I turned 30. It's supposed to help with my little heart, my little colon, my little blood pressure, and today your little hangover." She tapped Ashlee gently on the top of the head.

"I'll take this aspirin, but what I really need is another beer."

"A little of the hair of the dog that bit you? As I recall, we had this discussion last night. As I recall, we decided that we're going to slow down on that drinking; our livers will love us for it."

"Okay, no beer before lunch."

"That was good in the old college days when we were bullet-proof, but now I've decided to not drink until the sun goes down."

She walked to the big sliding door and opened the blinds, and the sun came streaming into the room.

"My, what agony," Ashlee said.

Mary opened the sliding door and stepped out on the deck. She stepped to the railing, removed the towel from her head and shook her long hair in the breeze.

She flung her head backwards and used both hands to straighten her hair onto her back.

"Mary Two," she said. "Oh, come here, dear."

The little girl came to the door.

"Yes, Mother dear," she said.

"Would you please go to my purse and get my big comb?"

The girl disappeared into the house and returned a short time later with a big red comb. Mary began to comb her hair from the bottom up.

"You've really got pretty long hair, Mom."

"This is mostly for your father, honey. Every time I get it cut or try something else, he gets this sour look on his face. He doesn't say a word, but I know what he's thinking. He's said many times that the best-looking hair on a woman is to just keep it clean and brush the shit out of it. And there was this time that I got it cut and old Mr. Jenkins at the pharmacy thought I was ten years older than I was. This makes me look younger, and we old girls need all the help we can get."

"I'll brush this mop when it dries," she said, laying the comb on the deck railing.

The back of her blouse was wet, but it felt good in the warm sun. She walked back into the house and to her purse.

"Okay, last chance," she said. "Anything besides aspirin?" she spoke to the room.

"Don't forget the blueberries, Mom," said Mary Two. "And the waffle mix, and hurry back. I'm starved."

"Got any juice? Look in the freezer door."

"Yep, here it is, frozen Minute Maid orange juice, two cans," said Ashlee. "I keep a couple of cans of frozen juice in the freezer door for screwdrivers."

We've got to work on this problem, thought Mary, as she closed the door behind her and walked down the steps.

Little did she know that she was walking into a completely new future.

"Thank you for the coffee," Ashlee said to the girl. "How do you like St. Louis so far?"

"Fine, but I still miss my horse."

"There are horses in St. Louis. They're at the racetrack. I could get a margarita at the racetrack," said Ashlee, a note of yearning in her voice.

"You know Mom's really worried about you," said the little girl as she jumped on the chair next to her aunt.

"I know that, she's played big sister to me all our lives. You all needn't worry about me. I'm going through a little spell of depression right now, but since I don't feel at all suicidal, I plan to pull out of it before too long." She patted the girl on the head.

"Do you believe in love at first sight?" asked the girl.

Ashlee thought a moment, "Oh, I suppose I do. Like fairy tale love, you mean? Puppy love?"

"No, real love," Mary Two asked. "Do you believe it's possible for two people to fall in love at first sight?"

"I suppose it's sort of like your parents."

Mary Two had walked around the counter and was dabbling her hands in the water faucet, turning the water off and on again.

After Ashlee had spoken, she turned the water off, picked up a hand towel off the counter and dried her hands.

She turned from the faucet and walked to the counter.

Ashlee was cradling a coffee cup in her hands with her elbows both on the counter. Mary Two walked to the other side of the counter, placed her elbows on the counter and put her chin in her hands. She was inches away from her aunt's nose, and she said.

"Tell me, dear aunt, how did my parents meet? I think I'm old enough to know."

"You mean your mother has never told you that story?" Ashlee sounded shocked.

"No, she always says she'll tell me when I'm older. I think I'm old enough now. That's the main reason I came along on this trip, to hear it from you."

Ashlee stood from the chair and walked across the room.

"Come on over here to the couch and sit down and get comfortable and I will tell you a story. First, please pour me another cup of coffee." She held out the empty cup.

Mary Two went to the counter and poured a cup of coffee and brought it back to the table in front of the couch. She took two coasters from the end table and placed one of them under the steaming cup and put the other at the opposite end of the table. Ashlee went to the couch, sat down and stretched her legs in front of her.

"Just a minute," said Mary Two as she hurried back into the kitchen. "I need a glass of orange juice."

She took a glass from the cupboard and filled it from the pitcher, brought it back to the living room and placed the glass on the coaster on the table. She sat down on the sofa, but jumped immediately back up and sprang into the kitchen to get a napkin, then hurried back to sit down in the chair and folded each of two napkins into fourths and handed one to her aunt.

"Now I'm ready."

"As you know, your mother and I are separated by 11 months. She was late and I was early, and there was just enough time between us that we were in the same grade. We had the same classes together and were pretty much like shadows of each other. We pretty much had the same friends, I was always a little prettier than her; I don't mean to say this in a bad way or anything, but she was always more studious, while I was wilder and looser, if you get my drift. She was, let's say, more mature."

"Does that mean you dated more?"

"Yes, it does."

"She made A's and I made B's because I partied more than I studied. She always helped me with my schoolwork, and I studied off her notes. She cared, I didn't. She took notes and I slept and wrote love letters.

"We were raised in a small town in Iowa, Waverly. We had gone through grade school and had crushes on certain boys, but she was never very serious. She loved the farm and the chores; I hated the farm and always wished we lived in the city. We were both cheerleaders. Mary was a candidate for homecoming queen. She didn't make it. But I had a lot more dates."

"Your father was a real scholar; he was in the top ten percent of the class. He never really seemed to try as hard as he could have; he never really brown-nosed the teachers like he could have to get the grade. He made A's and B's, and that was good enough for him. His father was retired military and they moved to Waverly when we were in the sixth grade. Mary never really paid any attention to your father. As I think back now, he was always a handsome boy, but not what you would call a heart-throb, not the kind of kid who went out a lot. We just never paid much attention to him. We always hung out with the kids we'd grown up with, and he sort of kept to himself or with a couple of guys he hung out with. He lived his life and we lived ours.

"He came into town after most of the cliques had been set. Mary and I had sort of dated the same two guys through grade school, and many of our friends are still with the kid they paired up with in grade school."

"I know how that goes," interjected Mary Two.

"One day toward the end of our sophomore year, it was in March, I believe, we were looking forward to summer. It was on a Saturday. There had been a Future Farmers of America convention in Des Moines, and Mary and I belonged to the Future Homemakers of America and we went, too. FFA and FHA were kind of tied together sometimes.

"We had left early that morning, and we came back on the bus that afternoon. I had wanted to go for a ride in Ted Thermond's new convertible, but your mother wasn't interested. She was going to walk that direction and find another ride. She thought Ted drove too fast, and he really did but I liked It. I liked Teddy.

"Your father, Tom Brown, had been president of the FFA. It was sort of unusual for him to take on that type of position. And your mother had been president of the FHA. They had become acquainted because of their involvement in this convention. Your mother had given a speech and your father had enjoyed it. Now this is what your mother told me.

"Apparently, they had struck up a conversation and they were both standing in front of the school. There was a sidewalk that circled the big old school building and a retaining wall made of concrete that was just high enough to sit on, and a lot of us would hang out in front of the school. He had asked her if he could have five minutes alone of her time to discuss a matter of importance to them.

"She thought he was going to ask her out, and she said she thought she would have said yes. They walked over together to the ledge, and he brought her to a spot and asked her to sit down. When she had sat down, he stood in front of her and told her to not say a word until he was done talking. During the FHA convention she had been chosen to give a little speech to the entire gathering. She had been elected to speak on behalf of all of the FHA girls. He told her that her speech had been exceptional and that it had really impressed him. He went on to say that he felt that she was certainly one of the smartest girls in the school and the prettiest, and that he had determined that she would make a very good mother for his children. She said she felt like getting up and running away, but she was in a state of shock. He told her again to not say a word.

"He had reached into his book bag and produced a single red rosebud and had placed the stem in her left hand."

"I've seen that rose," said Mary Two. "It's behind a little glass frame, and Mom has it on the wall in their bedroom."

"It gets better," said Ashlee.

"He then took her right hand and knelt down on his right knee and asked her to marry him.

"Out of the blue?" exclaimed Mary.

"Completely out of the blue," replied Ashlee. "They had not been on a date. He just out of the blue told her that he thought she was the best girl in the school and that he would do his best for the rest of his life to deserve her. And that he would do whatever it took to make her and her children happy. He went on to explain that he felt now was the proper time because at their age there was still time to head in a mutually agreeable direction.

"He had said that he would hold this offer open until the end of the school term because as much as he felt she was the one, he owed it to his children to be getting started. He had said that he would be faithful to her until the end of the school term. He then picked up his briefcase and walked away, and Mary hadn't said a word.

"She sat on that step completely speechless. She had until the end of school to make up her mind. He had said that she was his first pick and that any other choice after her was going to be second best.

"I don't know if you know it or not, honey, but your mother can be a real bitch when she wants to."

"I know that," said Mary Two.

"When I got home that evening, she told me that story and I just couldn't believe it. We laughed and laughed and decided that this guy was the biggest loser in the world. That next Monday in English class Tom had been standing beside his desk. Class had just gotten over, and some of the kids were still in the room. Remember she hadn't said a word to him, and she walked up to him and looked him straight in the eye and said, 'You know I can't stand boys that cry in public,' and she slapped him as hard as she could. The entire room heard it. And she just walked out of the room."

"She slapped him in the face?" asked Mary.

"Just as hard as she could. I was still in my chair, and I was shocked to death. We had decided over the weekend that her only option was just to tell him no. This behavior was unusual.

"The next day, walking down the hallway, she was on my right, and here came your dad walking with one of his friends. She stopped and waited for them to come even with us, and she looked at him and said, 'You know what I can't stand? Momma's boys,' and she punched him in the stomach as hard as she could.

"The first thing was a look of anger crossed his face, and if looks could kill, she'd be dead. You could see the tears just nearly well up in his eyes, and I thought this girl must really hate this guy.

"There was one class where they sat close to each other. It got so bad she would embarrass me. It was like she hated him; she kept calling him Mamma's boy and army brat and farm boy, to the point that during the next class period he sat way across the room. For all intents and purposes he began to ignore her. But I noticed that whenever he was in the same room she would be watching him. About a month into this, one day when your mother was having her period, your father was all alone in the hallway. She handed me her books and said, "Hold these." She walked over to him, spun him around and pushed him with all her might against the lockers. She pushed him so hard that his head hit the lockers and put a dent in them. She said what a pitiful human being he was, how he needed a haircut and a shave, and how he should throw that shirt away. That she would never consider kissing someone who chewed tobacco, that it was a foul habit and that it caused cancer, not that she gave a shit for his health.

"From then on he was always clean-shaven, he quit chewing tobacco, he got his hair cut and he bought some really nice shirts. And he had not spoken one word to your mother since he gave her that rose.

"She had been dating Tommy Edmonds off and on before he became the quarterback and dated a lot of the girls, and she had refused his advances. As far as your father was concerned, it had just come to the point where he ignored her and she ignored him.

"Tommy was a senior and was bound and determined that he was going to get in Mary's pants. It was the last week of school, and Mary and I were walking to the bus when Tommy and three of his football buddies came up to Mary, and he grabbed her roughly. He spun her around and told her that she was going to go out with him that Friday night and that he wasn't going to take no for an answer. She tried to break his hold, but he was hurting her.

"Out of the corner of my eye I saw that your father had been watching this, and he dropped his books and ran up to Tommy who was older and bigger and hit him three times really fast. He must have been stronger than he looks because it broke Tommy's nose, gave him a black eye, and as we later learned, broke one of his ribs. Those three other boys jumped on your father and beat him and kicked him, and your mother just stood there watching until it was like something snapped in her brain. She ran over to those boys and started kicking and scratching and pulling those guys off your dad. He had been whipped pretty good; he was all red and he was bleeding around his eyes and his nose and his mouth, and his good shirt was all torn. Those were some big old boys. They picked up their friend and started to amble off. She sat there on the curb with your dad's head in her lap and his blood just ruining her good dress. She was screaming and crying and she said, 'Stop hurting my husband.'

"And I about died.

"From then on they were inseparable just like peas in a pod. He would come over to the house, and they would plan things, how many kids they would have, where they would live. I used to sit out there and just listen. That's where your name came from, out on the front porch. They planned to have three kids with at least one of each, and they planned to try until they had girls and boys. They took all the same classes together for the next two years except gym. My grades suffered.

"They had picked out a little spot of land they wanted, and they figured how much money they needed to retire at 45. This was all in their junior year of high school, mind you.

"My parents had reservations about this relationship; they thought these two were entirely too young for this foolishness. But when they finally learned that Tom was honest and reliable and loved your mother, they grew to love him, too. As do I. Your parents were married the day after we graduated from high school. She wore a white dress at the wedding. That meant something in our day. It was a simple ceremony; there was one best man and I was the maid of honor. Our parents were going to spend a lot of money on the wedding, but your parents wanted to use that money and buy a tractor with it.

"We all went to college together. He graduated with a degree in Electrical Engineering, and she got a degree in human resources, and that, my dear, is the story of how your parents met."

"It's a great story," said Mary Two.

"One thing about your father, he's always loved your mother. He knows what he wants, and he gets what he wants.

"They bought that little piece of land, they bought that tractor and they had you, after they had three boys. Now I need something to sweeten up this coffee. I need a shower."

She had just stepped out of the shower when the lights went out.

9

TOM PULLED THE big blue truck onto the interstate, brought it up to 70 mph, set the cruise, and adjusted the rear view mirror so that he could see the trailer in the mirror. He tapped the brake lightly and turned the blinker signals one direction and the other. Looks good, he thought.

Carl was the perfect companion; he let Tom finish his routine before he spoke.

"And the adventure begins," said Carl.

"Times like these are when I really miss a cigarette, nasty habit, bad for your health, expensive. If they could make one that wasn't so darned addictive, one that you could just smoke without setting that monkey loose on your back. Oh, well. Lovely Iowa countryside. You know why I like this state?" asked Tom.

"No, old buddy why do you like this state?"

"You drive along and there's farmland and farmland and then a farmhouse with a barn and a corncrib, and then more farmland and farmland and then a farmhouse with a barn and a corncrib, and then more farmland and farmland, and then a farmhouse with a barn and a corncrib."

"Okay, okay," laughed Carl, "I get the picture."

They were headed east; Tom looked in the rear

view mirror and commented that there was a real storm coming, then looked ahead to the east and with the clear sky and thin cirrus clouds determined that they would possibly outrun the storm.

"Hope it rains," Tom said. "Now that the corn's planted it can rain all it wants."

"The last two years have been really hard," said Tom, "too little rain, too much drought. Welcome to farm life. This topsoil is 4 feet deep up here, some of the best land on the planet. This is why I chose to live here. I've been all over except for the Black Hills of South Dakota."

"The most productive land, too. If you're a city boy, you'd hate this," Carl said. "The city folks would cover that rich black dirt with asphalt and call it progress. They think their food comes from a grocery store."

Tom continued, "As you drive through this land, you feel that the earth can support any population, so long as we have grazing land for the beef cattle. Did you check the sack that the boys made for us. Look in the back seat and see if it is a little road food."

"Road food," Carl said, "my favorite kind of food."

Carl reached around and got the sack. Just like a kid.

"Yee ha, it's Christmas. This big old sack is full of jerky, peanuts, Pringles. That boy of yours is positively gold-plated. I ought to just give him that car. Better yet, why don't I just adopt him? I always wanted a boy."

"That's okay by me," said Tom with a laugh, "so long as I can borrow him back at planting season."

"Okay," said Carl, "you get him for planting season."

Carl opened the package of beef jerky and offered some to Tom, who took two large pieces.

"Home-made jerky," said Tom, "made with real wood smoke and no preservatives."

"Let's see if we can get a little music," said Tom. After a moment of trying to tune in a radio station, he got a puzzled look on his face. "That's funny," he said, "something's wrong with the radio or the antennae. I can't seem to get any radio stations."

"It's a brand new radio," said Tom. "Probably that's why it's not working."

"Just put on some Charley Pride music and let the miles roll by," said Carl.

They drove in silence for a few miles, enjoying the road food.

"I wonder if the power ever came back on?" asked Tom in a now worried manner.

"Of course, it did," said Carl, "what's the longest you all ever went without power, back in the '91 flood, wasn't it?"

"Yeah, '91, we were down for about three days when that flood water took out six miles of line. It wouldn't have been that long if the water hadn't stayed up, and it kept raining and we just couldn't get in there."

"If you're worried, call the plant," suggested Carl.

"I believe I'll do just that," said Tom, and took out his cell phone from his pocket.

"That's funny, no signal."

"Murphy's law of cell phones," said Carl, "they never work when you need them the most."

"We'll catch a repeater tower when we get closer to Des Moines. In the meantime, stop worrying. We're fine, the kids are fine, Mary's going to be fine. Enjoy the drive," said Carl with a laugh. "The kids have got some guns and know how to use them. We've got some guns and know how to use them. We've got a little money."

"How much money do we have?" asked Tom.

"Oh, I just threw a little folding money in the bag, about 50 G's," answered Carl in a matter-of-fact tone of voice.

"Fifty G's?" said Tom in an astonished tone of voice.

"With the price of cars the way they are today, that's barely enough to replace this truck. We might accidentally need to get back home."

"You know that's enough to get us arrested," said Tom. "The way they're able to scan these cars, they'll think we're drug dealers or something."

"Never happen," said Carl. "It's all wrapped in lead foil, nobody'll know it's here."

As they crested a hill, Tom exclaimed, "What in the world is that?" He pointed toward the horizon ahead. "Is that a building or what? It's in the middle of the road and it's getting bigger."

"That's an airplane," said Carl, "a big plane, and it's flying low. Is it going to crash? Never seen a big old boy like that flying so low."

"That must be a 747 or L1011, and it's coming right at us."

The giant plane quickly flew over at treetop height. The noise from the engines was deafening even with the windows rolled up.

Tom checked the rear view mirror and had changed to the inside lane. He hit the brakes and drove down into the median and onto the grass as the big airplane seemed to barely miss the truck.

"Did you see what airline that belonged to?" asked Carl.

"Couldn't see the tail markings because it was coming so straight on. If it weren't for that red stripe on the side, I'd say it was a military plane. I spent a little time working in Arizona, and those boys would come over that low and fast, and it always scared the bejesus out of me. They're probably just testing out their equipment or some sort of exercise," said Tom, looking for any excuse.

"Well," said Tom, "that sure is dangerous. If anything happened like a flock of geese or something, that big old boy would be a heap of smoldering metal."

"He's probably trying to get below the radar. It's lucky it didn't hit that little old tower up ahead."

"I think when we get back I'll report that son of a bitch." Carl was nearly speechless with rage.

There was a break in the traffic, and Tom brought the truck and trailer back up to speed.

The sun was beginning to shine through the clouds in spots; dark shadows lay on the road where the sun was peaking through.

"Does it seem like traffic is a little heavy for this time of day? Seems like all the traffic is leaving, not coming," Tom finally spoke as they neared the city.

As they drove around the city on the elevated roadway, they looked down on the shopping malls.

"Look at those people trying to get into that grocery store. That looks like my worst nightmare," said

Tom. "You know how much food is in a grocery store?"

"A lot," said Carl.

"Less than a week's worth," said Tom. "Believe it or not. Would you believe there was less than a week's worth of food in a grocery store? That's under normal operating conditions and doesn't include holidays like Thanksgiving. Some stores have to restock every three days. Under situations of stress such as hurricanes, tornadoes, etc., there's a hell of a lot less than three days' worth. If everybody decided at one time to go to the store, you could probably have a store emptied out in an hour."

"I suppose you're right," said Carl. "People in a panic would be buying things they didn't need. I was in Florida one time during a hurricane and happened to walk into a store they were boarding up. It was like a giant vacuum cleaner had come and sucked everything off the shelves. One other cause of panic would be a long-term power outage. Those people hit by a hurricane are really more affected by the long-term power outage than by the hurricane itself. Unless you got your whole house blown down."

Tom pointed to a crowd of people as they drove by. "Let's just say that those people we saw down there were in a panic over a lack of electricity. What do you suppose would be their first hurdle? Just getting in the door. Most grocery stores have electric doors that wouldn't open without juice. What do you suppose would be the hottest commodity on the shelves?"

"Well," Carl said, " I suppose the meat department. That's where I'd go, a bunch of big old juicy

T-bone steaks. About 20 pounds of baked potatoes and butter, and I'm good to go."

"Okay," said Tom, "now you've got 50 pounds of steak, but you couldn't eat it all before it spoiled."

"Now there's a challenge," laughed Carl. "We'll just have to cook it all up at once and eat 'til we can't eat no mo. Will there be beer to wash it down?"

"Depends on if you get to the beer aisle before some other son-of-a-bitch."

"I'm there."

"You know you could live quite a while without food, but you've got to have water."

"Or beer," laughed Carl.

"There is water," said Carl. "Just turn on the water tap."

"Sure, you've got water as long as you've got electricity, but if the power goes down, you've got no water."

"What about all that water in the water tower?" asked Carl. "They hold a lot of water."

"Unless people panic and start to horde water, if they start to fill up every jug and jar they have and all the bathtubs and such, and if the pumps quit working and no water goes in to the top of the tower, it wouldn't take long to empty one."

"Okay, let's say the pumps quit for some reason, let's say a squirrel gets into the line, will the water still come out of the bottom of the water tower or will it build up a vacuum that stops the water flow?"

"There would have to be a valve that let air into the top of the tower under normal conditions. Those pumps don't run all the time."

Tom continued, "This whole society has become

so dependent upon electricity that even a small glitch can cause major problems. That's why I got into the business. Of all man's inventions, electricity has got to be the most important. It's got to be at the top of the list because it has given power to the common man like never before in history. Surely we've had this conversation before."

"I might have been drunk," said Carl.

"Let's see," said Carl, "what is the most important discovery of the twentieth century? Television. Yep, television has my vote."

"Not electricity. It's television," said Tom.

"Let's see, the automobile?" Carl said hopefully.

"Can't make cars without power."

"Okay, how about medicine," suggested Carl. "Penicillin or aspirin?"

"No electricity, no drugs. No lights, no working till the wee hours of the morning."

"There must be something, I've got it, the love of a good woman."

"Well," said Tom, "there were good women dating back to the time of Adam, it's hardly an invention."

"You know that Adam and Eve story has always puzzled me," said Carl. "I always felt that Adam and Eve lived in New York in 1925."

"That has got to be the most hair-brained statement I have ever heard," laughed Tom.

"Okay then," exclaimed Carl, "let me ask you a Biblical question, did Adam and Eve have a belly button?"

Tom thought about this for a minute. "They sure as hell did if they were born in New York in 1925."

"Okay," laughed Carl, "let's get off this subject

before we go crazy."

"Let's see, where were we?" said Tom. "Oh, yeah, electricity being the most important invention of the 20th or any other century."

"Okay, I'll give you that one," said Carl.

"If we as a country have a weak spot, aside from the national debt, of course, it is the weak electrical system. It's old and frail; it's all exposed and being destroyed by the weather. Electricity has become way too important to our way of life. We must make it stronger and safer."

"Is there a quick solution?"

"You bet there is. Just shut the damned thing off."

"What?"

"The best thing that could happen to this country would be for the power to go off for four weeks. By that time all the food in the freezers would be spoiled, and people would get their heads out of their butts and start putting their priorities in order. Just pick a day or two or a weekend, give the country a month's notice and turn off all the electricity for two days. Do this every month for a year and you'd make real progress. People who live in rural areas are accustomed to blackouts and have adapted; people in the cities can do the same. In times past, Americans were a resourceful bunch; they may still be.

"Utilities like AC because it is easy to transmit, easy to transform, and can't be stored. We homeowners shouldn't like it because it's dangerous, the voltage is too high, and because we can't store it. We are dependent upon the utility companies, and that is a bad thing. Let the lights go out for a couple of weeks and you will see chaos in the streets. Our leadership should see this and press for an energy policy that rewards people for becoming independent from the utilities."

"So how would we do that?" asked Carl.

"Several ways, the first big thing would be to switch this country over to DC. Let the AC feed the home, but let the house be run off of batteries. These batteries could be charged during times of low load and used during the peak times to take the strain off the utilities. It could all be easily done with taxes. Use the old stick and carrot. Another thing that will help this country would be to simply raise the price of electricity. Back years ago we paid one-half cent per kilowatt-hour; today it's nearly 13 cents. The utilities fed us this line of baloney and told us we needed a whole bunch of new power plants and our leaders bought it. So we spent billions of dollars to construct power plants, and when the price of electricity went up, guess what, people started to turn out the lights. If you raise the price of electricity, people will find a way to use less; it's just that simple. It is that simple.

"Now we're stuck with these old relic nuclear plants that only had a life expectancy of 35 years or so. And now our kids will be stuck with these monsters, these nightmares that are 100 million tons of radioactive concrete that must be decommissioned. Who do you suppose will pay for the cleanup? Who always pays? What were they thinking? They weren't. Our leadership in this country has failed us so miserably it makes me want to just cry like a baby. Here are these giant radioactive relics, a testimony to man's greed, dotting our landscapes. And it was all unnecessary. You know that little red light on your TV set?

That baby is on so you don't have to walk over and push a button. That TV draws current 24/7 just so you don't have to walk across the room. You just wait; nuclear waste is already becoming a problem. Just wait 'til the bill comes due. The stockholders of these utilities will bail out and leave the cleanup to the government, mark my word. There are 103 nuke plants in this country; there is enough wind energy in just the state of Kansas, if it were harnessed, to replace them. Once you pay for the windmill, even if it takes 10 years, you have forever more free electricity.

"But let's get off this and return to the importance of the average power company worker to the continued success of America. We have become completely dependent upon the great electrical grid. There is almost no part of our daily lives that isn't some way powered by the grid. We get up in the morning with an electric alarm clock and go to bed with a soothing CD playing in the background. All of our necessities of life are powered by electricity, our water is pumped, our food is refrigerated, our cars won't start without batteries, and our nights have been made into days, all thanks to electricity."

"What about all the emergency generators scattered around," asked Carl. "I know I've got one at my house."

"Probably less than one percent of the country's power needs could come from emergency generators. The big ones like the hospitals use are powered by natural gas or diesel, so the fuel is dependent upon the electrical grid. Even if you had a thousand gallons of gas for your generator at home, how long would that last you? If the lights ever really went out, all the small generators would burn themselves up pretty quick.

"My concern is and has been that Americans have become so soft that the whole country has become vulnerable. You have to think small again — where was the strength in pioneer America? It was in the family unit. There is a concerted effort to destroy that strength. Our government has created an energy policy that is controlled by somebody who doesn't give a tinker's damn about you or me. If the power goes out, we're dead; it's that simple. People have become so used to getting supper at McDonald's or Taco Bell that they forgot how to cook. Back in the time of the great depression, people had a garden, they canned food and saved seeds from year to year. We have become so dependent on other countries for seed that one bad year could bring no harvest. Our society is hell-bent on turning farmland into Wal-Mart parking lots. One day, believe it or not, we may wish we hadn't destroyed all that farmland. One old boy farmer that I knew was concerned that with all these chemicals they use now that he felt it was only a matter of time before some combination of chemicals react to completely destroy the dirt. It's not so far-fetched an idea. They make a chemical that kills everything you spray it on; now they have come out with a soybean that it won't kill. So the farmer simply plants the bean among the weeds and sprays the shit out of the crop and kills everything but the crop."

"Let's get back to the power deal," said Carl.

"You mean to tell me that I could get by with a single 20-amp circuit; my house has a big old 200-amp panel. What's that all about?"

"It's just a luxury. People in America have had so much for so long that they take all this for granted. We are no longer the hardy stock that crossed the prairies in wagons burying babies along the way. We have become fat and lazy. And there is a whole generation coming up that doesn't have a clue about hard work. Almost every house has a computer or two or three. A simple program could be written to make them the center for load allocation. In a pinch we could take houses and make them get by with very little electricity. You can have light in one room, but only if the light in another were shut off. Your heater could work just enough to keep the house warm and could be cycled with the freezer and the refrigerator."

"One 20-amp circuit is a lot of electricity if you're in the middle of nowhere."

"This entire country would fold up and die if it weren't for electricity. Just think about it for a second," said Tom. "If the power goes out, first thing is you couldn't even get into the grocery store because the doors are electric. Once you get in the store, you can't buy any food. Back in the '80s all the grocery stores went to scanners that read that UPC code on the side of the package. This allowed the store to keep accurate inventory of what they sold and also allowed them to raise the price any time they wanted. Back in the good old days, each can had a little price sticker on it; I know you remember that.

"So now you somehow end up in the store, you've got yourself a cart full of groceries and you're at the checkout lane. Nobody knows how much to charge you, because the power is out. Hell, today most kids can't add anyway without a computer. So let's say that by some miracle the cash register and the scanner work. Let's say they were on some sort of battery backup. That's going to last maybe three hours tops. So now you have the total, how are you going to pay for this? Most people don't carry cash any more because of plastic and the ever-present ATM machines.

"While we're driving down this road, let's just think for a minute that the grid is down, okay? No power anywhere except for a few odd generators that will die soon due to lack of gas. I don't believe that to be the case, but just for the sake of argument, let's say that the grid's down. People are going to panic. They are going to realize that they don't have food for a week. Wendy's is closed. McDonald's is closed. Taco Bell is closed. Every fast food restaurant on the planet is closed. All the food is starting to rot in the freezers that are starting to thaw out. The refrigerators are thawing out and the food is starting to spoil. So the people are going to panic and try to run to the store to buy canned food, but when they get to the store, they can't even get into the door. And they don't have any money anyway."

"Not me," said Carl. "I've always got lots of money."

"Well, in your case maybe a little cash money would help."

"Not always," said Carl. "Remember a man named John Jacob Astor?"

"That name's familiar," said Tom, "that ought to ring a bell. John Jacob Aster, I remember him. He was on the Titanic, what was the deal with him?"

"He had like $5,000 cash on him. It would have been like having a million dollars today, and he

116

couldn't buy a seat on a lifeboat."

"Anyway, a week or so after the boat sank, they found his frozen body floating in the ocean with enough cash on him to buy the whole Titanic, and it didn't do him one damn bit of good."

"I can trump that though," said Carl. "Not only do I have enough money to buy the Titanic, I've also got a gun. I'll get me a seat on a damn lifeboat."

"Okay," Tom said, "you and your boat can go to the grocery store and figure out how you're going to get some food. What's going to happen is the more violent people are going to finally panic and bust the door down, drive their cars through the windows, climb in and steal everything they can, and basically in one day all the shelves will be empty except for the odd broken bottle of ketchup and stationery and cards and things that nobody's going to want anyway. But once these people get this stuff into the parking lot, there will be other vultures there to steal the stuff they've stolen."

"And then once you get to your house, you won't be able to take a shower because the water is pumped by electricity. So you can't drink the water, you can't take a shower, you can't go to the toilet."

"I guess we'll be screwed," said Carl.

"You bet we will. And it could happen so damn fast, we could go from the top of the world society back to the Stone Age in a matter of days. If that grid would go down, this country would turn to anarchy; it wouldn't take two weeks. In two weeks this entire country would be on its knees. People would be in the streets begging the government to please come take their knives and guns and please just do anything, whatever it takes, just feed them.

"There would be a few small exceptions, a few small cities that are self-contained that could be independent of the grid. There would be a few isolated instances where the people have had power trouble for years and have become used to living without it."

"Probably the whole state of Utah."

"How's that?" Carl asked.

"Well, it's been my understanding for years that the Mormon faith requires that its members keep at least a year's worth of food."

"There's your answer," Carl said, "all you need is a double-barreled shotgun and a membership list for the Church of Jesus Christ of Latter Day Saints."

"I guess that's right, but don't forget that they've got guns, too."

"So what do you think would happen?"

"Well, the people that had generators would have the power at least in the short term. Some cities are independent of the grid. Those people would be all right. It ain't going to happen, but let's just say for the sake of argument that it did and it was late winter. If it happened in the fall with winter coming on, it would be a real disaster, but not so bad if it was coming out of winter and going into spring. That would give people a chance to plant a little food. They could survive perhaps, maybe."

"So you think people would go out into their back yards and dig up their manicured lawns and plant potatoes?"

"Well, that or starve, I guess. Part of the problem is that our society has grown away from being self-sufficient. There are a few survival types out there who can be self-sufficient, but that is no large percentage of the population."

"Years ago during the depression people would preserve their own food for the winter; that was 70 years ago, about two generations. We are two generations removed from the type of people who survived the great depression. Our parents and grandparents would save seeds, now many of the seeds come from Mexico or other foreign countries. We couldn't get seeds without gasoline. No electricity, no gasoline; no seeds, no food. It's that simple."

"That's something I'd do," said Carl, "if I lived in the city. I'd just load up in my car and head out to the country and get myself a cow."

"Cows aren't in the country any more," said Tom. "They're all in feed lots and slaughter houses, and they probably would all be dead in a couple of weeks without water.

"No electricity, no refineries, no gasoline, no diesel, no semis driving down the road. There would be cars stalled all along the highways. I suspicion that within a week the highways would be clogged with cars."

"You mean like that car parked along the road right there?" Carl said as he pointed to a little red car parked along the side of the road.

"I suppose that would be one of the first signs," said Tom. "Do you suppose we're in the middle of a crisis?"

"I don't know," said Carl, "but let's try to find out."

Tom tried the radio with no success. He tried the telephone with no success.

"You know," said Tom, "seeing these stalled cars

makes me nervous."

"How much gas do we have?" asked Carl.

"Don't worry about that," said Tom. "We've got more than enough gas to get there and come back. What worries me is if that woman of mine took it upon herself to try to come home."

"Didn't you tell her to stay there?" said Carl.

"Yes, I did."

Two quail flew in front of the car, and Tom swerved to miss them.

"Holy smoke," said Carl, "you would get us killed over a couple of birds?"

"It's not just the birds," said Tom. "They would have messed up the grill or could have broken the windshield or any number of other bad things. You hear about these people that hit deer in the road and they suddenly have a couple of hundred pounds of hooves and antlers and bloody meat and broken glass in their laps. Nasty thought! There was some guy in North Dakota or some place up north just driving down the road with his wife and ran over one of those jack stands that was just laying in the road. This has been years ago, and I remember that that piece of steel came up through the floorboard of the car and came up through this guy's seat and into his crotch and killed him. Messy, tragic, scary."

"Aren't you a hunter?" asked Carl.

"I suppose I am, in season. It's instinct as much as anything."

The men sat in silence a very long time, finally, Carl spoke.

"About the time that those people's freezers started to drip and the food started to spoil, people would rethink their priorities. They ought to have six months' worth of food back on the shelves, at least. No more than a bag of rice and a bag of beans cost, every American could put back enough food to keep them alive for six months for probably a hundred dollars."

"Drinking water would be a big deal. Don't forget the drinking water. Talking about that makes me thirsty. Do we have anything to drink here?"

"As a matter of fact, we do," said Tom. "There is a cooler in the back full of ice and drinking water."

"Nothing sounds better right now than a big cold jug of clear, clean drinking water."

"About ten minutes ago I would have said a nice cold beer or a nice cold Coke or Pepsi, but right now nothing sounds better than water."

"And we Americans almost without exception take water for granted, because it has always been right there for us to turn on a tap and drink it."

"I suppose there would be people die if the power went off for good. Old people would die, young people would die. Sick people would die that couldn't get their medicine cooled. There would be a percentage of the population that would just naturally succumb to this sort of stress. I mean it would change our whole way of looking at life," said Carl.

"Okay, maybe it's not such a good idea to just shut off the power for six weeks," Tom thought out loud.

"Well, wouldn't it be the same if we had a voluntary power-off week?"

"How would you do that?"

"Well," said Carl, "you could challenge people to just go home on some weekend and turn off the breakers at their house. They could try to get by for just one weekend. We could drive through the neighbor-hoods with the power police, and if they had their lights on, we could give them a big old ticket."

"Yeah," said Tom, "we could tell people that we needed to work on the grid and that it was necessary to cut down the power demand for a period of time."

"We could start it with a little crisis, shut the grid down for a period of a couple of hours, and then tell people that the grid was weak and needed repairing."

The trip down the interstate had been rather un-eventful except for the mishap around Des Moines and the odd stranded car.

"See," Tom said, "It wouldn't take a very large crew of people to wreck the grid in this country. These power plants don't have much security, and by and large this country has not a worry in the world that anything like that could happen. The weakness of the power grid in this country is not so much at the gen-erating facilities, but in the very fact that all the wir-ing is overhead and exposed. It would be completely impossible to protect all those thousands of miles of wiring from a group of lunatics hell-bent on destroy-ing it. All that wiring is bare and exposed, and the voltages are so high that the voltage itself would do most of the damage."

"What about the military?" asked Carl. "Surely they could take over."

"Of course, as soon as the grid failed, there would be a state of emergency declared. But the army would be hard-pressed to feed themselves. Army bases prob-ably depend on civilian suppliers, and if the trucks quit rolling due to a lack of diesel, then the food would stop flowing in. I doubt that there would be any food left for the general population. Since the soldiers have the guns, they would fan out into the private sector and take the food. Our government is simply not set up to replace the electrical grid.

"Once the power's down, it's down. Until you fix the problem, those generators will stay off line. Oh, there would be a state of martial law declared. The local governments would stand up and take charge. There would be armed groups of citizens going from house to house collecting food from those smart enough to store it and giving it to the have-nots who were too stupid to plan for something like this. It's the American way."

"How would you do it?" asked Carl.

"That's easy," said Tom. "I'd just attack the grid at its weakest points, the places where the voltage is the highest, at the transformers and substations. See those big poles coming up here on the right," he said as he pointed. "Those poles carry three very large wires that are the power, and see those two big wires at the top? Those top two wires are grounds; they are connected to a wire that goes down to the base of the pole and wraps around the pole base. You can tell how much voltage is in the lines by counting the number of rings on the insulator. Usually the bigger the insulator, the higher the voltage.

"You can walk up on a hill under these big old power lines and hold a fluorescent light bulb in your hand and the thing will glow just from the electrical field."

"Surely those wires are insulated?" asked Carl.

"Heck, no," said Tom. "They're bare aluminum with a steel core. The best insulation is dry air. There is no reason in the world why those wires would need to be insulated."

"So now you and your merry band of criminals are hell-bent on shutting off the grid in this country, what do you do? Do you saw down the power poles?"

"You would have to cut down a whole bunch of poles to have any effect, although when a 100-mile-an-hour wind storm comes along it does a pretty good job.

"The thing for you to realize is that it takes electricity to make electricity. In order for these big power plants to function, they have to have a big source of electricity in order to create the electrical field that is needed to generate more electricity. This power comes from the grid; when you shut down the grid, you shut down the power plant, and it takes a whole lot to get it started again. This means that a well-timed and coordinated effort by just a few men could shut down most of the electricity in this country. The main thing that would do the damage is the electricity itself. You take a line that carries a couple of thousand volts of electricity and send all that to ground, and you've got yourself quite a spark, quite a little bang."

"Scary deal."

Carl slept for a long while.

10

MARY SWUNG HER purse gently as she walked along. Things were going well except for the car. She determined that this trip might not have been necessary since it seemed like Ashlee was not really in trouble. She had talked her into coming back home to visit. This was a nice little neighborhood, clean, middle-class, nothing really fancy. She would bet that her sister would have never walked to the store.

She passed an elderly lady working in a small garden at the front of her house. What was that pretty flower, a rose tree?

The lady spoke in a friendly manner and offered her a flower.

Mary accepted the flower, thanked the nice lady, and continued her walk.

As she passed the last house before the supermarket, she thought that this was the way things used to be. A grocery store had been located in easy walking distance from homes. One hundred years ago when the towns were first started, you could still find the remnants of these stores, nestled in the residential communities. The advent of the shopping center had destroyed all that. Even 50 years ago people didn't have cars; they depended upon public transportation or they walked.

Those were better days.

The malls had destroyed this old residential atmosphere.

This grocery store had been built within the last 10 years. The owners had built the building around several old and tall trees that shaded the parking lot, a very nice homey touch.

Several young people were stocking and facing the shelves. As she walked past the newspaper machines, she noticed that they all had the same headlines: five large airliners had been blown out of the sky by terrorists with a great loss of life. There were full-page pictures on each of the papers showing smoke and fire and pieces of wreckage.

Some new Islamic terrorist organization had already taken credit for it.

The President was contemplating declaring martial law.

The only exception was the local free newspaper that highlighted an article about growing award-winning cucumbers.

This was sort of out of the blue; the world had been at relative peace for a number of years except for the confusion in the Middle East that had been going on for thousands of years.

The fact that there was likely to be a state of martial law declared made her wish that her car was running and that she could get it filled up with gas and get back home. She hated the city; she had grown comfortable in the little nest they had built in the country.

She went to buy a newspaper and remembered that she was fairly low on cash. She stopped at an

ATM machine as she entered, took out her card, entered her personal ID number and thought for a moment about how much cash she needed. ATM machines had sprung up everywhere; they were in the mall, in grocery stores, at the airport, at all the banks. It was no longer necessary to carry great amounts of money, and people had grown into the habit of just getting small amounts of cash at a time.

Mary thought about it for a moment, something about those planes had made her nervous. She looked around and didn't see any stranger types lurking in the background, so when the machine asked for the amount of withdrawal she chose the maximum of $300. This should get her out of town if worse came to worse.

After reading several advertisements from the bank for car loans and student loans and after agreeing to pay an extra $1.50 to the bank for the service, she received 15 crisp $20 bills. She took $100 and folded it up and put it in the back of her checkbook; another $100 she put in her pocket, and the rest went into her purse. Men always kept some squirrel money in their billfolds; she thought it was a good idea. She went into the store and picked up a small hand basket, stood for a moment and thought about it and traded the little basket for a pushcart.

Grocery aisles all seem to be laid out the same; some genius figured out what priorities are and laid out the first store. She started in the fruit and vegetable aisle. She was looking for fresh blueberries for little Mary. She found them in the fruit refrigerator. Then she went to the pancake mix aisle and determined that she needed milk and eggs. She put a gallon of milk and a dozen eggs in the cart. She knew her sister was fond of butter, so she picked up a pound of butter.

Just as she picked up the butter, the lights went out, except for enough emergency lights to allow her to see the front of the store.

She had noticed that there were probably ten other people in the store.

There were two cash registers open. She noticed that the front doors had shut.

As she stood in line to check out, she looked into the parking lot and saw a late model red Chevrolet pickup truck pull up into the lot and a man get out of the truck and run to the front door. When he came to the door, it didn't open as you would have expected. He began to pound on the door. A young boy whom she had noticed earlier stocking shelves stood inside the door and raised his arms in a manner that indicated that he was unable to help. The man pried the doors open and by turning sideways slid his way into the building. He hastened toward one of the cashiers and interrupted her in a conversation with her customer.

"Do those things work?" He asked.

"What do you mean, sir?" asked the cashier with a look of fear on her face.

"Those cash registers?" demanded the man

"Of course, they work," said the woman. "We have emergency backup generators. This has happened before."

"You've probably got 90 minutes, maybe," said the man as he ran to the shopping carts and pulled one from the long line and then another, and he disappeared into the fruit section pushing one cart and pulling another.

Something clicked in Mary's brain. Think! she thought to herself. Is this man crazy or is he the smartest one here?

She and Tom had been of the same mind and had spent hours and hours discussing how important electricity was to the modern world. Possibly it was because that was Tom's line of work; probably it was not. Tom had always stressed that electricity was the most important event of the last 2,000 years because it put so much power into the hands of every man. He had always stressed that without electricity of some kind almost every other human endeavor would have been impossible.

Tom had always stressed to her that whenever the power went down it could be a simple thing or a serious thing. He had always stressed that if it ever went off there was no really good reason to believe that it was going to come back on right away. Tom had seen enough things in his career and had told her enough horror stories that she had no real comfort level with man's ability to fix it. He had always told her that one of his biggest fears was that he would be driving down the road and look into the parking lot of a grocery store and see it full of cars. And that in his nightmare he would finally find a place to park and that when he went inside the store all the shelves were empty except for the odd things. There at the cash register was a man pushing a cart full of groceries and pulling a cart full of groceries behind him. His wife was doing the same, and behind her were three children of varying ages, each pushing a full cart.

And the man was holding in his hand a credit card. As he walked down the aisle, all of the fruits and vegetables were spoiled, all of the meats had turned rancid, and all of the canned goods were gone except for two dented cans of stewed tomatoes which he hated and a broken box of minute rice, that in his nightmare turned to weevils. Tom had had that nightmare many times, and they had discussed the deep Freudian significance. Their final conclusion was that he had gone to bed too soon after eating spicy Mexican food.

Perhaps they had been wrong.

Seeing that man grab the two carts made something snap in Mary's mind; this was that man. She would have nothing to worry about if she were home. But she wasn't. The power went out from time to time on the farm and they were prepared.

She had never really bought into Tom's fears; she hadn't belittled them, but deep down she had always felt that everything would be all right and that Tom was just being paranoid. Tom, on the other hand, had always felt that it was a giant accident that things were all right and that it was only a matter of time before the little house of cards crashed down.

She regretted now that she had not brought her sister's car. She spun her cart back and got out of line, and she too got a second shopping cart. As she went back into the aisles, she ran into the man with the two carts, and he was busily filling one cart with five-gallon jugs of water.

"Have you heard the news?" he asked.

"No," she answered. "I haven't been listening to the radio or watching TV.

"It was just announced," he said in a breathless manner as he lifted the heavy jugs into his cart. "People are getting sick from the drinking water. Several major cities have lost their water supplies." He had filled one of his carts with five-gallon jugs of drinking water. There were two left on the shelf.

"Here," he said, and put two in her cart. "Do you want some gallons?"

"Sure" she said, and he put five gallon jugs of water in her cart.

The man placed his left hand on the handle of her grocery cart, looked her straight in the eye and pointed to her with the index finger of his right hand. "If you don't have a water filter, go immediately to aisle seven, middle of the aisle, bottom shelf. Buy the expensive one and all the spare filters they have."

"Now for the staples," he said.

She began to panic. "What the heck," she said out loud. She ran to aisle seven and put the water filter and all the spare cartridges in her cart. She then turned and found the man. He stopped in front of the dried beans, and she came right behind him.

He looked at her and smiled. "My name's John Sanders," he said, and held out his hand.

"Mine's Mary Brown," she said.

"Common name," he said. "I'm a Professor of Social Sciences at the University of Minnesota," he said. "I was here for the last two months working on my doctorate. I've rented a small place across the street where I can walk to class. I've taken a year sabbatical to study crowd behavior.

"You've got a little time. The panic won't hit until the story breaks on the evening news. I heard about it through a colleague who is involved with the CDC. We have been working closely together because our papers have similar qualities."

"How bad is it?" she asked.

"It depends on where you live," he said, "and how prepared you are for something like this. At home I was somewhat prepared, but with an apartment it was not feasible to stock up."

She thought about that game show where people rushed through a grocery store with a shopping cart and competed to see who could get the highest dollar amount of items in a certain period of time. Those people always rushed to the drug section, and she remembered she had come for aspirin. She hurried to the pharmacy through the darkened store. Normally she would have price shopped, but today she found the biggest bottles of aspirin, Tylenol, Advil and Motrin and threw three of each into the cart.

Then she came back and got another five bottles of aspirin.

She was now in panic mode; other people had joined in her panic and were filling carts.

She tried to put her mind on what she needed to buy, but she couldn't think clearly. Staples, she thought. What was it that the pioneers carried in their covered wagons? How long had she been in here? Would the generator last long enough to let her check out? She must hurry; she dashed to the baking aisle and put four large bags of flour in the bottom of the cart along with two packages of sugar, two tubs of shortening and five boxes of salt. Then she went to the bean aisle and picked up a large sack of pinto beans and a large sack of rice. On her way back to the checkout counter, she grabbed two boxes of tampons, six packages of toilet paper and three canned hams.

She had no idea how she was going to carry all of this, but figured she would borrow a cart.

She knew it was now or never.

She had pulled out of line first, and everyone else had followed suit. Now there was no one at the number one checkout lane. The professor was in aisle two; he had finished filling the first cart with groceries and had filled the other cart with large bottles of whiskey.

The total came to $362, but the credit card wouldn't work.

This seemed like a nightmare, the number of times Tom had talked about this exact scenario. He and his drinking buddies used to speculate about how important their jobs were, about how important electricity was. He always used to say that if the power went off the first problem was going to be just to get into the grocery store because of the electric doors. The next problem they surmised would be that once you got into the store the scanners wouldn't work and they couldn't tell how much things cost. The next theoretical problem would be paying for something in a world that had become more and more dependent upon plastic and the ubiquitous ATM machines. People didn't carry cash anymore; why would you when there was an ATM machine in every mall or where most superstores had banks right as you came into the door?

She paid with cash. "Don't bother to bag it," she said. "Just put it back into the cart. As she pushed the cart to the door, she was shocked to see that the parking lot was filling up with cars and there was a crush of people at the front door trying to get in.

"Let me help you to your car," said Professor Sanders; he had finally gotten through the checkout. He was carrying two small bags of groceries.

"Where's all the booze?" she asked.

"Damned credit card wouldn't work, and I had to spend all my cash just to buy food. Damned inconvenient."

"How do we get through this crowd?" she asked.

"Simple, Madam," he said. "You must realize that this population is not trying to keep you in, but rather is trying to gain entry. If we simply open the doors, they will flow past us where they will wreak havoc on the contents of the store.

"The larger this crowd gets, the more panic will develop until they begin to feed off of each other's fears, and when they get to the checkout and can't pay, they will simply fight their way out without paying. We are safe here for now, but in a very few moments we will not want to be standing here. Stand aside for a moment and I will release the hounds."

He set his groceries down beside the door and reached up and released the catch. The crowd of people rushed past them and into the store, nearly knocking the door from its hinge. The group of people fought over shopping carts as the manager tried to keep them from entering with no success.

Mary turned to go out the door and saw a very welcome sight. Ashlee and Mary Two had pulled up in front of the store in Ashlee's Buick. She had opened the trunk.

"Thank God we've found you," said Mary Two. "Let me help you." She ran into the store and began to pull the cart toward the rear of the car.

"What's going on? We decided to skip the waffles and eat at Denny's."

Mary pushed the carts to the back of the car and unloaded it into the trunk.

"This place is becoming a madhouse, let's go home," Mary said as she jumped into the back seat.

"Ashlee, have you got a couple of quarters?"

"I think so," said Ashlee, and shortly produced two quarters.

Mary took the money, said thank you and ran around the side of the building to where the paper machines where. She dropped three quarters in the *USA Today* machine and took out one of the middle papers. She ran back to the car and jumped into the right side passenger door.

Mary Two had had her door open, and they both shut them and drove off.

"Just a minute," Mary said, "drive way over there," and she pointed past the driver to a point in the parking lot farthest away from the building. "Turn the car around for just a minute and face the building." Ashlee did as she was told.

"Make sure the doors are locked," she said, "and leave the car running."

"Okay," said Ashlee.

"How are you fixed for gas?" asked Mary.

"Filled up last night," said Ashlee.

Mary Two piped in "What are we waiting for, Mom?"

"Just watch the doors for a minute. The professor said that it would only be a matter of a short time before all hell breaks loose."

It wasn't long before the first of the crowd began to emerge. The manager of the store was standing in the middle of the doors, and a tall red-headed man pushed him aside to let a woman push past with a cart full of sacks.

"You see," said Mary, "the electricity went out and they had enough gas in the generator to last 90 minutes, and we almost didn't get out in time. For some reason the credit cards don't work. It was lucky I had just gotten some cash from the ATM machine. Those people probably tried to pay with plastic and didn't have enough cash so they just barged out without paying."

"The electricity is out at home," said Ashlee.

"Well, that would explain why the credit cards don't work," said Mary. "Must be most of the town. Turn on the radio and see what you can find out."

Ashlee turned in the radio station and there was only static. "That's funny" she said. "I listen to KTRN every morning when I go to work. She pushed search on the dial, and they heard a country western station, a classical music station, a talk show that was unclear, finally a station with a man and a woman discussing current events.

* * * * *

The second man who tried to push his way past the manager was pushed back by the manager. The young man pulled a pistol from his belt and shot the manager one time in the stomach. The manager fell to the ground. The young man pushed past the body and out the door. He pushed the full cart around the side of the building and disappeared.

"We should call the police!" Mary Two said; she was nearly in shock.

"It won't do any good," said Mary.

"Have you got your phone, Ashlee?" asked Mary. "I left mine at the house."

"We know," said Mary Two, "we tried to call you."

"Doesn't work," said Ashlee as she handed her phone over the back seat. "Couldn't get a signal."

Mary looked at the screen on the phone and saw the bars on the right. "Are these bars on the right the battery?" asked Mary.

"The signal strength is on the left," said Ashlee.

She dialed in the number. "Just push send?" asked Mary.

"Yeah, send," said Ashlee.

Mary sat for a minute with the phone to her ear. "Doesn't work," she said.

"Drive back to the house" said Mary.

"Your slightest wish is my command, oh mighty," said Ashlee as she drove out of the parking lot.

Mary sat silently in the back seat staring at the picture on the front page of the paper. She opened a small bag that she had brought into the car. It was the last purchase she had made in her haste through the grocery store. She brought out three eight-inch butcher knives. Let's hope we don't need these, she thought to herself.

"Oh," said Mary, "don't drink the tap water. This man I ran into in the store told me that the water supplies had been poisoned."

"Poisoned?" Gasped Ashlee.

"It's probably nothing, but I bought some gallons

of water to drink until we can get some local news."

"Wish we had a cat," said Mary Two.

"What has that to do with anything?" asked Mary.

"The miners used to use canaries to test the air for poison; we could use a cat. You know, here kitty, kitty, have some nice water."

"Very funny," said Mary.

"Let's get back to the house and hunker down and wait for my knight in shining armor."

11

"SO WHAT YOU'RE saying," said Carl when he awoke, "is that security is probably lax at a power plant, and then you say that you don't really need in the plant to shut it down."

"Precisely," said Tom.

"Okay, you've got me scared, what do you see as the answer?"

"The best long-term solution, and I won't be making any friends in the power industry by saying this, is to get rid of the grid. Instead of those giant behemoth power plants, we need to go to a whole bunch of little ones. Nuclear energy was one of the biggest myths ever foisted upon the American consumer. They are just a great way for a few good old boys to get rich at the expense of the common man. Evil, I say.

"So we know that big power plants are too vulnerable, that big electric grids are too vulnerable right? Right?"

"Right," agreed Carl.

"So think small; if we make up our minds that we don't need big power plants, the American genius will prevail and we will get small. Americans need to be made to realize that with the way things are now it is impossible to keep the electricity on if someone wants to shut it off. We need to adjust our lives so that we

139

can get by without the electrical grid. It is not difficult; it is simply a matter of doing it.

"When it was cheap, people used a lot of it without giving any thought to it. The big power companies used these big usage numbers to justify the building of big power plants. So they built these big plants, and because of this the price of electricity went sky-high, and guess what?"

"Usage went down," piped in Carl.

"Exactly," said Tom. "When the price went up, people simply turned their lights out, and demand went down to the point were we really didn't need these dinosaur nuclear plants. That's the same thing that could happen now.

"If we want people to get off the grid, it will be a simple matter to raise the price. American ingenuity will kick in and Americans will find a way to use less power.

"There are all sorts of alternatives to the great grid. There is solar, and wind, and geo thermal, and fuel cells. Ever watch a hundred-ton ship rise and fall with the tide? Harness that energy. Ever watch a Kansas windstorm just blow and blow till it's scary? Harness that energy. Lay your hand on a steel roof in the summer. Harness that energy. Solar and wind power can break down water into hydrogen and oxygen. Store the hydrogen for later use. When electricity first came to rural America, farmers had windmills; the utility companies came and took the windmills and the generators. Build windmills next to ponds and lakes and use the free wind power to make hydrogen to run fuel cells for homes. Store up the hydrogen when the wind blows and use it when the wind quits. Nearly free power.

"Big oil spends millions telling America that this can't be done. We put a man on the moon, compared to that, this is easy. Shut the power off for a few days, make people nervous about the dependability of the grid, raise the price of electricity where people start to look for alternatives, and it won't be long before this country will be independent. Then let the lunatics do whatever they want to the grid and it won't affect but just a few people.

"Right now, most of this country would be completely screwed if the power went down. Big business likes that, but Americans can't afford to be that vulnerable. It is simply impossible to protect big generation facilities; it is simply impossible to protect all of the thousands of miles of power lines that run exposed throughout this country. If you tried to put these power lines in the ground, it would cost so much to change from bare wires to an insulation for that high voltage that the cost would simply be prohibitive. I don't even think they make an insulation for that high a voltage.

"Small generating facilities should become the norm and not the exception. You know, fuel cells are the answer; they have been around since at least the '50s. They have been used in space vehicles for years; they burn hydrogen, and the only byproduct is water.

"The only reason that fuel cells are not in common use today is because the last thing the rich bastards want is for the common man to get hold of a cheap source of power. There are two parts to being rich, keeping your money and keeping others from getting any. Every car should be fuel-cell driven, every home should be fuel-cell driven. Anybody with a windmill and a pond can generate hydrogen gas, but we won't see widespread fuel-cell use until the hydrocarbon industry can figure a way to monopolize the hydrogen market. It looks like they are trying to get a lock on the transportation system with a lot of help from our government.

"America has become fat and weak and vulnerable; we have been overrun with foreigners willing to work for no benefits in unsafe conditions. These Mexicans come up here and run jackhammers and saws and shit and don't wear eye protection or hearing protection or fall protection or dust masks, and every one of them is taking a job away from an American.

"The common man needs to have enough food to survive for a while and enough water to survive for a while. I would think a household should keep at least a six months' supply of food and water. This could be just a big old sack of beans and rice and a couple of big jugs of water.

"Let's say for the sake of argument, that the power went off, I'm satisfied that it's on by now, but let's say that it's off and that some calamity has happened and that the power grid has failed. If Americans as a group had expected that this might happen, then the individual would have more or less been prepared. There is a certain few 10 or 15 percent of the population that had ignored all the warnings and were always there with their hand out anyway for someone else to take care of them. The majority of the population would have stored a little food and a little water, would have bought a few candles to see by and would have weathered through this calamity without it becoming a crisis.

"Americans must be made to realize that electricity has made them dependent upon it for their very lives. They must be made to realize that this dependence has made them weak and vulnerable, and that the electrical distribution system in this country is old and frail and wrong.

"In the long term, the hope would be that the communities would develop small power generation facilities of their own that would be able to supply enough power to at least keep the freezers running and the heaters blowing, and whatever it takes to keep the water running and purified. This would free the majority of America from the large generating facilities that are so vulnerable and easily attacked and easily shut down.

"The ideal situation, of course, would be to have every home independent like these cabins in the mountains that have a little wind generator and a little solar and in the near future a big old fuel cell. They could all still be connected to the grid for emergencies, but would be independent of it.

"Look at those cars leaving the city. Notice that there are few cars going in, but the bulk of the traffic is coming out. This radio still doesn't seem to work. Look at those traffic jams in the outbound lanes."

Both Tom and Carl were leaning on their edge of their seats now, concentrating on the traffic coming out of the city.

"Maybe we're involved in a great event here," said Carl. "Maybe we are in the middle of the event you have just been describing."

"Just my luck," said Tom. "I've spent most of my

life preparing for this huge event, and where do I find myself — heading right into a damn city. How far do you suppose we have yet to go?"

"I imagine another 20 miles or so," said Carl.

"I think this highway changes to three-lane up ahead. I guess it would be six-lane if you count both ways."

"Thank God she lives in the suburbs," he said.

"It's almost evening, maybe this is just normal rush hour traffic. Since this is an elevated highway, look down among the buildings and see what's happening."

"Traffic seems a bit heavy, don't seem to see any street lights though. Look down there, another grocery store with a mob in front of it."

"That's great," said Tom. "I'm just starting to get hungry."

"We better save that jerky; it might be all we have to eat on the way back. Look up ahead at that traffic; let's stay close to the outside lane so we can get off this boulevard if we have to."

Carl began to chuckle.

"What's funny?" asked Tom.

"This reminds me of my favorite cartoon of all time."

"What was that?" asked Tom.

"It was a cartoon in one of those Sunday news magazines; it had two guys in a lifeboat, one a little guy and one a big old guy. The little guy was rowing the lifeboat, and the big guy was talking to the little guy. The caption below the picture read, 'Well, Weatherby, one of us just ran out of food.' " Carl began to laugh out loud.

"Very funny, Weatherby," said Tom.

"Let's get over to the right side."

Carl dug around in the glove box and looked at a map.

After a moment of looking, Carl said. "If you can get us as far as 103rd Street, we should be able to make it on the side streets."

"This is 125th Street, we've got 22 blocks to go. Let's get in the right lane."

Tom looked in the rear view mirror. The traffic was heavy, but they let him in. "It's starting to slow down. Can you see the exit from here?"

"I think it's that big green sign up ahead. We might have to get over on the shoulder, but I think we can make it."

Tom pulled over on the shoulder and pulled past the stopped cars. One semi had pulled too far to the right and caused Tom to pull way over and clip a couple of the little blue markers.

"This truck has seen a lot worse than that," said Tom. He finally drove the big truck onto the exit ramp and came to a stop at the stop sign. "Which way now, navigator?"

"Follow this road to Sunset, which should be about two miles ahead."

They passed the first light that wasn't working, and there was one wreck beside the road. As they came to Sunset, that light was also not working. The cars were pausing at the intersection and letting each other through.

"Now what?" asked Tom.

"Take a left on Sunset for about three miles," said Carl.

After they had turned the corner, Tom spoke. "See that intersection that is controlled by a series of lights? Look at it now; those cars are doing a fine job of taking turns. I don't understand why cities don't try four-way stop signs first before they go to lights."

Signs of looting were everywhere; people were breaking windows out of stores.

"Amazing," said Tom. "Have we entered the twilight zone? I wonder what this is all about. Reckon it had anything to do with that low-flying plane?"

"I have no idea," said a worried Carl.

Traffic was moving, but slowly.

As they passed a small shopping center, several people were carrying an armful of shovels through the broken plate-glass window.

Sure doesn't take long for society to break down, does it?" said Carl. "Take a right at this next intersection."

"I've got my bearings now," said Tom. "I remember this bank on this corner."

Traffic was light on the side streets.

"There's the old Buick; that must be the rear main seal. I can see the puddle of oil from here," Carl said in a relieved tone of voice.

Tom pulled the truck and trailer in front of the car and backed the trailer up to it.

"Let's go into the house and find out what's going on before we load this car," said Tom.

Tom went to the door and pounded on it.

"I thought I told you to go away," came a voice from inside. "I've got a gun and I'll use it."

At that time Tom looked toward the garage and

noticed that the pedestrian door to the garage had been torn from its hinges.

The door to the house slowly opened and Mary ran out. "Thank God it's you, Tom," she said, and ran into his arms."

Little Mary Two came running out and hugged Tom around the waist. "Daddy, Daddy," she said, I've been so scared."

"Thank God you've made it."

"They stole everything, some gang of young men," said Mary in a tearful voice. "We went to the store to get some staples, and they must have followed us home. They stole everything out of the garage and the car.

"They broke into the house, and we explained to them that they had gotten all of our food and they left. They said they would be back."

"Are you ladies all right except that you're shaken up and a little scared?" asked Carl.

"We're okay," Mary said, "just glad you're here."

"We need to figure out how we're going to get out of here. Looks like first thing is we better get armed."

Tom walked back out to the truck and unlocked the driver's door, and from under the floorboard of the rear seat he removed the floor mat and opened a small compartment. Inside the compartment was a steel box; he took the steel box, rearranged the floor covering and relocked the driver's door. He brought the box into the house.

The house was a wreck with furniture in disarray where the ladies had tried to barricade themselves in. Tom walked past the wreckage and set the box down on the table, then walked over to the sliding patio door and opened the windows to let in light. He returned to the box and removed a silver pistol in a brown holster. He also took out a box of shells and opened the box of shells and loaded the pistol.

Little Mary came up to her father and asked, "what is this all about, Dad?"

He gave her a hug and said, "This, my dear, is a 357 magnum pistol; it will shoot either 357 bullets or 38 specials. These bullets are hollow-tipped 357 magnums; they will deter any other looters. You've shot this very gun before, don't you remember?"

"Sure," she remembered, "that's the one that makes the loud noise, the one we shot the turtles with."

"That's right," said Tom. "Kids should be taught to handle guns safely at an early age. Kids are suspicious, and if they find a gun will want to play with it. Teach them how to use one safely and you will prevent many accidents."

He took another holster out of the box, a shoulder holster, and laid it on the table. He took off his coat and laid it on the back of a chair and put on the shoulder holster, put the gun in the holster, adjusted it for fit and put his jacket back on.

He removed another smaller gun from the box and loaded it. He turned to look at Carl, "You packin'?" he asked.

"Have been the whole trip."

"Never a doubt in my mind."

He reached down into the box and removed a can of pepper spray. "Here, Mary," he said as he handed it to the child.

"Do you have a pocket? Do you remember how

to use this?"

"Yes, I do, Daddy, and you've handed this to me several times and, yes, I will be careful with it and, yes, I won't spray myself."

"Mary," he said.

She walked across the room.

He handed the smaller gun to her along with a box of shells. Without a word, Mary took the gun and bullets and put them on a small table near her purse. "I sure wish I would have had this an hour ago," she said. Many times in the last hours she had wished that she had a gun.

He removed a small bullet holder from the box and fitted it to his belt. He closed the box and carried it to the front door and set it beside the door.

"Do the phones work?"

"No, I've tried it all morning."

"No power, no phones, no water," said Mary. "Oh, by the way, don't drink the water. A man I met in the store this morning told me the water had been poisoned."

"Great," said Tom, "my worst nightmare."

"We could sure use a beer right now, Mary," he said. "Is there any beer in the house?"

"There should be a 12-pack in the refrigerator," she said as she walked to the refrigerator.

"Don't open that door just yet," said Tom.

"Want a beer, Carl?" asked Tom.

"Love one."

"Okay, Mary, open the door quick and close it right back."

Mary opened the door quickly and removed the 12-pack and set it on the table.

He took two beers from the 12-pack. "Here's your beer, Carl."

"Be right there," said Carl. He had been looking out the front window. "Wish those little bastards would come back," he said as he walked back to the table.

"Me, too," Tom said. "We've got more things to worry about."

"How you holding up, Ashlee?" he asked. She had a drink in her hand; she raised it in the air and said, "Wish we had a little more ice."

"Let's make these the last ones for now," said Tom "we've got some serious work ahead."

"Have you got a road atlas in here?" asked Tom.

Mary brought him the atlas from the bookshelf.

"Do you have any radios in here, Mary?"

"No, we don't, they're all electric, and the one boom box we did have, the batteries are dead."

"Does anyone here have any reason why we can't just leave and get the hell out of Dodge right now?" asked Tom.

The girls were silent.

"Well," said Carl, "I sort have had an ulterior motive for coming along."

"I know you did," said Tom.

"Suppose that car of yours would last me till I get downtown if we put some oil in it?"

"The engine's got to be overhauled anyway," said Tom. "Put a couple of quarts of oil in it and it should last."

"How long do you reckon it will take you?" asked Tom.

"Under normal circumstances it would take me

about 15 minutes to get there from here. I imagine a couple of hours."

"If they're home, I should be back in a couple of hours."

"It's full of gas," Mary said as she handed Carl the keys. "How about oil? There are three quarts of oil in the trunk."

Tom and Carl walked outside to the car, and Tom raised the hood and checked the dipstick. "It's about a quart and a half low. Let's just put in one quart for now, and it should be good to go to the city."

Carl brought a quart from the trunk, and Tom put one quart in the engine and closed the hood.

"Don't worry about this, Carl. If it burns up, it's no big deal." Tom meant what he said.

"If I burn it up, I'll buy you a new one."

"I need my little box," said Carl as he walked toward the cab of the big truck. Tom threw him the keys.

Carl got his little box out of the cab of the truck, took a couple of pieces of jerky and put them in his pocket.

"You want me to come with you?" asked Tom.

"I'd appreciate it," said Carl, "but there are some places even I wouldn't take a white boy."

"Don't let no moss grow under your feet, Bubba," Tom said. "They'll be calling out the National Guard pretty quick and we won't be able to leave."

"You know, I've got to go," said Carl.

"I know, just be careful."

Carl started the car and drove off quickly down the street.

Tom walked back into the house.

"Where's Carl going?" asked Mary Two.

"He's got a daughter, honey. How old would she be, Mary?" he asked his wife.

"She'd be early 20s this year," said Mary. "She was living with her mother."

"Darned shame those two couldn't get along," said Tom. "Both of them are really good people, but their personalities just clashed; they were always at each other's throats. Carl told me that last Christmas was the last time he had seen his daughter. She was study-ing to be a nurse or something."

As Tom and Mary walked back through the door, Mary turned and locked the door.

"That's not something we do at home," said Tom.

"This isn't home," said Mary, "and I think from now on I'll be in the habit of locking the doors."

"Do we have any food in this house?" asked Tom. "I'm beginning to get a little hungry."

"I don't suppose you'd consider running down to McDonald's."

"I suppose you could," said Mary, "but I doubt it would do you any good."

They walked into the garage and forced the door open to let in some light.

"Look," said Tom. "They didn't get everything, they left the water bottles, and what is this? A big old sack of beans; this was probably the best food left and the idiots didn't take it. They probably thought food was a bag of potato chips."

He took the sack of beans into the kitchen and put them on the counter.

"Hey, Ashlee," he said to his sister-in-law, "do you have a propane grill?"

"Yes," she said, "it's outside in the little shed behind the garage."

"How about a big old pan?" he asked.

"In the lower cabinet to the right of the sink," she said.

Tom opened the cabinet and selected a large metal pot and set it on the counter. He selected a knife from the drawer and cut the corner from the sack of beans and began to put the beans in the pot a handful at a time. From time to time he would discard a bad bean or piece of rock. When he had finished, he took the jug of water and poured some onto the beans. Under normal circumstances he would have washed them, but water was scarce now.

He walked out to the patio and fumbled around with the grill until it was burning with a nice hot flame. He returned to the pot of beans and set it on the grill.

"Mary," he said, "would you please watch this water and just as soon as it comes to a boil shut the gas off and put this lid on, please."

"Okay," said Mary as she pulled a patio chair close to the grill. "I feel just like a pioneer woman."

Tom walked to the kitchen sink and confirmed that the water was not working. "Do you have a flashlight, Ashlee?" he asked. She brought him a flashlight from the cabinet in the living room. He took the flashlight to the basement and looked in each room and then returned to the laundry room. He selected two small towels from the laundry basket and placed one over the floor drain, and the other he stuffed into the drain hole of the washing machine after pulling out the hose. He emptied a laundry basket and put it on top of the drain and weighted it down with a jug of bleach and some laundry detergent.

As he was returning up the stairs, he was met by his daughter who said, "The water started to boil, so Mom turned the fire off."

"That's good honey, thanks," said Tom.

"What were you doing down there?" asked Mary.

"Well, sweetheart," he said as he led her back up the stairs, "every drain has a trap under it that fills with water. This water keeps nasty sewer gases from coming into the house and killing us. When the water stops running, the water in the P-trap dries up and lets sewer gases back into the house. I simply closed those two pipes to keep sewer gases out of the house.

"Now I need to run outside and dig a hole to use as a toilet," Tom said to Mary.

"No need," said Mary, "we've been using the guest bathroom."

"But it won't flush without water," said Tom.

"Oh we've got lots of water," said Mary, "the Johnson family that lives next door have a swimming pool."

"Really," said Tom, "let's go look."

They walked around the front to the neighbor's and knocked on the door. No one answered. They walked around the rear of the house through an un-locked gate and looked at a large patio with a large swimming pool.

"This is a gold mine," said Tom. "This was prob-ably filled before the water went bad. But just to be safe, we should only use this for bathing and toilet flushing. Let's get some buckets. They returned to the little shed behind the garage and selected two five-gallon buckets and took them to the pool and filled them with pool water."

Tom carried the two buckets back into the house.

When he had set them down inside the garage, Mary Two tried to raise one. "This is really heavy, Dad," she said.

"A pint's a pound the world around," said Tom. "Two pints to the quart, four quarts to the gallon; each gallon of water weighs eight pounds."

He carried the buckets through the house, sloshing a little out as he went. He set them outside the bathroom in the hallway.

"We can use this water for the toilet," he said. "Don't drink this water."

"Mary, I'm a little tired from this drive. If you don't mind, I'd like to take a little nap now."

Mary came over to him and gave him a big hug. "Sure glad you're here," she said.

"I'll take care of you," he said.

"Did you stir the beans?"

"Yes, I did."

"Good," he said. He sat down in the recliner and raised the footrest. He selected a page from a newspaper that was on a table next to the chair. He opened the paper and laid one sheet across his chest.

"Make sure the doors are locked," said Tom.

"I will," said Mary. He had already begun to snore.

12

AS CARL DROVE away from the house, he knew that he was heading into a very different world.

He had seen his daughter last at Christmastime. Just turning 22, she had been an A student, became a nurse, and was now studying to be a doctor. She was a beautiful girl by anyone's standards, and she had been the byproduct of a short-lived, tempestuous relationship he had had when he had been much younger with a young woman he had met at church. She had been part Hispanic and part white and he had loved her. They had been instantly attracted to each other, but had found it impossible to balance two careers and family at the same time. As it turned out, they had grown up just a few blocks from each other when they had been children. But they had never met. When they met in L.A., they found they had a lot in common. They had spent hours reminiscing about people and places they had shared. Back home.

Had Juliette been a boy, Carl would have kept him to raise, but they both felt that a girl needed a mother. He had always been more than generous with child support payments and alimony, this of his own accord. Neither had wanted to let the courts get involved. His investments had allowed him to be generous, and he had never found another woman who appealed to him the way she had. He had felt it a pity that they could never seem to get along.

Juliette had found a niche in the emergency room of St. Luke's Hospital. He was satisfied that this was where she would be, and he had determined to bring her back with him to the ranch. He was certain that she would want to stay, and he kept trying to figure a way in his mind to convince her to leave the city.

He had heard that she was dating someone, but he hadn't followed up.

As he drove down further into the inner city, the roads were cluttered with stalled cars and traffic lights that didn't work. Several times he had to actually pull off the road and onto the sidewalks. As he passed under the major highways, he noticed that many times there were traffic jams on these major arteries. He saw people climbing over guardrails and stumbling down the sloped grassy areas where the two roads met. People who had abandoned their cars on the interstates made the situation even worse.

He passed several gas stations, and the situation was always the same: several cars pulled up to the pumps with the hose from the pumps inserted into the car's tank and the driver waiting for some miracle to cause the pumps to come back on. They were out of gas and figured that eventually the power would come back on and they would be first in line.

Whenever he passed one of these stations, he instinctively looked down to the gas gauge and was thankful that the tank was nearly full.

He fought his way past one blocked intersection, and a man came running up to the car; he had a gas can in his hand.

"Please, mister," he pleaded, "could you spare just five gallons of gas? I've got a can and a siphon hose. Please, mister, I've got to get home."

The man actually tried to pry open the little door to the gas cap on the side of the car. Thankfully, the traffic jam had just cleared and Carl was able to drive away, leaving the man standing with his gas can and his hose. Carl began to notice several such people with red gas cans and hoses and pry bars working on the gas doors of parked cars.

He could just imagine that these people had broken the windows of hardware stores and had stolen these cans and hoses. He determined to never let his gas tank dip below half tank.

He'd never given any thought to this when he bought a car. He made up his mind that gas tank size would be a major consideration in the future. As he approached the inner city, there were more and more signs of looting. He saw people breaking into shops and carrying out stereos and TVs. A lot of good it will do them, he thought, without TV stations and electricity.

He was looking for G Avenue which was a large four-lane affair that would take him to the hospital. There was very little traffic on this large road, but then there were no shops. This was a four-lane, tree-lined road that led from one residential area to another; he was actually able to get up to speed. Eventually he saw a large blue sign that said hospital ahead, and he was able to see the large hospital buildings looming ahead.

He drove through the parking lots where cars were

parked at every angle except the proper one, as if the drivers had just pulled into the lot and abandoned their cars. He drove around until he found what he was looking for, a trash dumpster with a brick wall built around it. He drove the car alongside the wall till there was just a few inches between the driver's side and the wall. He turned off the engine and got out of the passenger's side door and locked the door. He walked around the back of the car and made sure someone couldn't get to the gas tank and then walked toward the first large hospital building.

He ignored the sidewalks that wound through the trees and shrubs toward the entrance. Instead, he walked in a straight line, up the hills and through the brush to the nearest back entrance. He could hear a generator running at the rear of the building. The back door had been left propped open by a large ashtray, the top of which was filled with half-smoked cigarettes. When he got inside, his eyes had to adjust to the dim lights. Only the emergency lights were burning, about every third light, down the long corridor that he had entered. He looked both ways, and the hallway seemed to go straight for a long way in either direction. He turned to the left and walked briskly down the hallway. The walls were white, the ceiling white, and the floors were a highly polished gray tile that reflected the glow of the ceiling lights.

He soon came to an intersection with another corridor. There was a sign hanging from the ceiling that pointed to the left that said ADMINISTRATION, another sign pointing left reading ADMISSIONS, and a sign pointing to the right that said EMERGENCY ROOM. He began to walk rapidly down the hall to the right. It wasn't long before he began to hear people's voices. He had not seen one living person since he had entered the building, but as he came to another corridor it was like a scene from *Dante's Inferno*. The hallway was filled with beds and filled with people in varying degrees of consciousness. Many had relatives or friends standing beside them. Most of the people in the beds appeared to be really sick. As techs and nurses walked past them, several of them would raise their hands trying to get their attention. The techs and nurses were too busy to bother with them, and the family members plucked at the sleeves of the medical personnel dressed all in blue as they hurried past. Many of the patients were coughing, and some were obviously too sick to move.

There was another sign that pointed to the left that read EMERGENCY ROOM and pointed to the right that said X-RAY/SURGERY. He hurried past the people in the hallway and down the corridor to the left. He stopped in front of a double swinging door with windows and looked out into the waiting room for the emergency room. It was filled with people, every chair was filled; there were people sitting on the floor and people standing. There was a mob of people at the admissions desk. Many of the people were coughing uncontrollably. He noticed that all the hospital personnel were wearing white masks.

There was a small room on the right side of the hallway that contained a bed, a chair and a small cabinet. On the cabinet, among other things, was a box filled with white masks. He grabbed four and put one on.

He returned back to the hallway; the air was filled with the sounds of people hacking and coughing. A young nurse came out of a room carrying a tray of medicines and walked toward him.

"Excuse me, Miss," said Carl, touching her arm. She looked up and pulled her arm away.

"How can I help you?" she asked through her mask.

"Do you know Juliette that works the night shift?"

"She's not here right now. She went home yesterday and didn't come in today."

He knew he would have to go to her apartment. Maybe she was sick, too.

He hurried down the hallway and out the door, tore off the mask and took a deep breath of fresh air. The loud hum of a machine caused him to turn to look toward the emergency generator. Hope that's on natural gas, he thought to himself. It would be a real mess in there if that quit.

The sun was beginning to set, and he had determined not to be caught out after dark. He needed to find a place to hole up for the night. He felt like he was in a scene from *The Omega Man.*

As he got in the car and drove out of the parking lot, he was thankful for two things. The first was the nearly full tank of gas, and the second was that he knew where Juliette lived and that it was close to the hospital.

He drove back to the main road and took a left on Jackson. In normal times there would have been a traffic signal working at this main intersection, but the lights were off. Luckily the streets were rather empty. He drove for two more blocks and turned right on Quincy.

The apartment was a three-story affair. With the money he sent her monthly she could afford better, but this was close to her work and she had friends living here. He drove through the parking lot and found an empty slot next to a fence. He pulled the car into the slot so that there was no space on the driver's side. He crawled out the passenger's side door and locked it.

The only sign of life that he had detected in this complex was an overweight couple dressed in identical yellow hooded sweatshirts and jeans and walking a teeny brown dog with a curly tail on a red leash. The dog was trying to keep up the pace with its little short legs working as fast as they could. There was also a group of young teenagers, three boys and three girls, playing a game of football in the grass. The girls were barefoot, and they seemed to be having a good time.

He walked through the parking lot and into the building. There were no lights burning in the hallways; only one exit light was lit and it was flickering. This would mean that the power had been out long enough so that the batteries had exhausted themselves.

He walked up the stairs to apartment 21 and knocked on the door; there was no answer. He ran his hand across the door to feel the number, and there was a piece of paper taped to the door. He took the note to the stair landing where the last dim light from the fading sun gave just enough light to read the note.

It read, "Dear friends, I have gone to visit my father, call me on my cell." It was signed, *Juliette.*

He carried the note back to stick it on the door. Just great, he thought. I'm here and she's there, maybe. Now he was anxious to get home.

His mind went back to all the sick people in the hospital, how they all seemed to have the same sickness. He hoped that she hadn't caught it.

He was suddenly struck by tiredness and realized that it had been a long time since he had slept. He decided to wait here in this apartment for the night because he didn't want to fight the traffic jams in the dark. He hurried down the stairs and back out to the car, opened the trunk and retrieved his little silver briefcase. The kids had quit playing football and were now just sitting under the trees in groups of two. He reentered the building, and placing the briefcase on the floor in front of the door, he opened it. He first turned on a miniature flashlight and opened a small leather case. He removed two small tools from the case and used them to open the lock while he held the flashlight in his mouth. The door opened easily; he replaced the tools and entered the dark apartment. The flashlight revealed a well-kept room with a fire-place, and the powerful little light cast long dark shadows from each piece of furniture. The fireplace mantle was filled with pictures, two candles and a long cylinder with fireplace matches. He used one of the matches to light the gas of the fireplace and used the same match to light one of the candles. The two logs in the fireplace began to burn, and the warmth felt comforting.

He carried the candle into the kitchen area. On the counter was a black wire stand with a hook that held two bananas. He peeled and ate one greedily and said to himself, I wonder if little girl has any real food here. He tore through several cabinets and came away with half a box of Ritz crackers. I guess this is better than nothing, he thought. He opened the door to the refrigerator, then closed it quickly. It was warm. He reopened the door and held the candle close. There was a gallon jug of water nearly full; he took that out and looked carefully around the appliance and closed the door again. "These people will have to replace a lot of appliances," he said out loud. He carried the water and box of crackers into the room with the fireplace. He sat for a minute on the couch and ate the crackers and sipped the water. The fire was burning now of its own accord, so he turned the gas off.

He set the food and water on the dining room table, wiped his hands on a napkin from the place setting, checked the locks on the door and returned to the couch. He carried the silver case to the table in front of the couch and removed a 45 automatic from the case, checked to see if it was loaded, then slid it under the front edge of the couch where it was just out of sight. He took off his shoes, lay back on the couch, pulled the coverlet over him and fell fast asleep.

The sun's rays awakened him. "My gosh," he said to himself, "how long have I slept?" He looked at his watch, and it was 11:30 a.m. "I've got to be going," he said, "but first things first." He was thankful that the restroom had a small window. He removed the lid from the back of the toilet tank. "Good," he said. "One good flush is all I need." He looked in the mirror and turned the water faucet on. No water, he thought. He took a handful of water from the back of the tank and splashed it on his face. He rummaged through the medicine cabinets and found a new toothbrush. He brought the jug of water in from the dining room table and brushed his teeth.

He looked at himself in the mirror. "You know," he said to himself, "civilization is great when it works;

when it's broke, it's a bitch."

Before he flushed the toilet, he washed his hands in the tank water. "Bye, bye, civilization," he said as he flushed it.

As he was preparing to leave the room, he heard an unusual noise by the front door. It was the sound of the door being forced open. The lock had shattered and was being held by the safety chain.

A pair of male voices could be heard in the hallway.

"She has to be home, how the hell else could that chain be on?" said the first voice.

"Hey, little lady, remember us, we just moved in down the hall, and you were too good for the likes of us?" said a second voice. "Come on and open the door, we'll show you a really good time."

Carl took the 45 from its holster and checked to make sure there was a shell in the chamber, then held the gun ready and waited by the restroom door.

The door shook with a violent blow, but the chain held. Another blow and the chain gave way, the door swung wildly open and two young Hispanic males in their early 20s entered the apartment.

"Come on out and play, Chiquita," said the first.

"Were going to show you a real good time," said the second.

Carl waited until they had entered the room, and then he stepped from the hallway and into the front room.

"Surprise," Carl said in a loud voice.

"Son-of-a-bitch," said the first of the two intruders, and he began to pull a pistol from his belt. The second already had a gun in his hand and raised it and shot one time at Carl.

The big 45 exploded twice, and both men lay dead on the floor, each with a bullet in his brain. Carl stepped over the bodies and looked both directions down the hallway. It was empty except for the blood splatter on the wall. He removed the wallets from the bodies and dragged the bodies to the large trash chute and forced them into it.

Carl locked the door and walked into the kitchen.

He looked through the cabinets again and found a can of tuna, better than nothing, he thought. Tuna on a Ritz, I'm the king of the world. He hunted through the drawers for a can opener with no luck.

"You mean the only can opener in this entire place is this Black and Decker electric gadget," he screamed out loud. "Civilization is a real bitch."

He set a breadboard on the counter and dug through the knife drawer until he found the biggest knife. He placed the can of tuna on the breadboard, covered it with a paper towel and with one violent motion cut the can in half. "Open sesame," he screamed, and quickly turned the two half cans so they would not drain out. He stood beside the window as he ate the tuna.

That's when he noticed that the car was missing. "Son-of-a-bitch," he screamed aloud, "somebody stole the damned car. Oh, shit."

He went back into the bedroom and tore through the closets until he found a ragged old suitcase. He put the holster in the silver case and the silver case inside bigger case and set it by the door. He slid the 45 into the large side pocket of his bib overalls.

The chain lock had been torn from the door, but

the lock in the handle still worked. He made sure the door was locked as he left. I guess I'll just hoof it, he thought to himself, reminds me of the old army days. It's probably not over 20 miles, just a walk in the park.

He looked down at himself, baggy shirt, old coveralls, work boots. Just another bum with his life's possessions in his bag.

He walked quickly out of the apartment complex, across the driveway and across the manicured lawn. The kids had left the football on the grass; he hoped they would be okay. The traffic on the road seemed less than the day before. He hurried across the road to the median strip and then, looking both ways, scampered across the other half of the road.

Here he was, what looked like a beggar, carrying an old bag. If he went the way he had come, he would be traveling through several middle-class neighborhoods. A small jolt of adrenaline went through his system thinking about all that danger.

Very likely a homeless individual would not be welcome.

He walked briskly keeping his head low, but his eyes were constantly looking for police or anyone who would cause him trouble.

A police cruiser came down the road on the opposite side of the median strip. There were two policemen in the car, and the one in the passenger's seat was pointing in his direction. Just great, he thought. If I stand I'm screwed, and if I run I'm screwed. He would rather meet up with a band of hoodlums than the police. The squad car had slowed, but now was accelerating toward the next intersection. That son-of-a-bitch is coming back, he thought.

He turned back to the road as he heard a late model Lincoln Towne Car pull to a stop at the curb.

The passenger window rolled down and a female voice with a slight Spanish accent said, "Carl, is that you?"

He lowered his head to look into the window and saw the most beautiful woman in the world.

"Alise, always a pleasure to see you. I thought you were out of town."

"Get your sorry ass in the car, plowboy," said Alise in an authoritative tone of voice. She was truly happy to see this man.

He tried to open the rear door; it was locked. He waited and threw the suitcase in when it clicked. He then quickly jumped into the front seat and lowered the visor. He looked in the visor rear view mirror and watched the police car as it began to make a U-turn.

"Let's go," he said breathlessly, "we're about to have some visitors."

The big car lurched forward.

"I've got to turn around and get Juliette," she replied.

"Don't bother, she's not there."

"Well, where is she?" asked Alise.

"There was a note on her door that said she had gone to see me."

"When was that?" she asked as she accelerated away from the curb.

"I guess it was yesterday or the day before. There was a note on the door. I spent last night there. Hurry up and lose these guys, okay?"

She sped up and turned right at the first intersection and made a quick left down an alley.

"We should have lost them," she said.

"I thought you had gone off to some island with Prince Charming," said Carl.

"He turned out to not be a prince and to not be very charming. I took the first plane back and ran into this. Just about didn't make it."

"What exactly is the this you're referring to?" he asked.

"The plane crashes? Haven't you heard?"

"What plane crashes? I've sort of been isolated the last couple of days, why don't you fill me in?"

"Terrorists or something blew up some airliners, because we were coming in to land and the next thing you know the pilot made a big left turn and circled around the airport, and we could see the two big fires where two airplanes had crashed. "

"Somebody had used a couple of missiles to blow up a couple of planes, and the pilot told us that we didn't have enough fuel to get anywhere else so they let us land. We circled right over where the planes had crashed. They both landed in residential neighborhoods, and a whole bunch of houses were on fire. It must have killed as many people on the ground as it did in the air. These planes were fully loaded with gas, and it created this giant fireball with a giant cloud of black smoke; it was like a scene from hell. Anyway, we circled around and landed, and I guess we were the last plane to land before they closed the airport. The airport was filled with people when they closed it, and it took forever to get my bags and get out of there."

She didn't say it, but she never wanted to get on a plane ever again.

"Do you have any idea what happened to the power?" he asked.

"Don't know anything about it; there was power at the airport. I don't think the power went out until this morning."

"Oh?"

"Let's see. I drove back to my apartment, watched the news for the rest of the day. I was tired from the trip, and so I tried to call Juliette and got no answer. I left a message on the machine and went to bed early. I slept in a little like I do from time to time, and when I finally got up the next day, the lights were out. I tried to get Juliette, but the phones quit."

"So how'd you get here?" she asked. "Did you have some sort of financial reversal. You look like a bum, and you smell like a bum. But I could recognize that gait of yours a mile away. I knew it had to be you."

"Do you make a habit of picking up bums off the street?"

"Only on rare occasions," she said. "Most of the bums I've picked up have been more polite."

"I've missed that razor sharp wit of yours," he replied.

"How do you happen to be here under these conditions?" she asked.

"I came down with Tom Brown to pick up his wife's car that broke down, see the city, eat a big old steak dinner, drink a few frosties, and get back in time for the late show."

"There won't be a show of any kind for a while, at least until the electricity gets back on. Why must you always adopt the Uncle Tom slave look?" she asked. "Where do we go from here, what's your plan?"

"How much gas have you got?" he asked.

"Just about a full tank," she offered. "I filled it right before I went to the airport, and I've just driven from there to my apartment and then to here.

"That's good," he said. "Gas is a rare commodity right now."

"Since Julie's headed to my place, and Prince Charming's not around, how would you like to come back to my place with me?"

"Oh, no," she said. "We tried that once and it didn't work out."

"We were young and stupid then," he said. "We're older and wiser now."

"Are you calling me old?" she asked in an alarmed tone of voice.

"Yes, older," he said in a diplomatic way, "but like a fine bottle of wine. You're still the most beautiful woman on the planet."

"That's why I pick up bums off the street, for the compliments."

"Now where do I go?"

"Go down about two blocks, take a left on A avenue. I don't suppose you know how to get to Tom's sister-in-law's house.

"How would I know that?" she asked.

"Never mind."

"Do you have a street map?"

"No such luck. We'll just have to wing it."

"This is not the sort of car to be driving through the hood with," Carl mentioned.

"Why not?" she asked. "I've got my can of mace."

"These days you'll need a machine gun. Remember the old joke about the guy that took a knife to a gun fight." He laughed.

They drove two blocks and turned right at A Avenue. As they drove, he couldn't take his eyes off her. God, she's beautiful, he thought. He remembered why he was attracted to her in the first place. No wonder Juliette was such a knockout, he thought.

They drove for several hours with the intersections being blocked, the constant looting, cars blocking the road. Several times they had to drive onto the sidewalk, and several times they had to push cars out of the way, with the help of bystanders.

People carried gas cans and hoses amid general chaos.

"You know, it would almost be faster to walk through this mess," he commented.

"As you will notice, I don't exactly have my walking shoes on. I just live about two blocks down this way. Let's go to my house and change my clothes and rethink this situation." She paused at an intersection, looked both ways, and drove quickly through.

"Fine by me," he said, "I'm getting hungry."

She had slowed down to let a few people cross in front of them. There was a sudden crash, and she turned to look and saw that a brick had been thrown through the window and that it had hit Carl in the head. He slumped forward in his seat, and she could see the blood pouring down the dash.

She accelerated into the crowd, and two people rolled over the hood of the car. She drove around the corner with the tires squealing; a hail of bricks and rocks from the crowd pelted the car.

She drove quickly two blocks and turned left into the parking lot of an apartment complex. There was a wooden blockade at the entrance, and she drove through it with splinters of wood covering the car. She pulled to a stop near the building and was by now in near hysterics.

"Carl, Carl," she cried, "are you all right?" His body was still slumped over and covered with pieces of glass and blood.

She opened her door and ran around to the passenger side. She opened the passenger door and began to brush the glass off of Carl's limp body. "Ouch!" she cried and pulled a shard of glass from her finger. She took off her sweater and used the sleeve to lightly brush the glass from Carl's face and folded the garment to apply pressure to the wound.

"Wake up, Carl, please wake up. There is no way I can carry you up those stairs," she pleaded through her tears.

The red brick was wedged in the seat, and she picked it up and threw it as hard as she could across the parking lot.

Carl was regaining consciousness. "God, my head aches," he said in a weak voice. "What happened?"

"They hit you in the head with a brick," she said. "Any other place and it might have killed you. Let me help you up to my apartment on the second level."

She helped him out of the car. "Stand still a minute," she commanded, and brushed some glass from his clothes. "Watch your head; it's still bleeding."

They got as far as the stairway leading upstairs, and he stopped and held onto the post. "Get my bag, please."

"Your bag can wait," she said, "we need to get you upstairs."

"Get the bag! Please," he said in a commanding tone.

"All right," she relented and went back to the car.

He lowered his head against the railing and slumped to his knee.

She ran back to the car and pulled the bag out of the back seat. It was heavy; she half-carried and half-dragged it back to the stairs.

"Here's the bag," she said,

"Thank you, dear," he replied.

She looked at him for a brief moment and dragged the bag up the flight of stairs as he staggered behind her. She fumbled for the key and unlocked the door, dragged the bag into the apartment, and he followed her in. Carl stumbled to the couch and sat down. She double-locked the door and ran through the apartment opening the windows shades to let in the sun.

She returned to the couch and removed the sweater from his head. "Let me look at that," she said. "Good, it's about stopped bleeding, I'll be right back." She hurried to the bathroom and returned with a folded washcloth. "Water's off," she said, "or I would have soaked this in warm water." She replaced the sweater with the washcloth. "Hold that tight," she said. She threw the sweater to the floor by the front door. "You owe me a $300 sweater, buddy," she said as she placed a couch pillow under his head.

She helped to pull his shoes off and got his feet up on the couch. "Let me get you some water," she said. "It's not cold." She walked to the refrigerator and opened it; the bottom shelf was filled with little plastic bottles of water. She opened one for Carl "Here," she said. "I'm sorry it's warm."

"That's okay, it's like liquid gold," he said as he took a drink. "Run back outside quick," he said, "and park the car close to a wall or something so somebody can't get into the gas tank."

"What do you mean?" she asked.

"Park the car next to something that makes it hard for someone to siphon the gas," he said.

"Oh, I get it," she said, and hurried out the door.

"Damn, this hurts," he said out loud and he staggered off the couch and into the bathroom to look in the mirror. He poured some of the water onto the towel and wiped off some of the blood. He dabbed the towel around the wound and shook his head slowly from side to side as if to clear the cobwebs.

She came back and stood in the doorway. "You need some stitches in that," she said.

"That's not going to happen," he said. "Just let me rest a minute."

He walked back and sat on the couch and watched her move around the small apartment. Like a big cat, he thought. He was foolish for letting her go. She was pacing from room to room without really doing anything.

She had not realized how much she missed this man. He had been a good father for their daughter. He had always thought highly of her. She had been foolish to let him go. She had always had dreams of first-class airplane tickets, big cities, fine meals and fancy clothes. She had come from a poor background and had spent the last several years in the fast lane. She looked at him in his bib overalls; that's how her daddy used to dress. This man wanted to get back to the basics in life, and she had not been ready. Now that she was older, she felt differently.

The fast lane was too fast.

On her plane flight home, before all of this chaos, she had decided to try to get this man back.

They now had one common goal, to find their daughter.

She watched him lying injured on the couch and decided that she would do whatever it took to get him back.

Carl sat up on the couch and cradled his head in his hands and moaned loudly.

She hurried into the kitchen, rummaged through the cupboards and returned with three pills. "Here, Carl," she said, "here's three Tylenol. It's the best I can do."

"Thanks," he groaned, and swallowed the pills with the water.

"Shall we have some food?" she asked. "That is, if you're up to it." She quickly moved into the kitchen.

"We have bread," she said triumphantly a moment later, looking out the door and holding the loaf in a triumphant manner. "We've also got tuna," she announced joyfully

"Please, not tuna," he groaned. "That was my last meal."

"Peanut butter and jelly," she said. "The bread's still fresh and the jelly has never been opened. Thank the Lord for peanut butter. This peanut butter cost $2.49 last week, wonder what it would be worth today?"

She made two trips to bring the napkins, plates and the sandwiches to the little table. She sat cross-legged on the floor in front of the end table and pushed a plate of food in front of Carl.

"Can you eat?" she asked.

"I'll be all right," he said, "just this terrible headache. I could use a good stiff drink."

"How about a beer? It's not cold though," she said. "They drink it at room temperature in Europe. Let's have one."

She stood up, stretched her lovely long legs and went into the kitchen and returned with two opened bottles of beer. She set it in front of him, and he drank about half of the bottle.

"Would you care for another," she said, "before I sit down?"

"No thanks, one's my limit, " he thanked her.

They ate their sandwiches in silence, but looked at each other as they ate.

"Remember that Christmas right after we were married," she asked, "when we came back to see the folks and all the restaurants were closed and all we had to eat were Doritos and bean dip?"

"Here we are again," he sighed.

"Better lie back down for a minute," said Carl as he wiped his mouth with a napkin.

She hurried to help him adjust the pillow under his head and covered him with a throw.

He awoke in less than one hour, and when he opened his eyes he saw that she was sitting cross-legged on a chair just watching him. She was wearing a very short white silk robe that was tied at the waist.

"Feel better?" she asked.

"Lots better," he said, as he began to sit up, he raised his head slowly and got to his feet.

She hurried over to him and took him by the hand. "Come with me," she said.

She led him down the corridor to a door with a large pane of glass. She opened the door and they stepped in; it was pleasantly warm and well lit. There were three skylights in the ceiling and one wall was glass. Against one was a rack that held 20 large candles, all burning. In the center of the room was a large pool of water.

"Solar-powered hot tub," she said.

She kicked her shoes off toward the wall, untied her belt at the waist, slipped out of her garment and laid it across the chair. She stood naked before him wearing only two gold chains around her neck.

"Let me help you get out of those clothes," she said as she began to unbutton his shirt.

"These clothes are in pretty good shape," she said.

"They should be; they were brand new yesterday."

"How anyone could be wearing brand new clothes and still look like a bum is beyond me," she said as she helped him remove his coveralls.

When he was completely naked, she took his hand and led him down the steps and into the water.

"Looks like at least part of you is glad to see me," she commented.

"All of me is glad to see you," he said as he took her in his arms and kissed her. It was a long deep kiss. She returned the kiss and hugged him tightly. Their hands played over the other's body as though trying to squeeze the other into one being. He laid her gently back on the floor while he remained in the water. He placed a folded towel under her head. She screamed with pleasure as he entered her.

"God, I have missed you," she moaned. "I bet those other women love you."

"You are the most beautiful woman I have ever seen," he said as he thrust into her again and again. "You ought to know there's never been any woman since you." She began to moan loudly with each thrust until she caught her breath with an intense orgasm. He waited just a moment and then he came, which caused her to climax again. He collapsed onto her and she wrapped her arms around him.

"I have been so unfair to you," she said as she began to sob.

"There, there," he whispered, "we're back."

* * * * *

They awoke from their night's sleep with the sun streaming into the window. It was the third day.

She was lying beside him. He removed the covers to look at her unclothed body lying next to him. He began to caress her body, and she awoke with a smile. "Come on over here, big boy," she said, and he obliged.

After they had finished making love, Carl held her for a long moment until she released him. He walked toward the window and picked up the phone, then threw the receiver onto the floor.

"I hate civilization," he snarled. "When it works it's fine; when it breaks it's the shits." He stood staring out the window. "I sure hope you left my sorry ass behind," he said out loud.

"What did you say, honey," she asked.

"Just hoping out loud that old Tom got the hell out of this town when he could and that he isn't waiting for me."

"Let's finish that bath now," she suggested, and led him by the hand toward the pool room. The water was still warm and the candles still burning. She saw him looking at the candles."

"Church candles," she explained, "they last for weeks."

"Hey, where are my clothes?" he exclaimed.

"I rinsed them out last night and hung them up to dry in the kitchen. They should be dry by now," she replied.

"Remember, I spent the better part of my youth in a state of poverty," she said. "We never had a dryer when I was small; we had a clothesline."

"I remember that, too," he said.

"These clothes are dry, but stiff as a board," he joked as he put the clean clothes back on.

"Let's get out of here," he said.

"Just about ready," she said as she came out of the bedroom. She was wearing hiking boots, jeans and a long-sleeved plaid shirt with a brown vest that had many pockets.

"Let's go to the farm," she said.

He carried the suitcase out the door.

The car was still in the parking lot where she had left it.

"Let's get out of this town." They drove out of the lot and onto the main road.

"We're at half a tank, and I bet we haven't gone ten miles," he said.

"Like you said, when civilization collapses, it's a real bitch."

They spent the better part of the day working their way back toward Tom's sister-in-law's house.

"We're going to need some gas," Carl said. "We've fought our way through this traffic for hours; we're still miles from where we need to be. Now here we are on some side street and we don't have a decent map." Carl had pulled the car over to the curb and was studying an old map. "You just never appreciate the convenience of convenience stores until they are gone," he said.

He had rolled the window down and heard a generator running in the distance.

"Somebody's got gas," he said.

"Wait right here a minute," he said, "I'm going to check this out." He leaned over the back of the seat and opened the suitcase. He brought forth a small pistol. He pulled the slide back to put a bullet in the chamber and snapped the safety on. He held the gun in front of her and said. "This is the safety, do you remember how to use this?"

"Yes, I do," she said. "I really don't want to be left alone."

"I'll be okay for just a minute, we need the gas," she finally agreed.

He again reached behind the seat and removed another pistol; he cocked this one, put the safety on and put it into his belt.

"Be right back," he said, and gave her a kiss.

Carl walked down the seemingly empty alley, drawn by the sound of the generator. The air was filled with a sickening sweet odor he had not smelled before. He was met by two dark-skinned men, one small, one large.

"What do we have here?" said the big one.

"What the fuck are you doing in our neighborhood, home boy?" He could tell from Carl's size and bearing that he was not to be messed with.

"I heard the generator, just thought I'd see what's

going on." These punks didn't faze Carl.

"None of your fuckin' business. Guess I'll kill you," said the big one in a threatening manner.

"I have no intention of messing with you, just settle down," said Carl as he stepped back a pace.

"Guess I'll teach you a lesson," said the big man.

"Last time I'll warn you," said Carl. It was a threat.

The big man took a step forward and pulled a pistol from his belt.

Carl used a sidekick to break the knee. The three men could hear the bones crack, and the big man fell to the ground. Carl spun once, and his left foot caught the big man under the chin and there was a sharp snapping noise. The big man lay motionless on the ground, and a small pool of blood began to form under his mouth.

Carl looked at the big man for a moment and then concentrated on the small man who was wearing a baseball cap turned backwards, a New York Giants' jersey, baggy pants and expensive new tennis shoes.

"Man, that was wonderful. You have motherfuckin' killed my motherfuckin' Benny. Two kicks, you are one mean brother. I can tell by those sloppy clothes you need a job."

He walked over to the body on the ground. "No problem, what's your name?" he asked as he dug through the pockets of the big man.

"Don't even think about it," said Carl in a threatening tone. Carl felt he would probably have to kill this man.

"Hey, I'm cool, man, I don't like guns. They get you killed, see?" he pointed at the dead man. He stood up clutching three packs of cigarettes that he had taken from the big man's pockets.

"These are better than gold right now," he said with a wink.

"Don't worry about him," said the small man. "I'll take care of the body. Yes, I will." He raised his hands in the air. "Hey, just pat me down, you'll feel better."

Carl patted him down.

"Benny was my bodyguard, used to play for the Giants. Got hit a couple too many times."

"Hey, you look hungry, come on over here," he walked back to a push cart, and there was a box there that he reached into and got out a couple of Ziploc® bags, packages of dried meat.

"Have one of these, life in the city without electricity," said the small man. "Some members of society have learned to adapt. I been selling the shit out of this shit. The old boy that owned this meat market sort of owed me some money, and me and Benny sort of took over when he didn't pay. Me and Benny, we love that jerky. Try some of this." He opened the bag and held it out to Carl.

Carl put a piece in his mouth, thought about it for a moment and then took another piece. He nodded his head in a positive way.

"You could trade this bag for a carton of cigarettes," said the small man as he put the bag back in the cart.

Jerky was always one of Carl's favorites.

"My name's Willy Davis, just like the famous running back, Willy Davis. No relation. This is a Willy Davis jersey, the one he wore last year in the playoffs."

"This is pretty good jerky," said Carl as he began

to eat the second piece.

"It's not the best we make, but it's been a pretty good seller. Named that recipe in honor of Willy, it's called Willy Davis jerky. Come on over here and have another piece; that whole bag's yours." He handed the rest of the bag to Carl.

"Look, I need you, you come to work for me you can have as much of that as you want. Besides you owe me, you killed my motherfuckin' Benny." He pointed to a larger box in the cart. "You like kosher food? There is a big population of Jewish types around this neighborhood, so we have to sell kosher food." He handed Carl a piece from another box.

"That particular box of jerky is all kosher. We call it 'Jewish white boy' blend of jerky. Had to get a Rabbi to come over so we could call it Kosher. Hee, hee, hee.

"Certain neighborhoods like that kosher food, can you taste that oregano?"

"Can't say I do," said Carl as he thought a moment. "Maybe a little garlic or onion."

"Those Jews like their garlic," said Willy.

As they walked, the noise that was the generator became quite loud.

At the end of the alley there was a large fenced in area that had been the parking area for a freight line company. There were probably 30 tanker trucks parked in the lot.

"Look at that," said Willy, "probably half of those are full of diesel, and there's five box trucks parked in the back that we liberated from Associated Grocers Supply. Those babies are full of stuff. We started getting our shit together about two months ago, and when the lights went out we were ready."

"See our generator? Benny used to be good with his hands. We've got enough diesel fuel to last us years."

"I'd like to see that generator," said Carl.

They went through a chain link fence and he noticed a large hose laying along the ground from the generator to the nearest tanker truck. There were rags packed around the hose where it met the truck, and there were little puddles of diesel fuel that had dripped off of the hose beside the diesel tanks.

"It looks peaceful and quiet, doesn't it, like no one is here," said Willy. "Just look up to the third window on the right."

The window was open. Carl could just barely discern a human and the barrel of a gun.

"Hey, Squiggy," Willy hollered. "Show that lazy ass of yours."

The man at the window moved closer to it. He was wearing a backwards baseball cap and carried an M16 military rifle. Carl figured that this man spent most of the day high on some drug.

"Where's Benny?" asked the man in the window."

"He's takin' a nap," Willy said, "yeah that's it, a nap. Run across the street and get Pete and bring Benny back here, he's in the alley."

The window shut.

The generator was setting on a large semi flatbed. The wiring had been temporaried to the top of a small shed. The wall of the building had been painted white many years ago. A fading red sign on the building said Meedeers Meat Market.

"Ain't that baby quiet? We found it down by the

docks. Benny was good with trucks and shit, and we dragged it back to here. We brought this baby back here, and we got a local electrician to wire it up. When he finished, he helped us with one of our first batches of product. Hee, hee, hee. Quite tasty product. Hee, hee, hee. We hooked that generator up to Meedeers Meat market, and now we're in the jerky business. Come on in, come on, come on. Long as you're with me, nobody hurt you. This is where you'll be working from now on. Come on in and see the bizness." He led the way up a set of crumbling brick steps and through an ancient doorway.

The sweet smell was overpowering, the smell of dehydrators. Along one wall were 12 dehydrators running full blast, and the smell of dehydrated meat filled the air.

"This here is the dehydrators, that's what old man Meedeer was good at; they sold a shit load of that jerky mostly back east. I come here by accident one day. I was their best customer, used to eat their shit by the pounds. Old man Meedeer and his wife were especially helpful in some of our first product. Hee, hee, hee."

"Sorry about the heat. Benny said not to turn on the air conditioning, something about the size of the generator. Said it might blow that baby up. These here are the dehydrators, and over here," he said as he turned to the left and pointed, "is the product."

There was a glass-fronted meat case filled with boneless pieces of meat; it looked to be nearly fat-free.

"In the morning, there'll be five cutters in here making this into jerky. It takes one day to make this much into jerky, and then when it comes out of the dryers we package it up and out the door. In this refrigerator this big old batch is put in spices; this batch goes in the dehydrators and a new batch goes into the spices. We trade this jerky for things of value — cigarettes, guns, knives, dope, shit, money's no good; nobody's got money, all the banks are closed. We got a warehouse full of them ATMs with as much cash as you could want and can't buy nothing with it.

"You have to barter cigarettes, worth their weight in gold, bottles of aspirin worth their weight in gold. You can't believe how fast the grocery stores were cleaned out. You can't believe how fast the drug stores were cleaned out. Man, that Tylenol went first. The medicine cabinet in the common house is worth a fortune. We trade that shit for jerky. Come on back here and see something."

He led the way into another room.

"This here is our product, this is where we keep our product," he said as he walked down a corridor.

There was a long wide hallway with several freezer doors on the left, and each door had a red and a green light burning beside the door.

"This here is our fortune."

Carl looked into the large freezer, and there were hanging rows and rows of headless gutted human bodies, skinless, handless and hanging by their feet. He couldn't tell which were men and which were women. Some were small, some were large, and the wrists of some had little puddles of blood on the floor below.

Carl had the urge to throw up. But fought back the urge.

"See that one there, that's going to be our special recipe of fat old white lady jerky, and that one over there will be our young Asian gang member jerky. And if that dumb Squiggy will hurry back, we will have our special mutherfuckin' Benny recipe. This is an amazing product. It delivers itself to our door; let me show you."

He walked out of the freezer and shut the door. They walked down the corridor and into an office.

"Let me show you how easy this works." He was very enthusiastic.

He walked to a TV set and turned it on. The picture was of a small table with a young man sitting behind it. On the table were bags of the jerky that Carl had already seen. There was a sign beside the table that read, " Trade jerky for ciggs and aspirin."

A young man approached the table in a suspicious manner. He walked to the table; there was no sound, but it was easy to tell that these men were bargaining. The young man behind the table stood up and motioned in a come hither fashion. Another man dressed in a blue jumpsuit entered the screen from the right and took possession of a paper bag that the new arrival was carrying. He shook the bag and looked at the contents, then smiled. He motioned for the man to follow him.

"See there," Willy said, "that there is a victim. It might be another Jewish white boy victim; these two old boys are really good at what they do. They'll lead him into that other room, and he'll get a good thump on the head. Next stop the meat locker, hee, hee, hee."

He dropped his feet to the floor from the desktop, walked over to the VCR and shut it off. Walked back to the chair and sat down. He motioned toward a chair in front of the desk. "Sit down, sit down," he said with a gesture.

Carl sat down to listen.

"I have here my prized possession. Remember the '72 superbowl when my hero, Willy Davis, caught the TD pass in the end zone just as overtime was running out. Remember how he broke his leg on that play and missed the first half of the '73 season. Remember how he was a hero?" Willy was so excited that he could hardly sit.

Carl did remember that game.

"Looky here," he said. He reached down in the desk drawer, and from the bottom of his right-hand desk drawer he brought forth a bone. This here is a fibula bone, not just any old fibula bone. See this line right here?"

Carl leaned forward to get a closer look.

"This here is the broken fibula bone of Mr. Willy Davis, my personal hero. Hee, hee, hee."

"And this here is the break that caused him to miss nearly the whole of the '73 season. Don't you think that hurt like a motherfucker?"

Willy rubbed his hand along the break in the bone as if it were a sacred object.

Carl had made up his mind that society had taken a terrible turn in the wrong direction.

"Looky here, here's the deal I'm gonna make with you. You can have all the women you can git, all the food you can eat, all the pills you want. I just ask one thing — protect my sorry ass, keep me alive. That's it. Keep me alive and well, 'til we can git out of this mother fuckin' city."

"How many of those guys in the window are there?" asked Carl.

"Tonight? Just the two."

"Well," Carl said, "today I've decided to do the world a serious favor." He reached into his pocket and brought out a nickel-plated pistol. He recocked it to make sure there was a bullet in the chamber. "This may be a dying world, but we don't need people like you," and he shot him three times in the chest. The explosion drove the chair against the wall, and Willy slumped to the floor.

Carl walked out the back door and past the generator. As he passed the generator, he reached up and turned off the switch, and the generator began to slow down.

As Carl was looking over the generator, he disconnected the wires going into the building. The man above the window had come down to street level. Carl placed his hand on the gun in his belt.

"Either drop that gun or use it, sonny," he said in a menacing tone of voice.

The boy dropped the gun on the ground. .

"Help me get this loaded," Carl commanded.

"It wasn't my doing," said the boy. "Ritchie made me do it."

"Okay," said Carl. "Just help me get this loaded. Are the keys in it?"

"They were yesterday," said the boy.

"This is an old World War II vintage truck." The GI green had been replaced by a psychedelic paint job.

Behind the machine was a large fuel tank. A sign on the tank said DIESEL FUEL. He checked a gauge on the side that showed it to be nearly two-thirds full.

Carl stepped into the big truck and started it.

He left the truck running, stepped out of the truck and walked to the gun lying on the road and put it on the floor of the passenger side of the truck. "You know, son, he said you better find another line of work."

"Yes, sir, I will," said the boy.

He pulled the big truck out the gate and down the alley.

He motioned for Alise to get out of the car. "Come on, get into this truck."

"But it's my car," she said.

"I know," he demanded, "but I'll buy you another one."

He took the suitcase from the rear of the car and placed it in the front seat of the truck.

She had difficulty getting into the side door, but once she was in she asked, "What are we going to do with this?"

"Were going home," he said.

"Look in that glove box for some paper," he asked.

"There's this," she said, and handed him a receipt from a tire shop.

"Do you have a pen?" he asked.

She rummaged in her purse and gave him a pen.

"Let's see," he said. "I'll date this two days ago." He handed the paper and pen back to her. "Please sign the bottom of that, use the name Shirley Thomas."

"Let's see," she said after signing. "You bought this truck and tank from someone named Shirley Thomas two days ago for $9,500. Nobody will believe that."

"Why not?" he said, "these are unusual times we live in."

He started the big machine and drove down the street. After the first right turn, there was a car stalled in the street.

"Well, Mrs. Thomas, let me show you how to use your machine."

He drove the big truck into the front of the car and pushed it out of the way. He accelerated down the road.

"Best damn purchase I ever made," he said.

13

TOM AWOKE FROM his nap.

It was dark and one candle was burning on the table. Mary was asleep in the chair beside him. He quietly lowered the footrest from the recliner and padded through the house. He stopped to pick up the flashlight from the table and quietly checked each room to make sure that everyone was asleep and safe.

He looked at the empty bowls by the sink in the kitchen and thought to himself, holy smokes, I've slept through the night. At least I feel rested. I'm really famished, he thought, as he stepped out onto the back porch and removed the cover from the big pot of beans. Mary had left a small flame burning under the pot, and the beans were still warm and smelled wonderful. He stirred the big pot one time and replaced the cover.

He walked back into the house and down the hallway to the garage door. He opened the door and looked into the garage. Satisfied that all was okay, he closed the door and walked back into the living room where Mary was sleeping.

He heard some loud voices outside and a car door slamming. He blew the candle out and went to the window. The air was filled with the strong cinnamon odor from the dying candle. He looked out the window and saw a late model pickup truck with a driver sitting behind the wheel. In the yard were two rowdy-looking young men, each carrying a bottle.

Tom overheard one thug speaking to the other, "This is the right house isn't it, June?"

"Yea, it is. I recognize the broken door in the garage. These ladies might have a little food left, but that's not what we want, is it? Let's wake these ladies up."

"Oh, ladies," the tall one said in a loud voice. "Wake up, ladies. We've been to the liquor store, brought you a little present. Yes, we did, a little present."

They staggered up on the porch and punched the button, but it didn't work. The tall one pounded on the door. "Wake up, ladies," he said. "Come on, ladies come out and play."

Tom walked through the room where Mary was still sleeping, removed his gun from the shoulder holster and waited behind the wall that separated that room from the front door.

"Come on, ladies." The big one took two steps back from the door and crashed into the door. The lock burst apart, but the safety chain held the door. He finished the bottle and threw the empty onto the porch. He felt the safety chain with his left hand and took a gun from his belt with his right. He stepped back another two steps and crashed into the door. The safety chain broke and the door burst open.

They both staggered through the broken door. "Ladies, oh, ladies, wake up. We said we'd come back, and here we are."

Tom had the flashlight in his left hand, and as soon

as he could tell that both men were in the building, he shined the light in the first one's eyes and put a bullet in his forehead. The man's face had a look of surprise as his body fell to the floor. The noise caused the second one to step back; he dropped his bottle and fumbled for his gun. Tom shot him in the chest. The force of the bullet caused his body to fly backwards against the wall.

Tom took several steps toward the bodies. He looked for a few seconds at the first man, then looked at the second, and seeing signs of life he put his gun to the man's head and shot him again.

He stepped over the bodies and out into the yard with the flashlight off. The driver had stepped out of the driver's seat and was relieving himself in the middle of the road. This third man was very drunk; he could not keep his feet under him, and weaved from side to side in the road, Tom waited until the man was finished and was zipping up his pants.

Tom held the gun up to where it was pointing at the man's head. The man turned and was surprised to see Tom.

"Do exactly as I say," said Tom. "If you don't, I'll shoot you where you stand, do you understand?"

The man nodded his head in agreement.

The crashing noise from Tom's gun had awakened the ladies, and they were huddled in the entryway looking at the bodies. Mary was still wearing her clothes; the other two were wearing night clothes.

Tom and the driver came up on the porch. "Drag this body back to the truck," Tom said.

"Yes, sir," the man said. He took the body by the feet and dragged the body across the porch. The head thumped on the stairs and left a trail of blood as he dragged it to the truck.

"Leave that one there for a minute," said Tom. "Let's get this other son-of-a-bitch."

The driver took the feet of the first man and dragged that body to the truck. Tom opened the tailgate of the truck. The bed of the truck was filled with an array of full bottles of liquor and wine. He selected a magnum of Riunite Lambrusco and threw it up onto the yard. They manhandled the bodies into the back of the truck and closed the tailgate.

The women were now standing on the porch.

Tom reached into the driver's side window and took the keys from the ignition. "Have you got a gun?" he asked the driver.

"Here," he said and handed it to Tom.

"Now get behind the wheel," Tom commanded, "you're driving."

Tom walked back to the porch and stepped into the house. He took the cover from the arm of the chair and picked up the other gun with it.

"Could you ladies wash this area down, please?" he pleaded. "I'll be right back."

He walked back to the truck and got into the passenger side door. He pointed his gun at the man. "Take me to the liquor store," he said to the driver.

The driver backed the truck into the driveway and then drove back the way they had come. He turned at the first block and then drove three blocks and pulled into a small shopping center. There was a large sign at the road that advertised it as Pheasant Run Mini Mall. Tom wondered how many hundred years had passed since a pheasant had run through here. They passed a day-old bread shop, a coin shop, a Laundromat; at the fourth entrance was a liquor store.

A sign said Thomas Liquor Store. The front door was broken. "Did you boys do some mischief here?" asked Tom.

"Well, the dirty son-of-a-bitch should have been more friendly. If he hadn't pulled that gun, we wouldn't have had to kill him."

"Which one of you sons-of-bitches killed him?" Tom demanded.

"Well, Clyde thought he got him, but I know it was my 45 that waxed the bastard. He was still movin' when I put that hole in his head. Pretty good shot, don't you think?"

They walked into the store. The shelves had been stripped bare; there were several broken bottles on the floor whose contents had spilled onto the floor. The looters had been thorough. The body of the owner, a gray-haired man of perhaps 65, was stretched across the counter, a shotgun still clutched in his hand, a large hole in his forehead. Tom walked over, avoiding the pools of liquor on the floor, and felt the pulse, but the body was cold and dead.

The shotgun was pointed at the belly of the driver. Tom laid his hand on the old man's hand that clutched the shotgun. There was a loud roar as the shotgun sent a blast that cut the driver in half.

"Well, old-timer," Tom said, "guess you got the one that got you."

Tom walked out the door, stepping over the body that was spreading a pool of blood on the floor, looked both ways and saw no one, turned left and walked quickly to the end of the mall along the sidewalk, keeping in the shadows. At the edge of the mall he turned once to look back at the truck. "Oh, brave new world," he said to himself. He walked to the rear of the building, across the driveway at the rear of the mall, across the street and walked the three short blocks home.

A few minutes later he walked to the front porch of the house and noticed that the ladies had used buckets of water to wash the blood from the front porch. He picked up the bottle of wine that he had left in the yard earlier. As he walked in, Mary told him to watch his step on the slick floor. The house was lit by a fluorescent camping lantern that was set in the middle of the kitchen table.

He sat down at the kitchen table and opened the bottle of wine. Mary reached into the cupboard and selected four small glasses and set them on the table. Tom filled all four glasses and said, "I think we could all use a drink." He downed his glass and held his hand in front of him and it was trembling.

The ladies each took a glass.

"Those were the same bastards that were here earlier," said Mary. "They said they would be back when they had more time. They got what they deserved. What happened to the driver?" asked Mary.

"Liquor storeowner shot him," said Tom in a matter-of-fact way.

"Are those beans fit to eat?" he asked. "I'm starved."

"I wish Carl would show up, I'm ready to get the heck out of here," said Tom. He looked at the front where Ashlee was trying to fasten the front door, but the lock had been destroyed.

"I'll get that," said Tom, as he hurried out the front door. He walked to the side bin of his truck and returned with a battery drill and a handful of screws. He shut the front door and attached it with three long wood screws that he screwed in at an angle.

"This will hold for the night," said Tom. "Why don't you ladies try to get back to sleep and we'll rethink this in the morning."

Mary Two said, "I'm scared, Mom, can I sleep with you?"

Mary looked at Tom and he nodded agreement. She set a bowl of beans on the table for Tom.

"I'll curl up on the couch in case there are any more surprises."

The ladies went back toward the bedrooms. Tom shut off the table light and sat in the dark eating his bowl of beans.

Mary was the first to awaken. She walked through the house opening the blinds; the sun was shining brightly and filled the room with new hope.

Tom was stirring on the couch, and Mary walked to him and sat down next to him. "Hey, baby," she said.

"Good morning, sweetie," he said, and gave her a hug with his hand fondling her right breast.

Mary took a deep breath, arched her back, and took a moment to enjoy the caress. She placed her right hand under the blanket and caressed Tom. "You know, Mary slept with me last night, and that means they're both at that end of the house, which would leave the bedroom by the garage empty."

"Lead the way," said Tom.

She led him by the hand down the corridor.

"Just a minute," he said as he stepped into the

hall bathroom to brush his teeth with a glass of bottled water. He quickly walked down the hallway, entered the bedroom and closed the door. Mary had removed her clothes and was lying seductively on top of the well-made bed. Tom looked at her for a moment and walked to the window and opened the blinds. The sun streamed into the room and drenched the bed and Mary with sunlight.

"Oh, that warmth feels good," she said, and luxuriated as though bathing in the sunlight.

Tom walked to the bed and knelt down beside it. He kissed her passionately and began to caress her body with his left hand.

She began to moan with pleasure. He kissed her harder and made sure that he caressed her breasts, her stomach, her thighs. As he caressed the inside of her thighs, her legs began to open and she arched her back. He kissed her on the neck and she fought it, but as he kissed her neck harder she arched her back. His left hand went to her pubic mound, and he caressed her until he found her stiffened clitoris. He gently applied pressure around that area and she began to moan. He began to kiss her on the mouth while rubbing her more intensely. Her body began to arch in a rhythmic way that increased in intensity until her body was racked with intense orgasmic spasms. Her screams were held in check by Tom's intense kissing. She pulled away from him and lay in a fetal state quivering.

Tom watched her with a smile on his face. It gave him great pleasure to give her great pleasure. He touched her breast gently and she pulled away. Good job, he thought to himself.

After a moment she took a couple of deep breaths.

"God, I needed that," she panted. "I love you so much." She sat up on the bed and gave Tom a hug. Her hand reached down between his legs. "Now it's your turn," she said.

He smiled.

* * * * *

Tom was standing by the sliding door looking out, while Mary was sitting at the table. "Do you have any idea what time it is?" asked Tom.

"Not really," said Mary "all the clocks in the house are electric."

"That's something," said Tom. "Just a couple of days ago if we needed to know the time we would simply turn on the TV and look to the TV guide channel, right there on top."

"Or," said Mary, "we could turn on the computer and the time would be right there. It even keeps track of daylight saving time. Or we could turn on the laptop, but the batteries are dead. "

"I would just look at the time on the cell phone, but it's dead and doesn't work anyway. We could tune in a radio station if we had a battery radio. Remember the old days when people had wind-up watches; you can't even buy them any more. Everybody has a battery strapped to their wrist, or they depend on their cell phone. The simple things we took for granted. I guess it's about ten."

"I wish Carl were back here, I'm ready to go."

"Ah, there you are," he said to Mary Two and Ashlee as they entered the room. "Since you're up, little one, would you like to go get a couple of buckets of water and see if the people next door are home yet?"

"I am flat starved," said Tom. He went to the refrigerator and opened the door. Are there any trash sacks, Mary?" he asked. Mary opened the doors under the sink and handed him a large black trash bag. He started throwing things into the sack.

He opened the freezer and water poured out. "Let's see," he said. "In happier times we would have a couple of TV dinners, a couple of pot pies, a frozen pizza." He tossed these into the trash bag. "What have we here? It is way in the back, and it is still frozen and it is a small ham with a ham bone. What a find! Who would have thought?"

"That was left over from last Christmas," said Ashlee. "We went out to eat instead." She didn't want to admit that she had stayed too late at the office party and hadn't made it home until breakfast. "I didn't want it to go to waste, but I really don't cook much."

"You and the rest of America," said Tom. "People are so used to eating fast food that we have a whole generation that can't boil water. I was in the store one time buying a soup bone, and the lady cashier said, 'That doesn't have any meat on it!' "

"Anyway, we can live for a week on this ham, with the beans Mary has, so we should do just fine for a couple of days if it comes to that."

"Let's leave this door open," Tom said. "If we shut them, it could mildew inside." He pulled the refrigerator out from the wall and unplugged it. "In case the power ever comes back on," he said to Mary with a wink of his eye.

"Surely you don't think this is permanent?" asked Mary.

"Since I have no idea in the world what caused this, we can't know if it will ever be fixed. Without any news, we can't know what's happening in the rest of the country," Tom said as he left the room.

"How much gas you got in that big old SUV in the garage?" he asked Ashlee.

"Just over a quarter of a tank," she said. "I usually fill it up on payday."

"Let's go get you some gas," he said. "Which way to the nearest gas station? You need to come and live with us for a while, and we need enough gas to get you out of this city." He looked at his wife and she nodded agreement.

"How do you intend to get gas without electricity?" she asked.

"It's magic" he said. "Come with me and I'll show you."

He turned to Mary. "Get a piece of paper and write a note for Carl, please, and say that we will be back and to wait for us. Thank you."

"Okay," she said, "I'll do it."

She went to the computer printer and took a piece of paper from the printer. One thing about the computer age, she thought to herself, it has been easy to get hold of a blank sheet of paper. She walked to the table, took a red pen from her purse and wrote a brief note.

Tom walked into the garage and pushed the up button. "This is going to take some getting used to," he said. He opened the rear door of the big SUV and stood on the doorsill as he reached over the top to grab the red ball that released the door. The door opened a few feet of its own accord. Tom stepped to the ground and finished the process.

"Mary, ride with your sister. Little Mary, come

with me. Now which way to the gas station?"

"Three blocks up the road and left one block," said Ashlee.

"Okay, you lead the way."

As they drove down the road, Tom thought about locking the house. What's the use, he thought, nothing to steal.

The filling station was at the end of the mall. It was obvious that someone had been trying to get gas. All of the hoses were lying on the ground, and several empty gas cans were scattered about. People had drained the hoses and left them lay on the ground and discarded the still empty gas cans.

Tom parked his truck near the building and motioned for Ashlee to park her truck near the pumps.

"Hang those hoses up," he said to the girls, and taking a flashlight Tom disappeared into the building through the broken front window. The station had been ransacked; the shelves were empty except for a few broken boxes and torn sacks of chips. He went into the back room into the electrical room and read the legend on the panel and turned off all the breakers except for three.

He walked back to his truck and told Mary Two to go wait with her mother. He backed the big truck to the back of the station and left the engine running. He removed a pair of lineman's pliers from the side of the truck and cut the seal to the meter and pulled it from the box and threw it on the ground. He took a large cable from the side of the truck and clamped the wires to the lugs at the bottom of the box. He then opened the door to the generator compartment on his truck, checked the gauges and flipped a switch. Nothing happened. Good, he thought.

He took his voltmeter to the front of the store and opened a relay cabinet under the front counter. By moving some wires around, the pumps in the front reset and were ready to run.

"They're on," Mary yelled.

"Fill her up," said Tom, with a look of relief on his face.

As the ladies began to fill the SUV, another car pulled up. "I'll give you $100 for five gallons of gas," said the man in desperation. "I have to get home."

"Fair enough," said Tom. He wanted to get home too. "But wait your turn."

Mary came to Tom and said, "Did you take money from that man? You can't sell gas to that man, it's not yours to sell."

Tom knew that Mary would worry, so he said, "Did you see the look on that man's face? He was going to get gas if he had to kill for it. Besides, Texaco won't miss a few gallons of gas. No, wait, it's Exxon; no, Shell. What the hell, it's all one big company anyway. It's like I tell the boys, it all makes sense when you realize that it's all one company. One insurance company, one oil company, one political party, the end results are the same."

"Mary, take this money and leave a note for the owner with our number on it and say that we'll be back to settle up when the crisis is over."

He picked up two empty cans and filled them up.

"Twenty-one point two gallons. No, wait. Add five more gallons for these little tanks, and five more for the tourist."

Just as they were ready to leave, a bald-headed

man in his 60s pulled in to the driveway in an im-maculate blue 1952 Chevy pickup. "Hey, you," the man yelled, "what do you think you're doing?" He seemed to be angry and upset.

"Getting a little gas," said Tom in a matter-of-fact way.

"My name's Petty, Virgil J. Petty, and I'm the owner. How did you get the pumps to run?" he said as he pulled the truck to a stop in front of a pump.

"A little Yankee ingenuity, with a little help from a generator. We didn't break your door down, by the way. We left a note with our credit card number, we are not thieves."

"Oh, I know that. Some thugs came in yesterday and were mad because I couldn't sell gas, and they kicked the door down."

"Could you leave that generator run for a minute and let me fill up old Bessie here? I'll pay whatever you ask." He began to fill the truck.

As if from nowhere, a line of cars appeared be-hind the old truck.

"I'll tell you what," Tom said in a helpful manner. "We've got a little time; I could leave that generator hooked up for a little while and you could help these people."

"I'd be much obliged, stranger," said the old man in a poor attempt at a John Wayne accent. He was thinking profit.

"My only fear is that I might not be able to re-plenish my diesel," Tom said honestly.

"Don't worry about that, son," said the man in a friendly tone of voice. "My brother Orville owns a station just like this one about three blocks down. His pumps are dead, too. He has diesel and lots of it. He went down there this morning to just sit with a shotgun to keep the bastards out. When you're done here, we'll go down there and get all the diesel you want."

"Thank you very much," said Tom in a relieved manner. He walked over where the girls were talking with a neighbor who had just come in.

"Find out anything?" asked Tom when their conversation had ended. He felt starved for news.

"Only that the power's still out. No one knows why, and nobody has enough food or gas or water. Joanie said that her cousin Bill has a ham radio set and that the electricity is down all over most of the country. The governor has declared a state of emergency."

"I reckon so," said Tom. "We've got to get home." He thought to himself that this was really bad news, but did not want to alarm the ladies.

The old man approached Tom. "Say, son," he said, "I brought an old generator from the house. It hasn't been run in a hundred years; I bought it right before January of 2000."

"You and 10,000 other people," said Tom. "Those stores sold those generators with the stipulation that they couldn't bring them back after the New Year." Tom had heard this story many times before.

"Do you suppose you could get it to work? I need to get this gas out of these tanks before it goes bad." Tom could sympathize with this problem.

"Boy, there's another thing that always puzzled me. Why would anybody manufacture a fuel that goes bad so quick? If we let that stuff set in our boats over winter, by spring you have to spend $500 to clean out the carburetors. Same with lawn mowers?"

Tom had his own idea but wanted to make light conversation.

"Well, son, I've been in this business a long time. This is only my opinion, and I may be wrong, but the way I see it is that gasoline, or benzene as it's called in Europe, is the carcinogenic byproduct of the kerosene refining process. The refiners have to make diesel for the big trucks and the trains and the planes. A by-product is gasoline. They have it, they can't store billions of gallons of the stuff, they can't dump it, they can't burn it; all they can do is let consumers dispose of it for them. That's why there are very few diesel cars and small trucks in this country. That's why the automobile industry makes cars that get five miles per gallon. If Americans quit buying gas, the oil industry would have to give it away or pay somebody to get rid of it. The refiners have got to be scared to death that people might wake up and buy only exactly the gas they need each day. You would see the price of gas fall so fast you would be amazed." The old man lit a cigarette and casually tossed the match on the ground.

Tom quickly stepped on the discarded match.

"You know we might get this thing to run," Tom said as he looked at the generator, "and it might be big enough to run these pumps. Let me drain this tank and we'll get it started."

A half hour later, the little generator was hooked up and Tom was free to go.

"Can we go see your brother now?" asked Tom. "I sure would like to get some diesel." Tom was worried that the diesel story might be just that, a story.

"Tell you what," said the old man. "Run back there

208

and shut that generator off, and I'll lead you to my brother's place." Tom was relieved.

"Fair enough," said Tom. He walked past the girls on the way to the back of the building. "Load up and get ready to go," he said. "We're going to follow the old guy to his brother's station so I can get some diesel, as soon as I turn off this little generator."

"Thank goodness," little Mary said to her mother. "I thought we would never get out of here."

The small caravan left the station, the old guy followed by Tom followed by the new SUV. Tom wondered how the ladies could all talk at the same time.

They pulled into the filling station. There was a man who resembled Virgil, only younger, sitting in a blue lawn chair with a shotgun in his lap.

That old boy looks just crazy enough to shoot us all, thought Tom.

Virgil parked next to the station and walked over to talk to his brother. Tom and the girls parked in the lot, and Tom walked over to the window of the SUV. "I feel it would be wise to wait just a minute, at least until the old man puts the gun down."

"Don't worry about us," Mary said as Ashlee eased the big SUV to the farthest spot in the driveway. Ashlee was thinking that she might have to escape quickly.

Orville stood up after a minute, walked into the station and returned without the gun. The two brothers, dressed alike in red Texaco shirts, blue jeans and tennis shoes, looked like twins. They walked toward Tom, and Orville held out his hand. "My name's Orville and I'm glad to meet you." He was sizing Tom up.

"I'm Tom." Tom shook the hand that was offered. The limp grip did not make Tom feel any safer.

"If you'll get this generator of mine working, I'll give you all the diesel you can carry." Orville had already sized up Tom's truck before he made that statement.

"Thanks," said Tom. "Let's get started." He walked briskly toward the blue truck.

Mary stepped out of the rear door of the SUV and walked up to Tom.

"Did you see what that man was charging those people for gas?"

"No, I didn't," said Tom. The number 20 flashed into his head.

"A hundred dollars a gallon," she said, "cash money."

"I knew I picked the wrong profession," Tom said as he stepped up into the truck. For just a moment a greedy thought passed through his mind.

"A few of the people put it on their credit cards, and he wrote it down as a battery or something. They were glad to pay it." Mary was truly shocked.

"We might have pumped 500 gallons in that short of time. No wonder the old guy is smiling."

The old man came running up with an old roll of wire. "Will this work? " he asked. The thought of profit had put a spring in his step.

Tom looked at it for a minute and nodded his head. "This might work, I may have to charge you for this one though."

"No problem," said Virgil, "whatever's fair." Fair to whom, Tom thought.

"I think about $8,000 would be fair in today's market."

"Eight thousand dollars is highway robbery and I won't pay it." Virgil stamped his foot and walked away.

"Then don't, I've got enough gas to get home. If you try to hook it up yourself, you'll probably burn the relays up and then you'll be screwed. What do you suppose you'll have to pay to get that fixed?"

The old man thought a moment.

"Okay," said Virgil, "I'll pay. Get to work."

"Good," said Tom. "Cash money, and in advance."

The old man shook his head, walked to his truck, leaned into the truck for a few seconds and returned with a stack of $100 bills.

"Here's half your money," he said as he handed it to Tom.

"Thanks" said Tom "this might be enough to buy lunch in today's economy.

"Maybe a can of beans," said the old man. "Food's scarce as gas." He walked back into the station.

It wasn't long before Orville came out of the station carrying his shotgun.

"Get behind me, Mary," Tom said. Tom knew if the man raised that shotgun with Mary this close that he would have to kill him. He let the man get quite close and drew the pistol from the holster. There was a look of surprise on the old man's face as Tom leveled the gun right between the man's eyes.

"Lay the gun down," demanded Tom. He was ready to shoot.

The man did as he was told. He had not expected to see that handgun.

"Now back away from it," commanded Tom.

The man backed away, Tom stepped forward and picked up the shotgun, holstered his pistol and checked the shotgun to be sure there was a round in the chamber. *Remington, my favorite,* he thought.

"Where's the rest of my money?" demanded Tom. He would have settled for half if the old man hadn't threatened Mary.

"I'll get it," said the man. "How much was it?"

"Ten thousand dollars," said Tom.

"Virgil said $5000." The man was angry now.

"That was before you were going to shoot me," said Tom. Tom wanted to leave right now.

The man went back into the station and returned with a stack of bills. Tom breathed a sigh of relief.

"That's all we've got," said the man. "It's $300 short." The old man had given up.

"That'll do," said Tom.

"Why don't you two old boys take your lawn chairs and sit over there by the curb until I'm finished?" demanded Tom.

He hooked the wires and generator up to the building. He started the generator, and the lights in the building flickered for a second and went out.

He motioned for Orville to come into the station.

"You've got too much stuff on. It's tripping the breaker on the generator. Lead the way to the panel and we'll take some load off."

As they walked through the station, Tom helped himself to some candy bars and beef sticks that he fit in his pockets.

"Hey," said Orville, "you can't take that food."

"Of course I can," said Tom. "You owe me $300, remember?" Tom was tired of dealing with these guys.

They found the panel, and Tom turned off all of the unnecessary breakers.

Mary was standing at the corner of the building, and Tom stepped out and told her to reset the breaker on the generator. She hoped she could figure that one out.

A moment later the lights on the control panel behind the counter blinked on.

"The pumps are on," he said to the man. "Reset the diesel pump and let's go fill up my truck." Tom was ready to check out of this new world.

The big truck was parked beside the diesel pump. It took only a few minutes to fill the big tanks. Tom got into the truck still carrying the shotgun.

"Lead the way, Mary," he said, "we're leaving."

The SUV pulled out into the road, and Tom started the big truck.

"Hey, what about my shotgun?" pleaded the man. Tom did not want to give this man a gun.

"I'll leave it beside the road about a block from here," said Tom as he pulled out of the driveway.

The man came running behind the truck.

Tom drove slowly, steering with his knee. He ejected the shells onto the seat and threw the five shells out the window. He aimed the gun out the window and pulled the trigger; it clicked. He pulled close to the left-hand curb, and slowing down he tossed the shotgun onto the grass. Tom had too much respect for firearms to damage this one.

The old man had stopped for a second to pick up the shells and came running up as Tom pulled away. He loaded the gun as quickly as he could and shot twice toward the now speeding truck. Tom watched in the rear view mirror and thought that he might have given the gun back too soon.

The pellets clattered harmlessly off the back of the truck. Tom shook his head and patted the wad of bills in the seat beside him. Maybe I did get in the right profession after all, he thought to himself.

He pulled into the driveway behind the SUV and stopped the truck. One day and this place feels like home, he thought. He walked to Mary standing in the yard, and they hugged each other.

"If you hadn't had that gun, he might have shot us all." Mary trembled at the thought, and Tom held her more tightly. He knew she was right.

"A hundred dollars for a gallon of gas, $25 for a bag of potato chips. We need to get out of this town. Hungry people are dangerous people," Mary said.

"What's going to happen to all these people?" she asked. Tom could tell she was having trouble.

"The government's bound to step in; maybe they already have. A lot of people will starve to death; a lot of people will be killed. I suppose there will be chaos for a while until the power comes back on. It should be soon," he lied.

"What if it doesn't?" she asked.

"It should, at least in parts of the country. I still have no idea what happened. But if it doesn't come back on for a few weeks, this country will have a whole new attitude."

"I've long said that the best thing that could happen to this country would be for the power to go out for a few weeks. Just long enough for all the food in the freezers to spoil. America thinks it is such a strong country. Wrong." Tom began to wonder if that had been such a good idea.

"Hey, girls, pack your stuff," Tom yelled. He started to worry that those old boys might have recognized Ashlee's car and might come back for their money.

14

...ALYN ANN WARNER looked across her empty
...k at the small Chinese man who spoke better En-
...h than she did. This was her first week on the job
...egional director of the Ladies for a Stronger
...erica. She doubted she would be here long enough
...ng pictures on the newly painted walls. This was
...f her first meetings, and she felt that it had great
...tial. Since her graduation from college she had
...ut hundreds of résumés. This job paid about
...hat she was worth, but it was a job. She loved
...wer that she felt when she had money to spend.
...d listened intently to the salesman's pitch. He
...plained to her that it was a good money-mak-
...ject for her organization. He had laid his brief-
...n its side on the floor and had removed a small
...box perhaps six inches to a side. He opened
...t contained a small glass cylinder. He laid it
...counter. Inside was a small, tightly rolled
...an flag. "Go ahead," he said, "unroll it." As
...lled it, small red, white and blue stars fell to
...

...me show you," he said. He picked another
...from the box, and holding the little flag by
...nd, he made a circle in a clockwise manner
...f him. The little stars flew in all directions,

"Where the hell is Carl? We've got to get out of this place before the shit hits the fan." Tom hated to swear in front of Mary and was sorry that he had.

"Could you hook the house up to the generator?" Mary asked.

"Well, I could, but it would be a lot of trouble and there isn't any food. Why do you ask?"

"Hey, Mary Two," Tom yelled.

"Yes, Daddy," she answered,

"Did you get those propane tanks?"

"Yes, I did, three new bottles." Dad was proud of her, and she could tell it.

"Good for you, dear."

"See, Mary," he said, "while we were busy in the back I had the child load up a few tanks of propane."

"What could those be worth today?"

"A million dollars," said Tom.

"We have a ham bone, we have some beans, we'll eat like kings, just like kings." Tom wished he had some cornbread, and that they were home, not for the last time.

"There are some people who won't even eat tonight."

The sun rose in the cloudless blue sky on the third day. Everyone was asleep except Mary and Tom, and they were sitting at the kitchen table. Both were so worried about the boys, but neither spoke of them.

The smell of fresh coffee filled the air.

"How much coffee is left?" asked Tom. He really didn't care.

"Enough for two or three more pots." Neither did Mary.

"Boy," said Tom, "we've got to get out of here.

We'll give him until noon. No later, he's a big boy."

Tom wanted to break something; now he was worried about Carl, too.

"I'm worried about the boys," said Mary with a note of fear in her voice. "Do you suppose they're all right?"

"A hell of a lot better off than we are right now." Tom stood up and nearly knocked the chair over. "They're probably living it up, having a party eating fish and steaks. With that generator running, they won't even know the power's off. I know they'll have enough sense to shut that generator down and save fuel." He feigned anger. "We brought them up right, they'll be okay." Tom was thinking about that big plane and had not told Mary; why make her worry.

"What worries me now is that it's been a couple of days without electricity. People are used to going down to the local pancake house for breakfast. No McDonald's, no Burger King, no Wendy's. Millions of people are going to wake up and realize that they don't have any food to eat. By now, all the grocery stores have been cleaned out. Most of the frozen food is rotting mush. Hungry people are scared and dangerous. Grocery stores have all been looted." Mary knew what that was like, and she was afraid.

"What you're going to have is a terrible state of martial law. With the radios not working, we don't have a clue what's going on. We can only assume that there has been a state of national emergency declared. We assume that this is nearly nationwide. There are some towns with their own generating facilities, and they would have disconnected themselves from the grid as soon as they saw it failing." Tom was on a roll.

"The National Guard will be called out, but they're

all out of the country. The police are on al
you will have is roving bands of people g
house to house looking for food. These an
of criminals, but common citizens, insur
men and dentists trying to feed their kids
be dangerous because they see it as them
will be hungry and afraid." Just like me, 7

"We need to find a warehouse, the
all the food is distributed to all the gr
As he was looking in the phone book
noise out front. Mary ran to the win
"It's a big pink army truck being driv
in the seat beside him is Alise."

Tom felt a wave of relief flow th

"What a sight for sore eyes!"
walked briskly across the yard. He
Carl and hugged Alise.

"We thought you died and wer
Tom. His voice showed emotion a

"Nearly did," said Carl.
Mary came from the house an
Carl.

"Where did you get that big
"Long story, tell you later,
Carl. "It's getting really weird
"Have you had anything to
must be starved."

"Hey," Tom interjected, "t
left from the trip, would you
you."

"No thanks," exclaimed
truck and threw up.

and when he was finished they took several seconds to settle to the top of the desk.

"Ooh," she said, "that's neat."

"We think so," he said. "Sort of gives them the old Fourth of July effect. You know I was born in Philadelphia," he lied. "We wanted to somehow get the end to sparkle, but we had too many problems with that, so we settled for the little stars. The only problem was that the stars stuck to the flags, so we added a little talcum powder, and now it works great."

"Now how much do these cost?" she asked.

"Our introductory offer is to sell these to you and ship these to any spot in the continental U.S. for around 25 cents each. You can sell these for $1 each, but you have to buy at least 4,000 at a time."

She did some quick mental math and unconsciously nodded her head.

He noticed.

"Our plan, as I said before, is to approach patriotic organizations such as yours that do fund-raisers. There's one more thing to see," he said as he took the tube off of the table and tapped it gently on the table. A small piece of wood fell onto the table.

"Watch this," he said. He snapped the two pieces of wood together, and it formed an X-shaped base with a little hole in it. He placed the little flagpole in the base.

"Oh, neat," she exclaimed. "I'm sold. Can I have one of these for my desk?" She really liked this little thing.

"Here," he said as he held out the carton. "There are 25 in each little wooden box. Please keep these with my compliments and pass them out to your friends. You will see in short order how very popular these are."

"Why," she said excitedly, "every teacher will want one of these on his or her desk."

"Exactly," he agreed, "everyone who is a patriot will want to display old glory."

"And the best part of this deal is that our parent company is willing to let you have as many of these as you can sell for only five percent down. The balance you can pay when you sell them." This was the finishing stroke. Take that, he thought.

"I guess I'll have to make a list of where to send these." She didn't want to make a stinking list.

"That's okay; we've got a data base. And for a small fee we will be glad to send these directly to your customers."

She sat back in her chair for a moment with her hands together in her lap. What do I want for lunch, she thought.

"You know this is an offer I just don't know how we could refuse." Pizza, yeah.

"That was our intention," he said. "We stand to make a good deal of money from this, but we need a front organization like yours that doesn't mind sharing the profits."

"Why haven't you gone to other organizations?" she asked.

"We felt that yours was the best for this effort, so we have come here first."

"So what you are saying is that if I say no then you will just find someone else to say yes?"

"Certainly, but you have first chance of refusal."

"Then yes. Is there something I need to sign?" It

would be rude for her to look at her watch. It must be 11:30. Chinese? Nah.

He removed a folder from his case.

"You will find this agreement to be most generous. Please feel free to have your attorney look over it before you sign it. When you do, place the document in the envelope enclosed. Keep the other copy for your files, and to speed things along, just fax a copy to this number. He handed her a business card. Of course, the sooner we get started, the sooner we can be making money."

"It will take us a little time to make these anyway," he lied. He knew full well that thousands of these were ready to be mailed at a moment's notice.

"We will be looking forward to hearing from you shortly," he said as he offered her his hand. He gathered his things and walked out the door.

After he had gone, she sat back in her chair, waved the little flag and said, "Whoopee."

Only after the meeting did his mind wander. He thought to himself as he walked out of the building that this lady didn't know that no matter how this meeting had gone, the packages were already addressed and the credit for them was going to her organization.

This little formality might save a little time.

She did not know that by signing onto this she was signing the death warrant for thousands of people.

Maybe tacos.

15

SENIOR STAFF SERGEANT Wilkerson of the National Guard sat outside his office and gazed out upon the high ceiling in the auditorium. Sunlight poured through the windows above the balcony seating; this was his domain. There were basketball goals attached to ropes and pulleys secured out of the way at either end. This room was used for recreation from time to time. The civilian population used this room for dances on Saturday nights, paying just pennies toward the enormous upkeep cost. Just last winter they had installed a very expensive air conditioning system so that the local community could be more comfortable with their Friday and Saturday summer dances. He looked at the giant American flag hanging vertically on the far wall; it was huge, perhaps 25 feet tall and 10 feet across. A plaque stated that it was a gift from the state. He was proud of that flag; he had drilled the holes in the concrete himself and helped to hoist the heavy treasure. He was proud to be a soldier.

He smelled chicken soup; someone must have used the microwave.

He looked upon the spotless wood floor and knew that people in his command had spent hours to put that gleaming finish there. Every surface had a polished look to it. It was all ship shape and he was in charge. Even when the lieutenant was here, which was seldom, and even the Colonel, which was less often, he was the one whom they came to for guidance, or when things needed done.

He had retired from the Marines after 20 years. He loved the service and so here he was in the National Guard. He was now drawing a pension. He would take off for the occasional fishing trip, but this was his job and he loved it. It was 8:30 in the morning, and in a half hour the floor would be scuffed with the boots of the men. His soldiers. He heard a door open and close at the opposite end of the auditorium; the noise broke the silence in the big room. He turned to see Corporal Smith carrying the mail. "Good, morning, Corporal," he said. "Just put it on my desk." Corporal Smith was a good man, but just could not get to work on time.

He walked back into his office and sat behind the desk. The mail was the usual assortment of bills and junk mail except for a small dark brown wooden box. What's this, he thought, what a cute little package.

"I have no idea what that is," said the corporal from across the room. "Let's have a look." The box was covered in plastic, and the Sergeant removed the one non-military issue item that he carried, a four-inch buck knife in a black leather case. He flipped the knife blade open with a flick of his wrist and made short work of the thick plastic.

Inside the box was another box about the same size that was taped shut. There was a letter folded on the top. "Let's see," said the Sergeant as he adjusted his reading glasses and sat back in his chair. "This says it's a bunch of little flags from our sponsor, the Ladies for a Stronger America. They want a dollar apiece, and we're supposed to pass these things out in two days. It's supposed to show our patriotism." He thought to himself that these pieces of shit were made in China, and a true patriot would only buy stuff made in the USA.

He opened the inner box and removed what looked like a small glass test tube. "Look at this, Corporal. It's a small American flag inside a glass tube." There was a stopper in the top of the tube, and he had to tug with all his might to get it open. It made the sound of a cork being pulled out of a bottle. He shook the contents out into his left hand and took the stem of the little flag in his left hand and shook the flag open. The air was filled with thousands of small stars and a white powder. "isn't this cute," he said just as he sneezed. The Corporal also sneezed.

"Look," the Sergeant said. "There's a little stand for the flag." He put the wooden stand together and stood the little flag up on the edge of his desk. He took a deep breath and blew the bits of white powder off his desk. He sneezed again and so did the Corporal.

"Who sent these?" asked the Corporal. He knew who would have to clean up this mess.

The Sergeant reopened the letter and said, "They are from the Ladies for a Stronger America, and they want us to peddle them for a donation. These ladies supplied us with those two new bar-b-que grills, as you will remember."

"What's this about two days?" asked the Corporal. "We're off for maneuvers next week, and then we disband for the summer."

"Let's pass them out today, Corporal."

Almost immediately, noises were heard in the auditorium as the men began to arrive. The large room was beginning to fill up. The noise level was increasing. They all knew where they were supposed to be. Within a 10-minute period all the men had arrived and the corporal went to the head of the crowd. "Okay, boys, let's get lined up," he said.

They formed a double row.

"Tenshun," said the Corporal as the Sergeant walked along the line.

"Hope you boys have had a good two weeks." The Sergeant meant it.

"Before you are dismissed today, we have one last item. These little patriotic flags are from our friends from the Ladies for a Stronger America. Remember those were the nice ladies that supplied us with the two new bar-b-que grills we got last year. And before that they helped us with the basketball goals. They want us to help them with a fundraiser. It's these little flags and they want a dollar apiece. I expect you all to help."

"They say they will give back to us 25 percent of what they sell in this area. I'll set this box by the door, and you all can put your donations in as you leave. This will be a sign of your patriotism; take these to your home and offices."

The Corporal was passing them out, and the men began to open them and wave them around. "Yee haw," the men said as they waved the little flags around. Several of the little bases hit the floor.

Many of the men began to sneeze.

"Don't forget the dance here Saturday; we have

the concessions. You all know who you are, so don't forget. Now, 'ten shun.' " The men came to attention.

"Dismissed."

The men broke ranks and began to mill around and head for the exit doors.

The Corporal had set the little vials beside the exit door, and the men filed past; most of them dropped dollar bills into the box as they left.

They didn't know that within twenty four hours the disease would have claimed the lives of 78 percent of them.

* * * * *

Tom Watson stopped at the grocery store to pick up milk and bread. He saw Jerry the barber. "Hey, Jerry," he said, and infected old Jerry with a handshake.

As he bought the jug of milk, he passed a $5 bill to Melissa Essington and infected her.

Then he went by the Phillips 66 station and infected old Jeremiah Thompson, as well as five other people who used the gas pump handle after him.

He got home to his wife, Sarah. She was waiting on the porch; he gave her a big old bear hug and infected her.

He went into the house and infected each of his four children. He patted the dog, and it later died.

He went into the bathroom to take a shower, and a little of the dust settled on the bathroom countertop. His mother-in-law was visiting from Dallas, and the dust infected her.

* * * * *

"Corporal," the Sergeant said as the last man went out the door, "why don't you run a quick mop over this floor and I'll clean off my desk and we'll go have a couple of frosties?"

He sneezed twice as he walked into his office. He heard the Corporal sneeze twice. Must be coming down with a cold, he thought, as he sneezed again.

Of the 49 men in the room that day, 38 would be stricken.

* * * * *

About midnight that night, the men began to trickle into the emergency room with high fevers and sore throats.

Since they had been on maneuvers, the doctors determined that they had all consumed some contaminated water and were treating this like an e-coli infection. It is not uncommon for people to get sick when they drink from streams.

The Sergeant and the Corporal drank way more than a few frosties, and they attributed their sickness to their having drunk way too much alcohol. They loaded up a fishing boat with tackle and bait and beer for a weekend fishing trip. They had built a fire on the bank of the river that evening, and by noon they were both too weak to move. By one o'clock the Sergeant had died and the Corporal soon after. It would be weeks before anyone found the bodies.

Several of the men who lived alone expired in their homes in agony. Most with families were brought to the emergency room at the hospital. It was now overflowing with men in the prime of their lives and the prime of their health who were suddenly dying. The director of the hospital brought the Center for Disease Control on board and explained the situation. They all agreed that they had all consumed contaminated water and started a search for the source.

The purpose of this contamination had been to infect these men just hours before the landing of the troop planes, which would mean that the law enforcement and military reservists and many in the military would be getting the symptoms at just the time when they needed to be at their peak.

16

THE GENERAL WAS the last soldier to board the big plane. He stood in front of the plane and looked to the left at the other nine planes and the lines of soldiers marching in single file into them. This was the culmination of a plan he had designed many years ago. He had waited until the political climate was just right, until several of the old guard had passed away, and he had gained the ear of Yea Yung. There was a fly in the ointment though; he had been unable to convince Yoh Wifong that this mission would be a complete surprise, and this coward had the power to prevent the Navy from fulfilling their part of the bargain. This all hinged on the ability of his old friend, Crocker Stuart, to assassinate Yoh Wifong. The death was to look like an accident, and Yea Yung would take over the Navy. This unfortunate death would occur just as the General's plan was unfolding, and his great success would swing the vote, and all would be well.

It was a beautiful day for this adventure, the sun was shining and there was a chill in the air. He waited until all the other planes were loaded, and then he carried his backpack up the steps and into his plane. He could hear laughing and talking among the troops as they adjusted to their seats, but as soon as he stepped on board, the plane became silent as a tomb.

The interior of the plane had been gutted. It was no longer a passenger plane. The seats had been removed and replaced with special chairs that folded out and allowed the soldier to sleep. He wanted his troops to be fully rested and ready to fight when they landed. The plane had been equipped with long-range fuel tanks and would be able to just reach their destination without refueling.

As he entered the plane, he removed his backpack and stowed it in the specially made compartment along with all the other backpacks and rifles of the other men. He turned to the right and made his way toward the front of the plane and his chair. He would be sitting behind the co-pilot and in plain view of the men. As he walked down the aisle, he recognized Corporal Sholing. She did not appear to be suffering over much from the torture. When this exercise was over, he would make it up to her.

An attendant closed the door behind him, and a small vehicle picked up the steps and pulled them out of the way of the plane.

The General sat in his chair and told the pilot to signal the other planes to take off and that theirs would be the last to leave. The big engines began to roar, and the General watched as the nine other planes rolled one at a time toward the runway. He watched the first two planes accelerate and take off until his plane began to roll and he could no longer see the others. He fastened his seat belt.

He hated to fly; whenever he got on a plane, he looked around at the people that he would die with if the plane went down. He hated this weakness in himself, but avoided flying whenever possible and took ground transportation. He couldn't help but think about the individual deaths in a plane crash; those people didn't die from the crash, they died because a piece of chair went through their brain. They died because a thousand pounds of luggage squashed them, or the fireball burned all the air out of their lungs, or they drowned trying to fight their way out of the sinking fuselage. These visions haunted him since he had been forced as a young man to pick up body parts at a crash scene.

The airliner had been fully loaded with college students on holiday. The pilot, it was rumored, had been drinking and flew into the side of a hill. The forest had ripped the plane to pieces. His platoon had been activated to search the huge crash scene for body parts. He had found the hand of a young girl on the first morning of his search, a beautiful little hand with red nail polish, severed at the wrist. For two days he placed body parts in bags, but he couldn't get the thought of that one girl from his mind. On the third day and on the other side of the hill he found the other hand with the arm attached; flies had been at work on the flesh. He had become physically sick and was unable to forgive himself for his weakness.

As the big plane attained altitude, the seat belt light went off. Soldiers began to move about the plane, and the noise level increased as they chatted with their comrades. He lowered his seat back and began to think about the plan.

For years China had killed their girl babies. Too afraid of overpopulation, the powerful government had been able to coerce the population into taking drastic measures to slow the population growth. Now there was a glut of young men, perhaps 20 million that would never have a woman. That is, unless those men were turned into soldiers and sent overseas to get their own women. The fear in the government was that these men would somehow turn their anxiety inward and overthrow the communist regime. This threat forced the government to take drastic measures.

America was ripe for picking, two generations of spoiled lazy, fat people with their eyes glued to the TV set. They had become so complacent they were no threat.

Thirty years before it was discovered that in order to get someone elected to public office it was a simple matter of spending more money than the opponent. The Congress and Senate and Supreme Court had been easily filled with people who were willing to disarm their country and send it into massive debt. This had been done early by forming sham corporations to support cooperative candidates. After the ranks had been filled with willing old-timers, it became far easier. Many people knew it was happening, but were powerless against the might of the incumbents. Everyone always hoped for the best.

The one key ingredient for the successful defense of a nation was money. The United States had now been stripped of its wealth and had been put in the clutches of an $8-trillion debt, much of it owned by China. The politicians had done their jobs well, without noticing it America had become powerless. The American media had been manipulated for 30 years. The Americans had been lulled into believing they were still the best, even though a casual observer could see that American children were no longer the brightest, and that the American school system had been controlled by forces that cared not for the education of the young. The Americans believed that China would never hurt a valuable trading partner, wrong. Why settle for a slice of the pie when you could have the whole pie? The American armies had been scattered all over the planet, the reserves had been called up and shipped out, and Americans had been stripped of any powerful defensive weapons in the name of national security. America was the weakest it had ever been. That was the beautiful part about democracy — you give the people a choice of two guys, but you own both guys — it's beautiful.

The attack was to come on many fronts, the General was to be the spearhead, and his army would enter the center of the United States and create devastation toward the coasts. A second spearhead was planned from the ocean. For years and years America was slowly made dependent on foreign manufacturing. America no longer built the machines that built the machines that made things. Rich, greedy, self-serving corporations made it impossible for America to compete. The bought-and-paid-for Congress refused to level the playing field with tariffs, and consequently, thousands of containers entered America each day. Many of these were sealed before they left China and never looked into until they reached the center of the United States.

The second wave consisted of several hundred specially designed containers. They looked the same from the outside, but inside was a hidden army. Each container had been equipped with battery-powered lights, toilets and bunks for 10 men each. These containers held small tanks and missiles and other war materials. They were shipped along the normal routes, and when they got to their final destination, surprise, a Trojan horse.

The greatest part of America's weakness was its dependence upon electricity. Electricity had become such an important part of every American's life that they took it for granted, as they did every other convenience. Without electricity, America would be on its knees in three days. The power grid that fed the nation was old and weak and vulnerable. A few well-trained men could easily shut down the grid for weeks, and this would cripple the nation. Because of this, coordination was vital; the containers must be at their final locations before the grid was destroyed. His planes must land and coordinate with the containers.

These were not the same Americans that won the Great War. The Americans that survived the great depression were tough; they raised their own food, sewed their own clothes, delivered their young and hunted their food. After three days without television, most Americans today would be on their knees in the streets begging the government to take their guns and knives in exchange for food.

It would be a long flight, perhaps 24 hours, 11,609 miles or 18,686 kilometers. It had been a long day. He unfolded the picture from his tunic pocket; it was the picture of the George Taylor farm. Soon, it would be his. He replaced the picture and fell asleep. He awoke twice to check on the progress of the planes; he ate two frugal meals, and left word that he was to be awakened when they entered U.S. air space.

All flights from the mainland had been cancelled

for three days because of a phony SARS scare. When the jets had finally been given clearance to depart at the same time, the U.S. was expecting a great inrush of planes, and appropriate actions had been taken to expect them. No warnings were sent, even when the big planes disappeared from the radar screen; that is how complacent America had become.

The General watched calmly as the big plane descended to treetop height. This last 100 miles would be the most dangerous. He fully expected to lose two planes to birds or wires or trees in this last dash to the target. The other planes had veered off to their respective targets, and now this plane was all alone.

It was quite a sight, those trees rushing along at over 200 miles an hour. This was quite a bit slower than the top speed of 604 mph, but at that speed a bird could tear the plane apart. The General was afraid; he gripped the arms of his chair until his knuckles turned white. No one else would dare to notice.

The pilot had maneuvered the plane to line up with the runway when it was 10 miles out. There would be one chance for surprise, to have a big plane come in fast and low and land before they knew what hit them. At the 10-mile mark the seat belt lights went on, the plane slowed and the flaps came down. The radio had been tuned to the appropriate channel, and all eyes had been watching the horizon for small planes. This was a quiet morning and there was no traffic.

The big plane sat down on the small runway, and the smoke rolled off the big tires as they strained to get the plane stopped. It slowed to a stop short of the end of the runway, and the pilot turned it, and using the engines rolled it toward the tower building.

When the plane slowed, the General jumped up out of his seat and called for a Colonel. A man stepped forward with the four gold stars and two gold bars of a senior colonel in the People's Liberation Army. "Please secure the landing zone, Colonel," he ordered. He sat back down in his chair to try to keep from shaking.

The Colonel walked toward the rear of the plane and spoke with a chief NCO3, who in turn gave orders for the first squad to prepare to embark. Those men stood up, recovered their weapons from the rack, checked them to make sure they were loaded and formed a line by a rear door. When the plane came to a stop, the rear door opened and a sort of slippery slide inflated. The men stepped out of the door and slid down the slide to the ground. The first two men held the straps at the bottom of the slide and held it firmly. The next two men ran toward the tower, the second two men ran to the office area, and the rest spread out through the facility. The orders were to break down every door and kill everyone in sight. The tower was a three-story affair with glass windows on all four sides. Two men were looking down at the big plane when the two armed men entered through the unlocked stairway doors.

"Hey," one said, "don't shoot."

The other stood in stunned silence.

They were the first gunshot victims.

The secretary behind the front desk, the flight instructor and a trainee were all standing at a window looking at the big plane. The door burst open and the two armed men filled the room with bullets.

The second squad left the plane the same way as

the first; their orders were to take control of the power and protect the communication network. They rapidly ran to the rear of the building, found the door to the electrical and communications, broke the door down and placed a guard over the contents of the room and the emergency generator.

The third squad had orders to take possession of all vehicles, preferably large SUVs. Half of the squad went to the automobiles in the lot, and the other half went to the bodies in the building to collect keys from pockets and purses.

The General finally slid to the ground. A man approached him with the three stars and single bar of a captain, and saluted. "Congratulations, General," he said. "The airport is secured with no casualties."

"Very well, Captain," said the General. "Get some men on those roads," he said, pointing to the roads leading to the airport."

The senior colonel walked up to the general and spoke, "The men are formed up and ready to proceed to the Syracuse building."

"Which direction is that?" asked the General.

The Colonel pointed in a southerly direction.

"Take the men that direction and unload the containers," said the General. "I need three vehicles."

The third squad had taken possession of three SUVs, two Fords and a Jeep. Wonderful things, these SUVs, thought the general, perfect for an invading army, big enough to hold four soldiers and all their gear. Your average city-dwelling American most probably never had occasion to use four-wheel drive, so the proliferation of four-wheel drives was a real testament to the effectiveness of the advertising industry. All these people willing to sacrifice fuel economy to be just like the Joneses. Secretly he was jealous.

The sound of automatic weapon firing by the road caused him to look toward the road. The land was fairly flat here; the road that led to the airport was visible for perhaps half a mile in either direction. A large black car had just crested the distant hill, and his men were firing at it. It was able to turn around and escape back over the hill. It would have been quite a long shot, but they would spread the alarm, pity.

The General left the Senior Colonel in charge, told him that he would be back in a few hours, and jumping into the passenger seat of the first SUV, led the three big trucks down the road. He had brought a map that he had marked on during his previous visit, and used it to navigate the roads. When the little convoy came to the main road, he told the driver to stop the truck. He stepped out of the truck, walked a short distance away. Taking out his cell phone, he dialed a number. In planning for this invasion, the government had launched a special satellite specifically designed to handle the special phones used in this operation.

The phone rang three times, and a voice on the other end said "Hello."

"Adam?" said the General, "this is Dad. How was the flight?"

"Bob never called," said the voice, "so Charlie called me; he's pretty busy right now. Henry and Ian are fine, George didn't make it; both Frank and Eddie are having a little trouble. David got lost somewhere. We're sort of busy right now, but as soon as I get free I'll call you back. We are all having a little trouble with the containers. Maybe you could look into that for us?"

The General hung up the phone.

This was not good, his plane had landed and been successful. Of the other nine, two were lost, one had crashed, one was fighting for their lives, three were in some sort of trouble, and only two were doing well. And what was this about having trouble with the containers? Each container had been equipped with a special phone. He had no way of knowing that the external antennas had suffered due to the heavy seas and salt spray. They could not have thought of everything.

The General could not have known that the pesky old Teamsters Union would pick this particular time to pitch a bitch about all that traffic coming across the Mexican border. Seems like for years the Mexicans had been bringing truck after truck across the border without inspections, and the drivers and rigs often failed to come up to U.S. minimum standards. A fully loaded semi with faulty brakes had turned a mini-van full of school children into a squashed mini-van full of young martyrs. The entire nation had been paralyzed by the truckers' reaction to the gruesome pictures that had leaked to the press. There had been a call for a Senate investigation, and most truckers were running at least a day late when the power went off, early.

The containers, the modern Trojan horses, had first been held up by high seas and now were still sitting on the docks waiting for semis to carry them inland. The containers were equipped with explosive bolts that would drop the big doors open from the inside, but they would do little good if they were packed together or if they were not at their intended location.

Timing had been an extremely important part of this operation; it would not do for a squad of fully armed soldiers to appear in the parking lot of a Wal-Mart; people would get suspicious.

The General had faith that this exercise would be a success, that even without the containers the plan could still be a success.

His men would take possession of the Syracuse building as planned and set up a communication center that would plant viruses in all databases that had not been crippled by the power outage.

He didn't have time for this; he wanted to visit his farm and post a sentry. He took his seat in the SUV and directed the driver to follow the road to the hill over which the black car had disappeared. They were accelerating along the road when over the hill a highway patrol car with its lights flashing crested the hill. The General used the walkie-talkie function on his phone to tell the last truck to dispatch the patrolman.

The first two SUVs roared past the patrol car, the pickup slowed, and the patrolman died in a hail of gunshots. The caravan crested the hill and came to the main road. The General noticed a small red sports car parked in the ditch, but thought nothing of it, as he directed the driver to speed through town. They drove through the town and came to the main road where they turned left. As they passed through the town, several citizens looked at them in wonder but kept on about their business. It won't be long, he thought, and these people will be saluting me as I drive among them. He would probably hang a few of them from the lamp posts just to get their attention.

The three trucks sped down the paved road and

turned off on a gravel road, the last two SUVs slowed down because of the cloud of dust that the lead SUV generated. They had gone 10 miles when the General told the driver to turn left. He had not noticed before, but this time the driver smiled and the General noticed that this man had incredibly bad teeth.

"Driver," he said, "we've gone too far. Go to the next intersection and turn back the way we came." After what seemed like hours, he said, "That house on the right about a half mile up, slow down and drive slowly into the driveway."

The driver did as he was told. The General turned to the two men in the rear, "Keep the damage to the house to a minimum; this is my farm now, this is where I am going to retire."

"Yes, sir," they replied.

The SUV came to a stop near the rear of the house, and the men jumped out and ran to the rear door of the house. They stopped a moment before they went in and listened, they heard the sound of gunshots in the distance. They had looked through the windows and had seen two old people at the dining room table. They only paused a moment, then broke the door open and ran inside. The big soldiers had no trouble doing the killing without harming even the chairs.

They dragged the bodies to the basement stairway and unceremoniously rolled them to the bottom.

A moment later the General came into the house and took a deep breath; it smelled of fresh baked cherry pie and coffee. He walked through the house, stopped in every room and looked slowly at every wall. "Check out the place," he said, "I don't want any surprises."

When he had finished walking through the house, he took a coffee cup from the cupboard, poured a cup of coffee from the pot, found the silverware drawer, and taking a fork, sat at the table and began to eat the rest of a cherry pie. He took a long time to eat the pie; he savored every bite and drank two more cups of coffee. He had secretly dreamed of this moment for years. The feeling was better than he thought it would be.

The men had thoroughly checked every building. They had sat down in the shade of a tree and were enjoying a smoke when a gray SUV entered the long driveway. The leader said, "Hide behind the building." The SUV came to a stop beside the others, and the Lieutenant calmly walked to the driver's door.

"Who are you?" asked the young man driving. Without a word the Lieutenant raised his pistol and shot the man; his body slumped over in the seat.

"Drag this body out of here," said the Lieutenant as he walked away from the car. Two men ran to the car, opened the door and dragged the body across the road and behind the barn.

The General had stepped out of the house to see what the commotion was about. He looked down the dirt road that led past the barns and saw a girl on horseback, riding back to the house. She had heard the gunshots and was coming to see what was going on.

"You men," said the General, "I want that girl alive."

"Yes, sir," said the Sergeant.

He spoke to two men, and they picked up their rifles and began to walk toward the rider. She stopped about 100 yards from the barn and looked at the two men walking toward her. She became afraid. She turned the horse around and began to kick its sides to get it to go. The horse was tired and wanted to go back to the barn and food and was in no hurry to run. Eventually, the horse began to gallop; the man in front raised his rifle and fired once. He missed. He fired again, another miss. The other man began to fire, once, twice, three shots, and the horse was now picking up speed. The third shot from the first man hit the horse in the rear leg, and horse and rider went down. The rider lay motionless on the ground, and the horse limped off.

The two men walked to the girl and roughly picked her up by the arms; she had hit her head in the fall and was not completely conscious. They shouldered their weapons and dragged the girl by her arms back to the house.

"What shall we do with this one?" the men asked the General.

"Strip her naked, and tie her to a bed," he said. The men looked at each other and smiled.

He walked to the Lieutenant. "Find the keys to that truck," he said, pointing to a Chevy pickup truck. Make sure it has gas in it. Get me a driver and have it ready in 10 minutes."

He walked back into the house and up the stairs. The two men were standing at the head of the stairs.

He stood at the door of the room and looked inside at the naked form on the bed. "Dispose of this when I am done. You are dismissed." He shut the door and began to remove his shirt.

A few minutes later he walked down the stairs, fully clothed. He stood for a moment on the back stairs of the house. "See that all the bodies are removed and disposed of," he told the Lieutenant. He pointed across the field to three tall silos in the distance. "Secure that farm," he ordered.

"That one is mine, sir," said the Lieutenant.

"Very well, secure your farm, Lieutenant. Neighbor." He smiled for the first time, as he walked to the waiting truck.

The truck drove down the driveway and stopped at the main road. The General got out of the truck and tore the name off the mailbox. He got back into the truck, and they disappeared down the road.

The Lieutenant picked three men. "You," he said, "come with me, we have a simple little job to do."

They all loaded into the gray SUV, drove down the driveway and turned at the road.

17

THE BIG BLUE truck and trailer were barely out of sight when the boys decided they had had enough fishing for one morning.

They knew that Albert and Juan were back at the house with a brand new Mercedes, ready to party.

As soon as the pickup was out of sight, Two said, "Let's get back to the house and plan this evening. The fish have really stopped biting." On any normal day these two boys would have hung around the creek bank until dark.

They loaded up their gear and put the fish in white five-gallon buckets. They had driven down to the creek in the green and yellow four-wheel drive John Deere lawn cart. They drove back along the edges of the fields to the house. They would have bet some serious money that they could make this trip blindfolded.

Albert and Juan were standing next to the black car, and they were in deep discussion. Albert was tossing the keys in the air. "That's a good excuse to drive this baby into town; we can wash it while we're in there."

"Did Carl really mean what he said about keeping the car?" Juan was walking around the car and checking it out.

"No." Only in our dreams, thought Albert.

"He's a good old boy and could probably afford a couple of these, but what I think he meant was that we could treat it like it was ours, but he would like to have it back, preferably in one piece." Albert walked over to his two brothers who had just arrived, and looked at the fish in the bucket.

"Let's call some girls and set up a party tonight," said Two, rubbing his hands together.

Albert walked past the car and up to the house. "Holy smokes," he said, "the generator is still on. I'd forgotten about that. Hey, Two, please drive down to the generator house and shut it off to save fuel. Power could be off awhile."

Both Two and Three began chanting in unison, "Heck no, we won't go; heck no, we won't go; heck no, we won't go …"

"Hey, Mexican, do you want a pop or something, Coke? Mountain Dew?" Juan and Albert had been fast friends since first grade.

"Mountain Dew, please."

Albert went inside to the refrigerator and returned with two bottles of pop. The two younger boys were still chanting, feeding off each other, "Heck no, we won't go; heck no, we won't go; heck no, we won't go …"

"Enough already!" He handed one of the pops to Juan. "If we leave," he said, "we need to leave a note for the boys to keep the refrigerator door closed."

"Let's go down to the generator," said Albert as he led the way.

The generator building was about the size of a single car garage, built of concrete blocks, with a man door on the south side and a roll-up door on the east.

It was well insulated, and as Albert opened the door the sound of the running generator blasted through the doorway.

Albert entered the building and returned in a moment.

"I thought you were going to shut it off?" asked Juan.

I killed the load and the generator will continue to run for another few minutes.

"What's load?" asked Juan as he sipped his pop.

Albert enjoyed playing the teacher.

"Load is all the stuff that the generator runs," said Albert. "In this case it is the house and the refrigerators and freezers and lights. We need to make sure that everyone knows that we've shut down the power, and we need to make sure everyone knows that we need to turn this back on every few hours to keep the freezers and what-not cold."

Albert stopped to think a moment, the weight of responsibility just became apparent. He realized that if he forgot to turn this back on, it would be a really expensive mistake.

"Please, please, please, do not let me forget to turn this on from time to time," he pleaded with Juan.

"Can I drive?" Juan saw his chance.

Albert was driven to use an expression that he had heard his mother use a hundred times, "Give me strength, Lord."

About that time the little green machine came rambling toward them with brother Two and Three on board.

They came down the driveway at a high rate of speed and turned it sideways in the road skidding to a stop nearly turning the machine over.

"What's happenin', big bro?" asked the driver.

"If Dad had seen you do that, he would have kicked your butt," said Albert.

"Hey, Dad's not here, and I know that because I am a genius."

"Let's party," said number Three.

The boys put the machine in reverse and backed all the way back to the house. The spinning tires made small ruts in the white rocks. They jumped out of the machine and ran into the house.

Albert and Juan followed closely behind them

"I need something cool to drink," said number Two.

"Wait just a minute," said Albert. "Don't open the refrigerator door just yet. The power is off."

"What about the generator?" asked number Two.

"I just shut it off, you moron." Albert was immediately sorry about what he had said. He would never hurt anyone's feelings on purpose.

Two and Three just looked at each other; they couldn't think of any wise remark to say, so Three said, "What the heck is the use of having a backup generator if you don't use it. Hello!"

"For your information, wise ass, the power has been out for a couple of hours, and I thought it best to save gas," said Albert in a commanding voice.

"Just trying to suck up to Dad again," said number Three."

"We'll be quick," said number Two as he quickly opened the door and brought out a gallon of milk.

He shut the door quickly and set the gallon on the counter, and taking two red glasses from the cupboard, he began to fill them.

"Just a second," Albert said. "If you're going to open that door, do it for just a second. The power's out for some reason."

"I wonder why?" asked Juan. For just a moment the four boys thought in silence.

"I don't know, but I shut the generator off, so don't be opening the refrigerators or freezers, and remind me to set it to sleep mode," said Albert in a testy tone of voice.

"Sleep mode, what's that?" asked number Three.

"It's a little relay setup that Dad hooked to the generator that turns the generator on for just a couple of minutes in an hour. He spent hours one winter night calculating just exactly how much time it needed to run to just keep the house from freezing and the food from spoiling. He was running up and down the stairs turning off breakers, and the house was near freezing, and Mom was ready to kill him. It was funny." Albert laughed at the thought.

"You guys want any of this milk?" Three asked as he filled the glasses again.

"No thanks," said Albert and Juan in unison.

The two younger boys got serious and came over to the table.

"How much gas is in the generator?" Two asked.

It was amazing that these boys would become serious over this. Their father had brought them up to realize that electricity was vital for their survival and that it was a very fragile thing.

"Well," Albert said, "I think it's a full tank. Remember, last week we found a little yellow ticket in the handle of the diesel tank."

"Oh, yeah," said number Two "you had Three run it into the house and give it to Mom."

"If that was last week," said Albert, "it would be nearly full."

"How long did it run this morning?" asked Albert.

"Probably an hour, maybe two," agreed the brothers.

"We better get it topped off then so dad won't be pissed." Albert decided.

"Two, would you please call Horscheimer's and see if they could come out and top off the tanks, the book's by the phone."

Number Three ran to the phone and picked up the receiver. "Phone's dead," said number Three. "No phone, no power, we are isolated from the world."

"Road trip," yelled number Three. "We're going to town, and I've got first dibs on the shower."

It won't take these boys long to appreciate electricity, thought Albert. Showers don't work without water, and the water doesn't flow without the electric pump. Albert walked out the door toward the generator building.

Albert was just about to the generator house when he heard the boys yelling to turn the pumps on.

A few minutes later both boys emerged from the house cleaned and dried.

"Well, you smell good," Albert said. "Have you got a girlfriend? "

"Not yet," said number Two, "but I'm fixin' to. Let's go to town."

Albert called to number Three before he left the porch. "Hey, lock the door, and while you're at it, run through the house and lock all the doors."

"Why?" asked Three. "We never lock the house."

"Because if you don't I'll whip your ass, that's why," said Albert in a playful manner. He was beginning to dislike this new responsibility already. No wonders parents get gray, he thought.

A few minutes later number Three came out the door and made sure it was locked. "Tight as a drum," he said. "Let's go to town."

Juan and Albert were in the front seat with Albert driving. Number Two and Three slid into the back seat, and the car pulled away.

They had gone about a mile, and Juan looked up at the sky. "What in the world is that?" said Juan. "Is that a plane?" He couldn't believe his eyes.

"No" said Albert in disbelief, "that can't be a plane."

"Holy shit!" said number Two, "that is a plane and it's coming right at us."

The realization put them all in a state of shock.

"Stop the car!" exclaimed number Three, and Albert pulled over to the side of the road. The four boys jumped out of the car and watched the plane.

It was a huge blue airplane at treetop height screaming overhead. They had to put their fingers in their ears because the noise was unbearable.

The wind from the plane nearly knocked them down.

"What kind of plane is that? It's huge!" screamed number Two.

"I do not know," said Juan, "but it is flying low. Goin' to the big show. And it's a big old boy. And I've never seen one that low that big before."

"Where could it be going?" asked number Two.

"I have no idea," said Albert, " but let's go find out. Did it have its landing gears down or up?" asked Albert.

"Down," said Juan.

"Up, said number Two.

"I don't know," said number Three.

They drove as fast as they could, trying to catch the plane. The road took them to the edge of town, and they pulled into the local convenience store. They stopped beside a shiny new red Ford pickup truck with a license plate that said simply "red," and all four boys bailed out of the car.

"Hey, Bill," asked number Two, "did you see that plane?"

"What plane?" asked the astonished young man with the mop of red hair. He had a soda in one hand and a bag of chips in the other, "I didn't see no plane, I was in the Quik-Trip. What plane?"

"There was a giant plane treetop high that just about ran over us," said number Two breathlessly.

"Well, let's see," said the red-haired Bill as he got into his pickup. "You fellas are looking for an airplane, I believe I'd try the airport; yessir, that would be a good place to start. Have a nice day."

The boys had already jumped back into the car and were driving through the town with reckless abandon.

The car made a right turn at a little blue sign with a picture of an airplane with a white arrow. As they drove down the asphalt road, there were more of these signs.

"Slow down a little," said Juan, "the airfield is about a mile beyond this next hill."

As the car topped the little hill, the airfield was laid out before them. The runway was off to the left of the road, and beyond the airstrip could be seen the numerous buildings that had been built as an industrial park. As the weather was halfway decent and the road asphalt, the boys had rolled all the windows down. As they approached the field, they heard a series of small explosions.

"What is that?" Juan asked.

"Don't know," said Albert "sounds like somebody's shootin' at somebody."

On the edge of the runway the large blue plane was sitting with two doors open and the bright yellow emergency slide deployed. Men were sliding down the slide and were running toward the hangars. The two men in the front of the pack were firing their guns into the windows of the airport office.

Albert hit the brakes and began to look for a place to turn around. "Let's get the heck out of here!" he screamed, "I don't like the looks of this. He pulled into a small side road. The road was blocked by a locked gate with a big red sign that read: AIRPORT PROPERTY — KEEP OUT. As he put the car into reverse, they heard a sound like a beer can opening; a small hole had appeared above the right passenger window and another on the hood of the car.

"Holy shit," said number Two, "those guys are shooting at us, step on it." The boys in the rear seat lay down as low as they could get.

Albert put the car into drive, pushed the pedal to the floor, and the big car sped forward. The rear tires screamed in protest as they gained speed up the hill. After the car crested the hill, the boys sat in stunned silence for just a moment.

Juan, who was obviously shaking, said, "Look, I don't know what that was, but it could be our worst nightmare coming true."

"Let's just think about this for a minute," said Juan. "The power goes out for some unknown reason, a large airplane full of fully armed men comes in at treetop height and lands, and they start killing everyone in sight. Why here, why now? We need to tell someone because that shooting meant that they have killed anyone that might have spread the alarm, and for all we know they might be right behind us, so step on it."

Albert started to go a little faster after this, and as they approached the main road into town, he nearly sideswiped a small red sports car coming from the east. Both cars came to a sudden stop, the red one in the ditch. A young olive-skinned girl stepped out of the red car.

The young girl had missed her turn and ended up driving all the way through town. Now she wished she had paid a little closer attention to the map her father had sent her. As she passed the city limits, she knew she must turn around, and what a stroke of luck, here was a car coming toward her that she recognized. It was not stopping or slowing down, and it forced her into the ditch.

She stopped the car in the ditch, got out and walked to the big black car that was now stopped in the road.

As the window was rolling down, she said, "Hello, Daddy. Wait a minute," she said in disbelief, "you're not Daddy. What have you done with Daddy?"

"Whose daddy?" Albert asked. Why was he stopped? They were running for their lives.

"Carl Stoneman," she said.

"You mean Uncle Carl, this is his car."

"Well, where is he?" she asked, beginning to be irritated.

"He went to St. Louis," said Albert.

"He what?"

"He went to St. Louis." Under normal circumstances Albert would have felt shy around a girl he didn't know, but he was scared.

"Why in the world would he have gone there?" she asked.

"Well, he went to get my mom. It's a long story. Look, get in the car right now. There are some guys shooting at us, and they may be coming over that hill right now. So leave your car here, get in with us and we'll tell you all about it." Albert was becoming anxious.

"Just a minute," she said. " She ran back to her car and got her purse. "I need to move my car."

"Leave the damn thing where it sits," Albert said as he jammed the Mercedes in reverse. The tires squealed as he backed into the road. He drove forward, and Juan reached behind the seat and opened the rear door.

She jumped into the car and it sped down the road. She wondered what she was getting into.

"Who are you guys?" she asked.

"We know who we are," Juan said. "The question is, who are you?"

"I'm Carl's daughter," she explained.

"I didn't know he had a daughter," Al said. "Maybe

I did, who knows, what's your name?"

"Juliette," she said.

"I'm Albert and this is Juan." Albert had the car going as fast as it would go.

"Back in there are brothers Two and Three."

"Is that it?" she asked. "Two and Three?"

"Works for us," said the boys in unison.

"You guys are weird," she said. She wished Albert would slow down, but his fear was contagious.

"Let me tell you the story," said Two, as the car sped down the paved road. "Carl went with our father, Tom, to St. Louis to pick up our mom's car that broke down. Now it looks like the shit has hit the fan and we are very confused, and you smell really good."

The girl blushed, "Thank you."

They told her briefly about the plane.

"Where did you come from?" asked Two.

"I just came from St. Louis," she replied.

"This is too strange," said Albert.

"All we know now is that a plane full of armed men has landed at our airport for some reason, and they shot everyone in sight and they shot at us and we are playing Paul Revere," said Three.

On the outskirts of town was a large three-story red brick building that housed the highway patrol department.

Albert pulled in at high speed, and the brakes locked and the car screeched to a halt.

"You guys wait here," he said.

"I don't think so," said the girl as she stepped out of the car.

"Already I'm sorry I didn't leave you beside the road," complained Albert. He didn't mean it.

They hurried up a set of steps and into a large well-lit room with white walls and six cubicles at the back. The front desk was chest-high and prevented entry without a key. The lady behind the desk was talking on a radio microphone.

She had seen the car pull up in a hurry and said, "I should give you a ticket right now for reckless driving." She wasn't in a very friendly mood today.

"Never mind that," Albert said out of breath. "A plane load of armed men has landed at our airport, and they are shooting people."

"No," she said. "We would have heard something about that."

"You just did!" screamed Albert at the top of his voice. The lady at the counter looked at Juliette, who shrugged her shoulders.

When Albert raised his voice, it caught the attention of two officers who were in the back of the room, and they looked up from their desks and one got out of his chair and came to the front.

"What's that you're saying about some shooting?" the officer asked.

Albert lowered his voice and took a deep breath. "As we were coming into town, a big plane came in at treetop height, we went to the airport and saw many men getting off the plane and shooting people."

"Can I see some ID, please?" asked the officer.

Albert hung his head for a moment and then took out his wallet and showed it to the officer.

"Please take it out of the billfold," the man said calmly.

Albert patiently removed the license from the billfold and laid it on the counter. He was very sorry that he had come into this building.

"This shows that you live way on the other side of town. Why was it you were coming into town?" asked the officer. Albert thought of a dozen wisecracks to make, but thought better of it. He did decide that he had better get out of there.

"Will you please listen to me? There is a bullet hole in the back of this car where they shot at us," Albert pleaded.

"Okay, who shot at you?" asked the officer.

"The men from the plane!" Albert spoke slowly. "What is it going to take to get you to listen?"

"Hey, don't use that tone of voice with me," demanded the officer.

Another man came forward; he had three stripes on the arm of his uniform. "Okay," he said, "tell me quickly the whole story; start at the beginning."

"First," the man with the stripes said, "what is your name, son?"

"Albert Brown."

"And you, young lady?"

"Juliette Stoneman," said the girl. Finally, she thought, how in the world could any person be this stupid?

"You're Tom's boy, aren't you?"

"Yes, sir."

"Good man, Tom. Now what is your story?"

"We live about three miles out of town. We were coming to town to order some diesel fuel because the power is out and the phones don't work."

"The power has been out for over three hours," said the sergeant. "Do you know why?"

"No, we don't," said Albert. He had started to pace

the floor. "We were coming into town, and this giant blue plane came flying over at treetop height. It landed at the airport. We followed it to the airport, and when it landed a bunch of armed men got out of the plane and started shooting everyone in sight. They even shot at us, and if you don't believe us, come out and look at the hole in the car." It was all he could do to keep from screaming.

"There were a lot of them, they were armed to the teeth, and they are probably headed this way, and I'm going back to the house to get my guns. I suggest you call the National Guard or the Governor or the President or your mother or whoever the hell else you're supposed to call before we all get killed." Albert had worked himself into a lather.

"Don't take on that tone of voice with me, young man," said the sergeant.

"Don't shoot the messenger," said Albert as he dragged Juliette out the door. "I'm tired of trying to talk to you morons." Both Albert and Juliette wanted to strangle these guys. She was thinking about a rope, and he was wanting to use his bare hands.

"I'm going down to the city police department and tell Bill, he'll believe me. I just want you to know that there are a whole bunch of mean motherfuckers with guns who just landed at the airport. They are a whole lot better armed than you, and it's only a matter of time before they get their hands on some vehicles and drive down that road and kill you."

He walked quickly to the car and opened the driver's door. The other boys were leaned against the trunk. He looked at them and said, "Get in the car, please, let's go."

Juliette called out, "Shotgun," and got into the passenger's seat.

The boys all crawled into the back seat.

He backed out and squealed the tires and drove down the street.

The sergeant turned to the man at the radio. "Get on that radio and see if there's any truth to this. Wilkinson, get in your patrol car and drive down to the airport and see what's going on."

The man on the radio called the state headquarters. "This is Timberlake Station," said the man. "Has anyone up there heard anything about some armed men landing at the airport?"

"Not a word about that," said the voice on the other end of the radio.

"Those kids must have been lying," said the sergeant angrily. "They must have been on drugs. I think I'll go arrest them."

He got in the patrol car and drove in the direction the Mercedes had taken.

Wilkinson, in the meantime, had driven as fast as he could in the direction of the airport. His lights were flashing, and as he crested the hill he saw the big plane, but saw no one else. There were three trucks coming in his direction. The first was a late model SUV. The second was a white pickup truck, and the third he couldn't make out what it was. They were coming in his direction at a high rate of speed. He turned on his lights and siren. The SUV drove past him; the windows were heavily tinted so he could not see who was in the truck. The white pickup truck followed the SUV, and Wilkinson saw that the driver was an Oriental. The third truck was also driven by an Oriental, and he saw that the passenger was pointing an automatic weapon at him. The barrel flash was the very last thing that Wilkinson saw on this earth.

In the meantime, the Sergeant had caught up with the Mercedes. They had turned down Walnut Street that led to the local police station and into the parking lot of the big white wood building. The highway patrol car pulled in behind them with his lights on. The Sergeant got out of the car at the same time as Albert and pulled his gun and said, "Hold on there. Just one minute, son, you are under arrest." Albert was no fool, and he raised his hands. Albert thought that it would be impossible to hate anyone worse than he hated this man at this instant.

"You other kids get out of the car, too, and get your hands on the hood of the car," he ordered.

The others got out of the car and put their hands on it.

The Sergeant reached into the side window of his car and took the radio microphone. "Wilkinson, this is Henry, come in, Wilkinson." There was no response. "Dispatch, this is Henry."

"Go ahead, Sergeant," the dispatcher replied. "What have you heard from Wilkinson?" asked Henry."

"Not a word since he left," said the dispatcher.

"Wilkinson, answer me or it's your ass," said Henry angrily.

"Dispatch, this is Henry. Get hold of Wilkinson for me and let me know."

Two whispered to Three, "Bet that stupid bastard got his ass shot off."

Juliette heard that and agreed.

Henry threw the microphone down in the seat of his car and turned back to the kids.

"Okay now, you kids stay right where you are." As he was saying that, the door to the police station opened, and an officer dressed in a brown uniform with a green stripe down the leg stepped out of the building.

"What is all this?" said the officer. It seemed like at least once a week he had to deal with Henry.

Albert stepped forward and said, "Bill, will you please get this guy to listen to reason."

"What's going on here?" Bill demanded.

"These kids are under arrest," said Henry.

"What are the charges?" asked Bill.

"I'm not sure yet, but I'm sure they're guilty of something."

"Hey, Albert," said Bill, "how's your old man doing?"

"Just fine, Bill. Mom's car broke down in St. Louis, and he and Carl went over there to get her."

"Did you kids do anything wrong?"

"No, Bill, we didn't."

"Henry," Bill said, "put that gun away and why don't you get back in your car and drive your bony ass back to your own office and leave these kids alone before I throw you in jail, you prick."

"There's something really fishy going on here, Bill," pleaded Henry.

Bill looked at Albert and asked, "What's going on, Albert?" Bill was thinking that even a broken clock is right twice a day.

"A big plane landed at the airport, it was full of armed men and we saw them shooting people, and they shot a hole in this car. Show him the hole, number Two."

Number Two stuck his finger through the roof of the car.

"Could you tell me why we would make up some story like this?" Albert asked.

"It doesn't make any sense," said Bill. "You must be telling the truth."

"Why, look here," said Bill, as he walked around the back of the car. "There's two more holes in the trunk of the car; you kids are lucky to be alive."

"So there was a bunch of shooting at the airport," said Bill. "I wonder how come I haven't heard about it."

"Could be the phones are out?" asked Juan.

"Could be all the witnesses are dead," exclaimed Julictte. "Could be the reason old Wilkerson never called back."

"Wilkinson," said Henry

"Whatever," said Juliette. She was beginning to scream, "Somebody better call the Army."

Albert thought he might be beginning to like this girl.

Bill had turned and was quickly walking back into the building.

"Can we go now?" asked Albert.

"I guess so," said Henry as he walked back to his car. He picked up the microphone and tried to call Wilkinson again with no luck. He called Dispatch, and they explained that they too had been unable to contact Wilkinson.

Albert and the rest followed Bill into the station house. It was a spotless room that smelled of floor polish. Bill got on the phone and called the office of the Governor. He explained that he was the Sheriff of Culver County and that many people had been killed and that the National Guard should be mobilized.

This man doesn't mess around, thought Albert.

"That's the best I can do," he said as he hung up the phone.

"Matilda," he called,

"Yes, Bill," said a young lady with braces who looked up from the filing cabinet.

"Do me a favor, please, and contact all the sheriff's departments in all the surrounding areas and let them know what's going on."

"Sure thing, Bill." She hurried to her desk.

He turned toward Albert, "Well, son, I know you, but who is this young lady?"

"She claims to be Carl's daughter."

"Didn't know he had one," said Bill. He turned to Juliette and said, "Carl is a fine man, and my friend."

"Thank You," said Juliette as she blushed.

"She's kind of lippy, but good-looking," said Albert.

Juliette looked at Albert, opened her mouth to speak, closed it again and walked out the door.

"We better get to the house and load our guns," said Albert. "Let me know if we can be of help."

At that time a middle-aged lady in a pink dress rolled her chair out of an office and said, "Bill, you better listen to this. Brian just called and said he was investigating the report of some shots being fired by the airport, and when he got there an officer was down."

Bill walked across the room to the radio.

"Brian, this is Bill. What's going on out there?"

A voice and static was heard on the radio.

"There's a whole bunch of guys down here with automatic weapons. They shot a bunch of people and they shot at me, and there's a highway patrol car in the ditch with its lights on and a body hanging out the door. I have no idea what their intention is, but there were three truckloads of them, and they're headed toward town."

Bill raised the blinds and looked out the window and watched the highway patrol sergeant squealing his tires and driving rapidly back toward the airport.

"Well, kids, we've got a pretty situation going on here. I suggest that you get back to your houses and let us take care of this."

He hollered to the lady at the door, "Glenda, would you please call the Governor's office and the National Guard and tell them this is the real thing and no drill. Tell them to be ready to repel a plane load of well-armed men." He knew that he had not seen it all, but he knew if he could just stick around he would.

He turned to Albert. "Okay, Albert, how many of them do you think there were?"

Albert thought a moment. "There was a plane load of them, and it was a pretty big plane, like a 747 or something. We probably saw maybe 30 guys with guns before we high-tailed it."

Bill tried to think, the last time he flew it was that vacation to Mexico. How many people could a big plane hold? Maybe 500?

"You kids get on home now," said Bill as he hurried back into his office.

Juliette looked at Albert, "What are we going to do now?" she asked.

He remembered an old quote; something about if you were in charge, take charge.

"Let's go," he said to her, and he reached down with his left hand and grabbed her right hand. "We have to get back to the house."

"I need to get my things out of the car," she begged.

"Not this time," he said. "The guy on the radio said there were at least three truckloads of armed men coming into town. They will be driving right past your car. It would appear to be suicide to try to get back to your car right now."

As they jumped into the car, she asked, "What do you expect that we are going to do against a bunch of armed men?"

"I don't rightly know, but it strikes me that I'd be a lot better off armed than unarmed at this time." He couldn't answer her question because he didn't know the answer himself.

He backed the car out into the road and went toward the house.

Juan asked, "Where are we going?" He had a pretty good idea.

"Thought I'd go by Old Mike's to get a little ammunition." Juan had guessed right.

They drove about 10 blocks, and there was a large old brick building with a large parking lot in the front. The sign above the door read "Old Mike's Shooting and Archery Supplies."

"Just what we need," Juliette said. "This means that we are going to get shot." She was beginning to feel afraid.

Albert looked at Juliette for a second and shook his head.

Albert parked the car near the entrance and walked into the building.

Juan followed Albert into the building. A moment later Juliette came into the building and let her eyes travel over the interior.

The walls were lined with racks of shotguns and rifles. There was a glass case that separated the customer from the wall racks, and these cases were filled with handguns. A rack in the back right corner was filled with archery equipment. In the back left corner was an ancient desk piled high with papers. The left wall had a large window near the door that allowed customers to see into the gunsmith area where a man was intently bent over a firearm locked into a bench vice.

Juliette was talking to the stuffed animal heads on the walls, telling them she was sorry that they had been shot. Two and Three were making fun of her.

There was one man seated near the desk and two men standing near him. They were all eating roasted peanuts and throwing the shells toward a single wastebasket.

The seated man looked toward the door as they entered and hollered at Albert. "Hey, Albert, is that old man of yours with you? That son-of-a-bitch owes me $5."

"The way I heard it, you owe him $5, Mike," laughed Albert, "and no, he's out of town."

"Tell him 'Hi' for me," said the man.

"We were just talking about that rotten son-of-a-bitch," said Mike. "One of the best shots on the planet.

Doesn't hold a candle next to me, but what the heck! Seen any deer yet this year?"

"We've got a big old buck spotted out there. We have him chained to a tree until season opens."

"Say, how's my credit?" This was the very first time that Albert had seriously thought about credit.

"Well, Albert to be quite honest, your credit's not worth a bucket of warm spit. But your old man could have this whole building on credit. Whatever it is you need, we'll work something out. Where's your old man?"

"He and Carl went to St. Louis, and we haven't heard from them." Albert had not been worried about his parents until just now.

"We need some ammunition, we kind of have a problem."

"What kind of problem?" Mike asked as he rose from his chair.

Albert quickly told him the story about the plane and the airport.

"What do you think about that, John?" Mike asked.

One of the men stepped forward. He was dressed in Army fatigues with shiny black boots; he had the insignia of lieutenant on his collar. He spoke.

"Sounds like we've been attacked, and I better get back to my post. Hell of a bad time for my guys to be sick."

"What are you fixin' to do, Albert?" asked Mike.

"I guess we need a little extra ammunition," said Albert.

"What do you want?" asked Mike.

"We've got a little at the house," said Albert. "Let's

try 10 boxes of 357 magnum. Another 10 boxes of 30-06 about 150 grain. Probably six boxes of 12-gauge in double oht buckshot.

Mike walked behind the counter and quickly set the boxes of ammunition on the counter. "Anything else?" he asked. Mike knew that Tom would approve of anything Albert wanted; he had said as much just the other day.

"Well, I could really use a gun right now," said Albert.

"Sure thing, do you suppose your old man would approve if I gave you that gun he ordered?" he said as he walked into the back room. He returned with a small box that had been opened. "I've been showing this off to people." He shook the contents open, and there was a box inside the box.

"This is a 1911 Colt 45," Mike said. "They don't make them any more, and they don't make a more dependable firearm. The old 45 took us through the Second World War. It uses this 45 ACP ammunition," he said, and he set five boxes of shells on the counter.

"Is this gun new or used?" asked Albert.

"Almost never used," said Mike. "Shoot it all you want and you won't hurt it."

"You take care of yourself. I would feel real bad if you got killed."

"Hey, I can't sell you kids any guns, but I could hire you to take these guns home and clean them for me."

"I'll pay you, oh, minimum wage, will that work?"

"Works for me," Al said.

"Who you got with you?"

"Juan and the two brothers."

"Whose that girl that came in with you?" he asked.

"She's Carl's daughter."

"I didn't even know he had a daughter."

"Kept it a secret," said Albert.

"Bring them over here," he said.

Albert called for the others to come to the front.

"So you're Carl's daughter," said Mike. "Quite a looker you are."

"Thank you, sir," said Juliette. "Do you know my father?"

"Lost 50 bucks to the son-of-a-bitch two nights ago," said Mike.

"And," she said, "this is just the kind of place he would like to hang out in."

"You know, I bet those guys are headed this direction." There was a hint of worry in old Mike's voice.

"You boys get behind the counter there and get those Remington 30-06's. The boys walked behind the counter and looked at the tags hanging from the trigger guards of the guns.

They selected four similar guns all with scopes.

"714 Remingtons, semi-automatic in 30-06 caliber, best all-round gun on the planet," Mike said. "I like that 308."

"Scope's been sighted in on these rifles?" asked Two.

"Bore sighted is all."

He handed shells to the other three boys. "Check the caliber on the guns," he said.

Mike walked into the back room and returned with four plastic bags. He threw the bags on the counter. "Take these," he said.

Albert opened one of the bags and said, "What

have we here, it's a 10-round clip, how handy! I thought they made these illegal."

"Those are merely experimental, they don't exist."

"Good thing," said Albert.

"What about me?" said Juliette. "Don't I need a gun?"

"Can you use a gun?"

"Let me think, you know my dad, what do you think?"

"Well, young lady, what would you like?"

"How about something in 9mm?"

"Just right for me," she said.

"A Glock in 9mm parabellum. Good choice."

He tossed two boxes of ammunition on the counter.

"How many does it hold?" she asked as she released the clip and laid it on the counter. She was afraid that she might say the wrong thing and look stupid. She could feel all the eyes in the room focused on her.

"Thirteen," said Mike. "If you're man enough, or rather woman enough to load it."

She opened a box of shells and began to load the clip. The last two bullets went into the clip with difficulty.

She picked up the clipless gun and forced the loaded clip into it.

She aimed the gun at the floor and pulled the slide back to load a bullet into the chamber and put on the safety. At this time she was grateful to her father for the gun safety training he had given her as a child.

"This lady likes them fully loaded," said Mike. "Need a holster for that gun, little lady?"

"No thanks, I'll just drop it in my purse."

"Do you have a holster for this 45?" asked Albert.

"Just the thing," said Mike. He reached under the counter and brought forth a green holster with a web belt.

"Army issue," he said," kind of old, but made for that gun."

"That'll do, Pig," Al said.

"Could you keep that box for Dad?" Albert asked.

The other boys had loaded the ammunition and guns and were seated in the car.

"Thanks, Mike," Albert said. "Hope we don't need this."

"Me, too," said Mike.

Albert got into the car.

"Looks like you boys have handled guns before," said Juliette. She was trying to not be afraid.

"Folks around here sort of feel like they were born with a gun in their hands," Albert said. "It's the only thing that keeps this country free."

Albert backed out and quickly drove down the road.

"What now?" asked number Two.

"Better see if these guns are accurate. Let's get to the house," said Albert.

Number Two asked, "Why did we get these guns? We got our own guns."

"They were there, and I just took them."

"How did you pay for them?" asked Juliette

"I didn't," said Albert.

"That man let us walk out of there with several thousand dollars' worth of guns and ammunition?" She had never seen anything like this before.

"Such is the credit of our father," said number Three. "Always wanted one of these. Hey, Two, trade me, would you, this barrel is two inches shorter than yours."

The boys got in the back seat and had loaded the clips. Number Two looked into the box, "What in the world is this?" he asked and reached into the box. "There are two of these in here," he said. "It appears to be a hand grenade."

"Holy shit," said Albert. "Don't mess with that. Old Mike must have thought we were out for bear."

"Surely that can't be real?" questioned Juliette.

"Do any of you need to do anything before we go?" Albert asked the group.

"I need my car," said Juliette.

They all ignored her.

"We're fine," Juan said.

Juliette said, "I need my car."

They ignored her

They drove about three miles east of town and turned onto a well-used gravel road. There was a sign alongside the road that read Sunflower Archery Range — Members Only.

"Are you guys members of this club?" asked Julie.

"Heck" said number Two, "we are the club."

"What do you suppose we ought to sight these in at, Albert?" asked number Three.

"Probably 200 yards."

They drove down the rutted path surrounded by dense undergrowth until they came to a clearing on the side of a hillside. The view to the left stretched for perhaps a mile, and the rolling hills were shaded by several full-grown trees. To the right of the road were a series of benches lined up to face the side of the small hill perhaps 300 yards away. There were six benches, and at the base of the hill were six wooden targets. The dirt was mounded behind the targets, and fresh dirt was exposed where the bullets had torn through the target paper and disturbed the earth.

Albert stopped the car near the benches, and the boys brought the guns and laid them on the tables.

"Come on, number Two," asked Juan. "Help me get the targets set up at 200 yards." The two boys walked to the base of the hill and began to carry the targets back to a spot on the ground that lined up with a stake that read 200.

Number Three went to a metal gang box and took out three targets and carried them with a staple gun to the 200-yard mark. When the other boys had set the wood frame in place, he stapled the large target to the wood.

"Hey," Albert said. "I need a target at this bench."

"You got it, boss," said number Three, as they began to drag a target in a different direction."

Albert walked to the number four bench and picked up a piece of carpet eight inches wide and two feet long and shook out the dirt and beat it against the table.

"Juliette, could you come and help me, please?" he asked.

"Sure thing," she said. "You can call me Julie." She had been feeling useless and was glad to be of help.

"Okay, Julie," said Albert. "Could you come and help me, please?"

"What do you want me to do?"

"See that old crank handle? I want you to tighten up the handle when I put the gun in the vice, but not too tight."

The boys had placed the new paper on the target and were walking back.

"Would you people please hurry," said Albert with a note of worry in his voice. "I feel those guys breathing down my neck.."

The boys began to walk more quickly out of the line of fire.

Albert had placed a shell in the chamber and was holding the rifle in the vice.

"Tighten this down, please," he said. She did as she was directed.

Number Three had produced three sets of ear protectors from the green gang box and brought them to Albert, who put one pair on. He handed one pair to Julie, who looked at them in a funny way and then put them on her ears.

"These look like headphones, but without the wires," she said

Albert made a few minor adjustments on the rifle, made sure that it was secure and said loudly, "Ready on the left, ready on the right, ready on the firing line." He then took one last look through the scope and pulled the trigger. The air was split with a loud blast, and the smell of gunpowder filled the air. Number Two, who had seated himself on the second bench over and who was looking through a spotting scope, said, "Two inches to the left and a half-inch too high."

"Not bad," said Albert. "At least we cut paper."

Albert reached into his pocked. "I need a dime,

anybody got a dime?"

Juan brought one over. He took the dime and removed two black caps on the side of the scope and
began to make adjustments.

"What are you doing now?" Julie asked

"Well, this here is the simple man's way of sight-
ing a gun. What you do is, you take the gun and sort
of aim it at a target and pull the trigger. The barrel of
the gun is lined up with where the bullet went, but
the scope is pointed somewhere else. Since we know
where the bullet went, it will be a simple matter to
adjust the crosshairs of the scope to line up with where
the bullet went. One bullet and your gun's sighted in.
The trick is to not let the barrel move." How clever,
Julie thought.

He made two more adjustments on the scope and
slowly squeezed the trigger. The gun again exploded,
and number Two said, "Dead on at 200 yards."

"Next gun," said Albert.

"If you don't mind," said Juan, "I'd like to sight
my own gun in."

"Me, too," said Two, "and me," said Three.

"Have at, guys," said Albert, and walked toward
the car with his gun. Julie followed him to the car.

"When was the last time you saw my father?"
asked Julie.

"This very morning," said Albert.

"How was his health?" she asked.

"He appeared to be in fine shape," said Albert.

"What's your story?" he asked. He was listening
to her, but all the while watching the other boys.

She closed her eyes for a moment and began to
speak.

"I was born in L.A. Mom was a model and Dad was a policeman. He always dreamed of moving to a farm, and she wanted to go to the big city and pursue her career. I think that's what pulled them apart. Their dreams pulled them in different directions. Dad always had to work late and Mom wasn't getting any younger. I was about eight when we moved to St. Louis, where Mom had family. Dad stayed out in L.A. That was probably the low period of my life. Right after the separation, you know, I'm not so sure they ever got a divorce. Dad always sent money to Mom, and whenever we needed anything extra Mom never hesitated to call on Dad for some help."

"We lived well and Mom was doing good in her modeling career. I graduated from nursing school and took a job in St. Louis. Daddy would come to see us every chance he got."

"So how's your love life?" he asked.

"That's kind of a personal question, but not so good. I dated a few guys, but they never came up to Daddy's expectations. I've always denied the fact but deep down I seem to have always wanted to find a young man that my daddy would approve of."

"How is it that you have not come out here to visit?"

"Well, I was never really asked to come. He came into the city a couple of times a year. I always felt that he was sort of ashamed of his little ramshackle farm and his poor circumstances." Albert wondered if Julie really thought her father was poor.

"He's sure doing better than a ramshackle farmer. He's got a few thousand acres, and he's one of the most well-respected men in the community."

"That's good to know," she said. "I always loved my daddy."

"Me, too," said Albert.

"Excuse me?" said Julie in a shocked manner.

"He's always been like a second dad to me," said Albert.

"So what brought you here this day?" asked Albert.

"I was working at the hospital in St. Louis about three weeks ago, and people started coming in with strange ailments. It was stuff that doctors couldn't cure. And the doctors didn't know what to do. The hospital was filling up with sick people all with the same thing. It was obviously contagious."

"Then they started to die. A lot of them."

The air was split by an explosion as the boys sighted in another gun.

"It became such a burden cleaning these people up, and then the other nurses started getting sick and then the doctors."

"Dr. Willey finally took me aside and told me that I better get out before I caught it. He had taken an oath, but he said I wasn't getting paid enough to die, and there was nothing I could do for these people anyway." She was ashamed to think back to that sudden feeling of hopelessness and the fear that turned to panic.

"I thought it was time to get out of the city. I tried to get in touch with Mom. She was out with some new boyfriend, so I just decided to get into the car and head this way. I just got into town and saw Dad's car, and the rest is history."

"How did you know this was your dad's car?" asked Albert.

"I helped him pick it out last Christmas. See the little decal of the red lipstick that looks like a kiss right there in the lower windshield. I put that there for good luck."

Albert looked at the little decal on the windshield. "Lucky glass," he said."

"What?" asked Julie. Had she heard him right?

"Never mind," said Albert. "When my dad and your dad left for the city, your dad tossed me the keys and told me not to get it shot full of holes. I sure didn't think we would get it shot full of holes."

"What about high school?" he asked.

"It was pretty normal and boring. I was on the swim team and I was a cheerleader. I never studied very hard, but got passing grades."

"Same with me," said Albert. "Never could really see a reason to work any harder than just enough to keep my parents off my back."

"Does your Mom work?" She could check him out, too.

Bang.

"No, she pretty much stayed home and took care of the home place. The folks moved out here about the time I was born. Dad is sort of a supervisor at the local utility company. We've got a few hundred acres and some cattle that I help with, but I always wanted to go to the city and work for awhile."

"Not now, you don't," she said. "The city is smelly and dirty and full of mean people." And now they are dying, she thought. She looked around at the beautiful green scenery and smelled the clean fragrance of the country.

"Dad always used to say, 'There is no shortage of

people willing to take advantage of someone willing to be taken advantage of.' " Albert stood up preparing to leave.

"I think I'd like to meet your dad, and mom for that matter," Julie said. "Is there any food around here?"

Bang!

"That should be the last shot. They will be coming back now. See, I have finished loading the 10-shot clips. The electricity has been off, and so no restaurant is open, but we can rustle something up at the house."

The boys came walking back to the car carrying their rifles. They were talking excitedly.

"Got 'em sighted?" asked Albert.

"This one's a little off, but it might have been a wind gust." Juan held up a rifle.

Albert handed each of the boys a 10-shot clip. "Make sure those guns are unloaded when they go into the car; remember Jimmy Dorsey."

"Who is Jimmy Dorsey?" asked Julie.

"Jimmy nine toes," laughed number Two. "We were quail hunting, and he had the gun barrel resting on his right foot. The gun was loaded, he forgot to put the safety on, I hit a bump, and boom, nine toes. Blew a hole right through the floorboard of Dad's pickup; damn near made me deaf. I know it's not funny, but I laughed till I cried and still laugh when I think about it.

"Here's one that's not funny. A couple of years before, Bobby Martin was hunting with his dog and his brother-in-law, and he forgot the safety and the dog was messing around and pulled the trigger on the gun, and we buried old Bobby. Killed by his own dog."

"And you boys still mess with guns?" asked Julie.

"Holy smokes," said number Three, "hundreds of people get electrocuted, and nobody suggests we stop using electricity. Doctors kill thousands of patients each year, and we still have doctors. Cars kill way more people than guns, but it's the driver, not the car. The gun has done way more good for mankind than bad."

"What got him so wrapped up?" laughed Julie.

"He's scared they're going to take our guns away. He's afraid there is a group of people out there who never give up. He lost a baseball game one evening; they ate Mexican food right before he went to bed and he had a nightmare that the other team showed up in front of the house with baseball bats wanting to rape and pillage his mother. He woke up screaming, and the only way we could get him to go back to sleep was to give him a shotgun to hold. Dad took the barrel off so it was completely safe, but it helped dispel those demons," Albert explained.

"I guess he has a point though. It is every man's duty to protect his home. Suppose a mob of guys showed up in front of your home and wanted you and your mother. How would you stop them?" Albert had walked over to the girl and placed both hands on her shoulders.

"That won't happen." Secretly she thought it just might.

"Suppose it did?" continued Albert. "The safest countries and the most free are countries that train all their citizens to use guns at an early age. Teach gun safety at an early age, and there will be fewer Jimmy Dorsey stories. You can only go so far in protecting man from himself."

They all five had loaded into the car and were driving back through the winding gravel roads.

"I wonder where those guys at the airport were headed?" asked number Two.

"I can't even imagine what they have in mind all the way out here in the boonies," said Albert.

"That one guy in the gun store said it was an invasion," said Julie. "Do you think it's possible? The big city is in chaos and has been for several days. When I left, there were sick and dying people everywhere, and then the power went out." She had felt lucky to have gotten out in time.

"Wait a minute," said Albert. "Did you say the power was out in the city? Hell, I thought it was just around here, and I figured it was because Dad left for a day or two. It always seems like the stuff hits the fan whenever he leaves, even for just a couple of days."

"You know Dad has long said that the best thing that could happen to this country would be for the power to go out for about six weeks. That would be long enough for all the food in most of the freezers to start to melt. That would change everybody's perspective." They all sat in silence to let that thought sink in.

Albert turned around to speak to the boys in the back, "Are you getting hungry?" Albert had heard his own stomach growl.

"You bet," said number Three. "We were planning a big fish fry and a cookout, and we still have to clean those fish. Looks like our plans have changed."

They pulled into the driveway of the house. The

car slowed in front of the generator building. "Start that generator, number Two."

Number Two jumped out of the car and ran to the generator building.

"One of my all-time pet peeves," said Albert as he drove slowly down the driveway, "he always leaves the door open."

He drove the car to the back door of the house, and they all got out of the car.

Juan had just closed the door to the passenger side rear of the car when he said, "Wait a minute, did you hear that?"

"Hear what?" asked Juliette.

"Gunshots, coming from that direction," he pointed toward the Taylor farmhouse."

"Wait," said Albert as he stopped beside the car and cupped his hands over his ear. I hear them, too, two more shots. Hey, number Three, run into the house and get the field glasses and run up the side of the silo and see if you can see anything. Please."

Number Three ran to the door of the house, and the door was locked. "Keys," he hollered, "I need keys, whose got keys? This door is never locked. What is the world coming to?"

Albert reached in his pocket and tossed them to number Three, who opened the door and ran into the house. He left the keys hanging in the door.

"This may be happening quicker than I thought." Albert sounded worried.

Three ran out of the door carrying a set of binoculars. He ran across the parking lot to a large silo that had a staircase spiraling up to the top of its 60-foot height.

As he was halfway across the parking lot, the big generator kicked on.

"Holy shit," said Albert, "Juan, run over there and shut that generator off. Use the emergency shut-off. It's the big red button inside the door. Hurry."

"Why are you doing that?" asked Juliette. There was a note of worry in her voice.

"Because our little invading friends for some reason may have decided to come our direction, I think. If they have, I don't want them to know we are home."

"Good idea," she said.

Moments later the generator was silent.

They all stood and watched number Three ascend to the top of the silo.

Number Two came running from the generator building. "What in the world is going on? Juan said you told him to shut the generator down."

"We heard gunshots coming from over there. We think it is our little invading friends, and I didn't want to arouse suspicion."

They stood in silence as number Three descended the stairs and came running to them.

Three said breathlessly, "Looks like the same guys with guns over at the Taylor house. That's a long way to see though, and there's trees in the way." None of them doubted that it was the same people.

"It's getting ready to get dark. Let's wait till dark and sneak on over there. My stomach thinks my throat's been cut. Let's get a quick bite to eat." Albert had carried one of the guns to the porch. "Let's get armed."

"Number Two, get up the ladder there and keep a watch on the road to the house. Everybody else, let's get some food quick."

"Wait," Juan said. "I just had an interesting thought. Smoked turkey."

"That's right," Albert said. "I forgot about that."

"What do you mean by that?" Juliette asked.

"Yesterday we caught a few trespassing turkeys eating the newly planted corn crop, and we claimed them for the cause. A few turkeys can just ruin a crop; they pluck the baby plant right out of the ground, hundreds at a time."

"Is there a turkey season?" asked Julie

"Yes, there is," said Juan. "It opens in about two weeks. When we saw these birds, we opened it for just a second, but we closed it right back."

"Anyway, we thought we would have a little party, and we put those birds in the smoker and they would be just about ready now."

"Get 'em out quick, Juan," said Albert. "Julie, can you run into the house and get some plates and napkins, nothing fancy. We have to eat quick and get over there."

"Juan, peel off a leg for Two and Three. I've got to run in here for a second."

Juan returned from the area of the barn with a large pan that held two medium-sized birds.

Albert returned with four small radios, two handguns in holsters and a double barrel shotgun. He laid the handguns on the table and walked with the shotgun to the backseat of the car. There, he opened the back door and dug around in the sack for a box of shotgun shells. He carried the box to the table, took out two shells and loaded the gun.

He carried the radios to Juan and gave three to

him. "Take one of these to Two and one to Three, please. Tell them we're on channel 4."

"Roger," said Juan.

Julie was back at the table by this time and asked, "How is it that you guys have all this stuff?"

"What stuff?" asked Albert.

"All the guns and stuff," she said.

We hunt to live, and we live to hunt."

As if to prove a point, he reached into the pan and tore off a turkey wing and began to gnaw on it. He looked at the girl, "It satisfies a deep primal need. Have some, it's good." He stood up and walked away. "Watch out for the bird shot in that meat," he said. "Take little bites, you don't want to break a tooth."

She picked up a knife and carved a large piece of breast. She sprinkled salt on it and ate it with her fingers as she followed Albert.

"What do you use the radios for?" she asked.

"Usually we use them to talk about the weather; sometimes we use them to help spot deer."

As he stood holding his radio, it beeped.

"Go ahead," he said into the radio.

"It's Three," said a voice. "There's a gray SUV leaving the Taylor place and headed down the road, fast."

"You hear that, guys?" he spoke into the radio. They all responded that they had.

Juan walked out of the house with a semi-automatic Remington 12-gauge shotgun, went to the table and put four shells in the magazine and cocked one into the chamber, then loaded another in the magazine. He took five more shells and put them in his pockets.

"Just our luck," he said. "We sight in big guns and it's almost too dark to use them."

"These old boys might have night stuff or infra-red stuff or grenade launchers, so let's be careful," said Albert.

The radio beeped again.

"It's Three. I'm in these trees out front. Looks like I can see two people in the front seat and maybe one in the back. They're coming up the driveway."

"Is that the Taylors' SUV?"

"Looks like it," said Two.

"Oh, hell," said Albert. "Julie, get your gun."

"Juan, hide over there by the barn."

Albert walked along the side of the house and peeked around the corner.

"I see four men and guns," he said. He talked quickly into the radio. "Two, get with Juan. We don't want to shoot each other. You, too, Julie."

Julie and Two ran to the barn to be beside Juan.

"These guys will shoot first," Albert said into the radio. "I'll be inside the house."

The SUV came rapidly down the driveway and scattered white rocks with its tires.

Two's voice came over the radio, "They're getting out of the car with guns. They're pointing at the black car. They're splitting up, two guys are going around the front; you should see them in a second, Three. The other two are going up to the house. They'll be there in a second, Albert."

"I see them," said Albert. He tried to keep the fear out of his voice.

"One guy is going to the generator house," said Two. "The other's coming around the front."

"Juan, can you get the generator guy?"

"He's in my sights."

"Can you get the front door guy, Three?"

"He's in my sights."

"Shoot when I do. Don't miss."

The soldiers walked onto the back porch.

Two said, "They're going to shoot into the house. Get down, Albert."

The two men stood before the back door and opened fire with their automatic weapons into the house. The glass shattered as the bullets crashed into the building.

After firing several rounds into the house, one of the men walked to the back door and forced it open. Albert stepped into the doorway and pulled one of the triggers on the shotgun. The shot was high, and most of the pellets hit the man in the head and shoulders.

Two pellets hit the second man, one in the forehead and one in the neck.

As soon as the shotgun went off, there was a shot from the barn; generator man fell dead.

The radio hissed and Juan's voice said, "I can just see the guy coming around the front."

Number Three had fired three times at the man coming around the front of the house. "I missed," he said over the radio. "He's coming around the side of the house."

"I'll get him," said Juan. He fired two shots at the man. One shot hit him in the leg, and he began to limp down the driveway. Juan shot again with no results. The man began to limp faster down the driveway and toward the main road. Albert opened the front door. He leveled his pistol at the running figure and emptied his gun. The last bullet hit the man in the lower back, and he spun around and fell to the ground. His gun fell to the ground, and he lay paralyzed on the ground.

Albert ran back to the kitchen table and reloaded the pistol and ran back out the front door. Juan was walking slowly toward the man with his rifle aimed at him.

Albert called back into the house, "Make sure those bastards are dead." There was obvious fear in his voice.

"Will do," came a voice over the radio.

Two pistol shots came from the house, and shortly thereafter one shot was heard from behind the house.

Albert and Juan walked up to the man in the driveway. He was whimpering in obvious pain. His legs were not moving, and he was dragging himself along using his hands. There was a trail of blood about 10 yards long that showed how far he had dragged himself. As he lay in one spot, there was a large pool of blood forming under him. The man saw them coming, and he tried to pull himself further. He rolled over on his back and raised his hands in the air and spoke in a language that neither boy could understand. He finally said the word "doctor" in English. He said it over and over again, "Doctor, doctor."

"Doctor," said Juan, "he wants a doctor."

"Let's see," said Albert, "this dirty son-of-a-bitch just tried to kill us and he wants a doctor. Here's a new word for you," he said as he approached the dying man, "undertaker," and he shot the man in the forehead.

He took out his radio, "Three, get the tractor with

the loader, and let's get these bodies out of here. Save their guns and ammunition."

"Julie, hop in that truck and park it back behind the barn between those bails of hay. Park it out of sight."

They walked around the house to the back where the trucks were parked. Julie was just getting into the SUV. She jumped back out of the car. "There's blood all over this car," she said.

Juan and Albert walked to the car and looked into the passenger side window. The dash and front floor were covered in blood.

This was the Taylors' car," said Juan. "They must have shot someone in the car."

"Probably the Missus," said Albert. "She almost always drove this, and old George drove his pickup."

In the barn was heard the loud noise of a tractor starting, and soon thereafter the large green machine with a front loader, driven by number Three, came out of the barn and toward the body lying near the generator building. He dropped the scoop to the ground, and without slowing very much he scooped the body off the ground. He spun the tractor around and drove right up to the steps at the rear of the house. Number Two was dragging the second body from the house; Three jumped off the tractor and helped Two to load the bodies onto the scoop.

"Still room for one more," he said, and mounted the tractor and backed away from the deck. He stopped beside Albert and Juan and slowed the big diesel down and asked, "Do you have any special spot in mind for these?"

"Well," said Albert, "the coyotes been pretty thick

down by the creek. I'd think if you dumped them in the tall grass down by the low water bridge they'd be pretty hard to spot."

"Sounds good to me," said Three.

"Just hurry back here," said Albert.

"Righto," said Three, and he increased the throttle on the big tractor and drove around to the front of the house.

Juan hurried along the driveway to help load the last body.

Julie drove the gray SUV back behind the barn.

Juan, Albert, Julie and Two were sitting in silence on the deck of the house and watching the tractor finally making its way back from the creek. They were all in a mild state of shock.

Three brought the tractor to a stop beside the porch and shut if off. He jumped out of the cab and deposited several pieces of paper onto the table on the porch.

"I thought I might as well pick these old boys' pockets and see who they were," he said. "It's a little dark out here, so I didn't look at them."

Two came out of the house with a Coleman lantern. He set it on the table and lit it and adjusted the flame to the best brightness. He then hung it on a hook on the side of the house, and its light illuminated the table.

"Let's have a look at these papers," said Albert, and he passed them around the table so that each one could help.

After a few minutes Albert asked, "Are you finding anything?"

"It's funny," Juan said, "look at this." He laid a piece of paper on the table that was a copy of a photograph; the paper had been folded. "What in the world? That's a picture of our house. When was that taken?"

"Well, I don't know. Hey, isn't that that old '84 jeep you had sitting in the driveway? Yes, it was. That was last summer. See that sign in the window, that's when it was parked in the driveway for sale."

"Look what I found," said Julie. She threw a picture on the table.

"Why, that's a picture of the Jones' farm," said number Three. "Why in the world would these guys have pictures of our farms in their pockets?"

"I don't know," Juan said.

Number Three came out of the house. "Let's look at the guns these guys had."

He picked up one of the rifles and played with it and learned how to cock it and fire it and where the safety was. "Cheap gun," he said.

"Maybe cheap," said Albert, "but it's good enough to kill us with. If they are Chinese, they have a billion-man army and we have pretty guns. They have a surplus in their budget every year, and we have an increased national debt that they own a big piece of."

"Suppose we went to war with a country that had a billion-man army, and suppose it takes 20 bullets in a war for each casualty. We don't have 20 billion bullets."

"Somebody knows these thugs came over here, and in an hour or so they'll be expecting them back. When they don't come back, they'll be coming over here looking for them, and they'll be ready for us and they have more firepower than we do. It's almost dark now; I say we pay a visit to our friends next door," said Albert.

"Hey, Three, that was some pretty piss-poor shootin' back there. What's the deal?"

"Look at this dumb scope," said Three as he held up a rifle. "It's loose as a goose. I knew I bumped it going up the steps, but I didn't think I hit it that hard."

"We'll have to resight it. Want to use one of these machine guns?" He handed it to his brother.

Albert and Juan walked back into the house to find that Julie had completely set the table by the light of the Coleman lantern and that she was just about done eating.

"What's the deal?" Albert laughed. "You didn't wait for us?" He was glad that she had eaten. The excitement had taken his appetite, but he did not want to admit it.

"Not a chance! If I had waited for you lunatics, I might never get fed and I was starving. Besides, we'll all be in a lot better mood after we've eaten."

"What's your plan now?" she asked. She had just started bringing water glasses to the table.

"I guess we'll finish eating and then sneak over to the Taylor house and exact a little revenge," he said.

"How in the world did you kids, growing up in a small town, get to be so bloodthirsty? How can you be so cold-blooded like this?" she asked.

Albert explained between bites. "Part of it is the way we were raised. We have sort of expected this sort of thing our whole lives. We also spent a lot of our lives involved in paintball; that's a game where we use air guns that throw plastic balls filled with paint at the opponent. They're like war games, and it can be quite painful. We've done this since we were about eight years old." He didn't want to admit that it was fear that was driving him, that he was scared to death.

"What's the object of the game?" she asked.

"You dress up in camouflage and run around through the woods and try to attack or defend a spot, and when you get shot it's like you're dead. We've done this for years. So we're sort of ready for the real thing." The words came easily, but the reality was that he was feeling pretty badly.

"We've all been living off the land here for all our lives, just like our ancestors have done for centuries. We shoot deer and turkey and all kinds of birds, and we fish a lot and we raise cattle and we see things die all the time, so it really isn't any big deal. Maybe after this is all over we'll think about it, but for right now I can tell you, at least from my perspective, that I'm pretty darned scared."

"We've been shooting foxes and turtles and snakes and coyotes and mad dogs and rabid skunks for all our lives, and there's not a whole lot of difference from what went on today. It's just another piece of shit varmint to be exterminated. The vermin come in and kill your crops and your little animals, your chickens and your ducks and your geese and your pet cats; these bobcats come in at night and eat the little kittens you've grown attached to. There are hawks and buzzards and every imaginable type of animal that's preying on the little animals. All these years we've sort of been in the habit of destroying the vermin that have been destroying the little animals that we like. There is not a heck of a lot of difference between that and killing a two-legged vermin."

"But a man has a soul," she said. She couldn't

imagine why she was giving Albert a hard time right now, maybe because she was scared herself.

"I want you to prove that to me. Prove to me that those vermin had a soul. 'Til you do I'll just shoot 'em all and let God sort 'em out."

He sat at the table and began to eat. "This sure was nice of you to set this table."

"Don't mention it," she said as she got up from the table and walked to the sink.

He watched her as she walked to the sink. "You know," he said, "you're mighty easy on the eyes."

"What?" she said. There it was again, a compliment that she missed.

"You're easy on the eyes, you're good-looking."

"Never heard it said that way," she said, "thanks." She felt herself blushing.

"Just set those dishes in the sink," he said, "we'll get them when we turn the power back on."

"Hey, boys, come in and get it, and wash your hands first, and don't use all the water. The pressure tank is about used up." Albert didn't bother getting up from the table.

"Yes, Mother," said Three as he walked to the sink.

They ate in haste and in silence. Julie walked past Albert and took his plate to the sink.

"You know you are right handy to have around," he told her.

She turned and looked at him and didn't say a word.

"What's next?" the boys asked.

"Let's get the night gear," said Albert. "How much of that is working?"

"Let's see," said Three. "We had two and one

broke, so we were down to one. Then we got another one, so we have two. Let's get them out, please, and check the batteries."

Three disappeared into the back hallway and returned with two boxes, each containing night vision goggles. He set them on the table and began to check the condition of the batteries.

"Check this out," said Three, producing a rifle with a large scope on it and a box of shells. "Remember this?"

"Oh, yeah, Dad got that for coyotes. It's a 25-06 with a 4-power night scope. Good job, we can use that baby."

"These check out good," Albert said, and gave one to Three.

"Okay," said Albert, "let's get going."

Julie walked toward Albert, "What shall I do now?"

"The best thing would be for you to just stay here, keep your gun handy, and watch the front driveway. If they come here, just run out the back door and into the woods, and we'll be back as soon as we can."

"You might check that last turkey in the smoker," said Juan.

"I think I'll just take a little nap. I've had a long drive," Julie said.

"Come with me," said Albert. "Let me show you something."

He led her by the hand outside and across the wide parking lot to the back of the big silo. They walked around the back of the silo, and he led her to a spot in front of a door with two handles. "Now reach down there and turn both of those handles," he said. She did as she was told. The door swung open. "See back in there to what looks like a big airway?"

"Yes," she said. She couldn't really see in the dim light, but she could imagine what it looked like.

"That's the airway for the fan that dries the grain. If you go in that door, you can close it from the inside. You can crawl past the fan. It is a tight squeeze, but I can do it, so you can, too. Past the fan is a plate. You can hide behind that plate, and they couldn't see you unless they knew where to look."

"So if someone, anyone, comes down the road to the house, you run down here lickety-split," he cautioned.

"How was that?" she laughed. She was making fun of him.

"Lickety-split — it's an old term that means fast."

"So you run down here fast and hide in here, and we'll come and get you."

He reached down and closed the latch. "Now you should be safe 'til we get back, take care of that turkey."

He started to walk back. With her left hand she took hold of his right hand. He stopped and turned around. She pulled him closer to her. "You boys be careful, you hear?" He pulled her closer and took a deep breath through his nose.

"You look good, and you smell good, too."

She kissed him quickly on the lips and said, "You be careful."

He smiled and said, "I'll be back." He was thinking how glad he was to have something to come back to.

He held her hand as they walked across the driveway, and squeezed it one time hard as they got to the other side.

"Load up," he yelled.

Number Three drove silently up in a battery-powered, four-seated cart. The boys got in.

"We'll go across the pasture here to see if anyone's home."

"But how can you see in the dark?" Julie asked.

"Let's see. Moon's about full, we've been hunting possums and coons in the dark all our lives, we could get across that pasture with our eyes closed."

Two said, "In about an hour you'll be able to read a newspaper by moonlight. Look, no clouds."

They disappeared down the path that led into the field.

"Let's park this by the last gate; we'll walk the last little bit," said Albert.

When they had stopped the cart, Albert whispered, "Load your guns and check your safeties, no accidents. We'll sneak up on them if anybody's there."

They all did as he said.

"I'll lead the way," Albert whispered. "Then Juan, then Two, bring up the rear, Three." No one questioned his authority this time.

They walked slowly and silently down the road, Albert opened the fence gate and left it open while the others followed.

When they got within sight of the house, Albert whispered, "Two and Three, sneak around past the hay bales and come up on the other side of the big barn, over by the gas tanks. Don't go past the gas tanks, they've got a pig lot over there; you want to stay away from those boars. We'll get there first; we'll wait right beside the garage, so we'll wait till you're ready. Give us one short whistle. Have you still got the radio, Three?"

"Yes, I do," said Three.

"Good," said Albert, "turn the beeper off."

Juan and Albert reached the garage quietly and quickly, and Juan was looking through the night glasses.

"What do you see?" asked Albert.

"There is one man standing guard; no, wait," said Juan. "There is a man taking a leak beside the house. He's going back into the house now. I don't see anyone else."

"What's that car in the driveway?"

"An SUV of some kind," said Juan. "Never seen it before."

"Just one?" asked Albert.

"Seems to be just one. Wait a minute, there might be a different pickup in the driveway."

Soon they heard a low whistle. Two and Three were in place.

Albert was on the radio, "What do you see, Three?"

"We saw one guy by the back door."

"We can see in the front window, looks like one guy sitting at the kitchen table. He's got his back to us. There's one guy by the back door."

"We'll get the guy by the back door," said Albert, "and anybody else who comes through that door. You guys get the guy at the table and anybody who goes out the front door. Click the mike twice when you're ready."

Number Three sneaked across the driveway and

across the yard and took a place outside the dining room window. He placed the barrel of the shotgun on the windowsill and aimed it at the man sitting at the table. Number Two hurried across the front yard and waited on the front porch.

Albert flipped the safety off the rifle with the night vision scope. He aimed the gun at the head of the man by the back door. The radio clicked three times; Albert shot the man in the head.

When the shot was heard, the man at the table stood up, and Three shot him through the window. The big glass exploded.

Albert laid his shotgun down and drew the Colt 45 from its holster. He ran past the dead man at the back door and into the back door of the house. He ran through the back porch area and through the kitchen area and into the living room area where there was a stairway leading upstairs.

As Albert entered the kitchen, a man came running down the stairway and toward a pair of rifles leaning against the wall in the dining room. He was wearing a shirt and no pants. Number Three shot at this man, but at such close range that he missed him, but two pellets pierced the man's leg and caused him to stumble. Albert was standing over the man with the 45 aimed at his head. "Stop right there," commanded Albert.

In perfect English, the man said, "You wouldn't shoot an unarmed man now, would you?"

"Yes, I would," said Albert, "lay down."

The man did as he was told.

Juan came into the back door behind Albert.

The front door opened and number Two came in.

There was a noise from upstairs and the sound of footsteps coming down the staircase. Three guns aimed that direction. A man, completely naked, came running down the stairway. He stopped at the base of the stairs when he saw the guns.

"Bad luck," he said in broken English, and he stopped in his tracks. When the man spoke, Albert noticed that the only remarkable thing about him, aside from the fact that he was naked, was that he had incredibly bad teeth.

Albert stepped back and leveled the 45 at the man's head. "Lie on the ground."

The man did as he was told.

"Watch these two," Albert said. "I'll check the rest of the house."

Number Three came in the back door. "Look what I found on the shelf, a roll of duct tape. Let's tie these guys up."

Juan set two kitchen chairs in the middle of the room, and they lifted the first man into the chair and tied his hands to the chair arms and his legs to the legs of the chair. In short order they did the same to the second man.

Albert began to walk through the house with the 45 at the ready, a room at a time. When he got to the basement door, he took the steps quickly, and when he returned he had a look of grief on his face.

"They killed the Taylors and dumped their bodies down the stairs. The bodies are in a heap in the basement."

He walked to the bottom of the stairs leading upstairs. "Back me up," he said. Juan followed behind him with a shotgun.

Up the polished wood stairs he ran and went to the left. He opened the first bedroom door and checked the closet; he did the same with the second bedroom, and then the third. There was a fourth bedroom, and as he opened the door, he said, "My God, Jenny." On the antique bed and tied spread-eagle to it was a girl of 19. She was bruised and bleeding from her nose and her groin area. Her arms and legs were tied with ropes to the four bedposts. She had a washcloth pushed in her mouth that kept her from making a sound.

A wave of relief passed through the girl as she recognized Albert and Juan standing in the doorway. For a moment the pain went away.

Albert took a knife from his pocket and cut the ropes that tied her ankles, and then her wrists. When he had done this, her body curled into a fetal position, and he pulled the cloth from her mouth.

"Thank God you've come," she said in a weak voice. "They said they killed my parents and were raping me."

"Wish we had come sooner," said Albert. He didn't want to admit that they had waited until dark.

"It wouldn't have done any good," said the girl. "Mom and Dad were eating supper and they killed them quickly."

"Take care of her, Juan," said Albert, as he walked out of the room.

He returned to the dining room and looked at the two men who were taped to chairs. He walked to the first man and slapped him hard. "How many of you are there?"

"One hundred forty two today, but tomorrow a

million," said the man through bleeding lips.

They heard a noise at the bottom of the staircase, and they all turned to look in that direction. It was the girl, completely naked, walking as though in some pain. She had the physique of a body builder, complete tan with no tan lines, zero body fat, tight muscles and small breasts. Albert remembered that she had placed highly in the state body-building competition. Juan followed right behind her.

She stopped in front of the bathroom door and turned to Juan. "Would you please bring a bar of soap and a wash cloth, Juan?" she asked. She pointed toward a cupboard. Then she took two more steps and turned to face the others. "Where's the first guy?" she asked.

"What guy?" asked Albert.

"The General or whatever?" she said.

"Where's the General?" Albert asked the first man.

"He had his way with this peasant girl and then went back to the camp. He should return any minute. This will be his new home," said the man with a grin.

The girl looked at the first man, and without blinking said, "Revenge!"

She walked out the back door, and Juan followed behind her, carrying a towel and soap.

She went to the outside water faucet that had a hose attached. She turned the water on a small amount and held out her hand for the wash cloth and soap. Juan held the cloth and soap out to her. She wet the cloth and rubbed the soap on the cloth and then washed her neck and body with the cloth. She used the hose to wash her groin area.

"I've got to get those bastards out of me," she said.

She did not seem to object as Juan watched her. She rinsed the soap off after a minute and turned the water off. She turned to Juan and said, "I'm sorry," and she walked back into the house.

She walked to the wall in the kitchen that held an assortment of cooking utensils and selected a wooden rolling pin. She walked to the naked man with the bad teeth.

"You know," she said, "all the while these bastards were raping me, all I could think about was knocking this guy's rotten teeth back into his head." Saying that, she swung the rolling pin with all her might. Her muscles rippled with power and shattered the man's teeth and jaw. Rotten teeth and blood flew everywhere. His jaw hung open, obviously shattered. Thank you, Lord, she thought to herself.

She dropped the rolling pin to the floor and walked back into the kitchen. She opened the knife drawer and selected a steak knife with a wooden handle. She turned and walked to the first man who was wearing only a shirt. "You know what we did all day? We castrated little pigs, all day. You're going to help me answer a question I've always wanted to ask them." The man tried to bounce the chair away from her. Two and Three held the chair in place.

"Whenever we cut these little fellows," she said, "we take a knife a little sharper than this one, and we cut their little sack open just like this," she said as she made a quick movement with the knife at the man's groin. "Then," she continued, "we grab the little jewels just like this," she reached down with her left hand and pulled up two gray objects the size of walnuts; each had two tubes the size of pencils attached."

The man screamed.

"We always cut these little tubes, but I always wondered what would happen if we just pulled them till they come out?" She stretched the tubes until they snapped. The man screamed again and passed out. She threw the gonads on the floor.

"Now for you, Toothie," she said. She walked to the second man and with a slow sawing motion of the knife removed all of his sexual organs. A pool of blood began to form below the chair. She dropped the bloody mass and the knife and walked to the bathroom. "Could you please feed these to the pigs?" she asked. She walked to the sink and washed her hands.

After drying her hands on a towel, she opened a cupboard door and removed a large bottle of wine. "I really don't want to remember this tomorrow; I want it to be just one big fuzzy nightmare." She stopped in front of Juan. "I don't want to remember these guys; I know I'm in shock. What I would like to do is go upstairs and wash real good, get really drunk, have a couple of you American guys make love to me, and pass out. Hopefully, when I wake up I won't remember these," she spat in the direction of the limp bodies.

She turned to Albert, "My parents built this house, and I don't want these slime balls to have it. Would you please see that I'm carried out of here when I pass out, put my parents' bodies in their favorite chairs and burn this house around them?" She didn't wait for a reply, but turned and walked upstairs.

Juan followed her upstairs. "I'll take care of her," he said.

The second man had bled out and was dead. The old house had settled and the dark red blood had run to the corner of the room and formed a puddle. The first man was coming back to consciousness.

"Shall we shoot him?" asked Two? "I'd sure as hell want somebody to shoot me."

Albert spoke, "Let's see, these guys invade our country, kill our friends and rape our women. Let's save the bullet." He walked into the kitchen and removed a white trash bag from under the sink, walked behind the semi-conscious man and pulled the bag over his head. He then took the duct tape and wrapped it around the man's neck. In a moment the body began to convulse and shake, the trash bag became the image of the man's face as he gasped for air. After a few minutes the head fell forward.

"Let's do like she asked," Albert said, "get the tractor out of the barn, the one with the loader, and we'll feed these guys to the pigs."

Two went out the door to get the tractor. Albert and Three dragged the chairs with the bodies attached out the back door and let them fall off of the steps to the ground.

"Come help me get the old ones out of the basement," Albert said to Three. They carried the bodies into the living room and set them in their chairs. When the bodies were set in place, both boys burst into tears and left the room. They had known and loved these people all their lives.

"As soon as Two drops those bodies in the pigpen, let's get some of that old hay and fill the front porch with it. We can pick up that 200-gallon diesel tank and drop it on the front porch among the hay bales and it will burn forever."

It wasn't long before Juan came down the steps

carrying the limp body of the girl, wrapped in a white terry cloth bathrobe. "She said she took a nerve pill along with a half a bottle of wine," he said. "She's out of it. I packed a bunch of her clothes and threw them out the window. Are we going to burn the place?"

"That's what she wanted," said Albert.

Two went ahead of Juan and opened the door for him. He led the way toward the family garage where a green Jeep Wagoneer was parked. The keys were in it, and Juan laid the girl in the back seat and drove the Jeep back to the Brown house.

Three had brought the battery cart from the woods, and it was parked and ready in the driveway. As Albert stepped from the house, Two was fitting the last of three giant hay bales on the front porch. He drove the big tractor to the fuel tanks, and using the big front loader lifted the 200-gallon diesel tank from its stand. He drove the tractor around the front of the house, the long hose trailing behind. He stopped the machine for a minute and jumped down to remove the cap from the big tank. He looked over to Albert and asked, "Are we ready?"

"Let's get out of here before they come back," said Albert.

Two put the tractor into low gear and drove the big tank of diesel fuel into the large front plate glass window. Leaving the tank buried in the window frame, he backed the tractor up, and lowering the blade he drove slowly forward, the sharp bucket teeth cutting holes in the big fuel tank. The fuel began to fill the house. He backed the tractor down the driveway and parked it a distance from the house and ran back to the green machine. Albert was carrying an old oil lantern from the mantle in the house. It was lit; he threw it into the broken window hole and ran to the machine.

"Let's go," he said.

There was a whoosh and flames erupted from the front of the house. The other windows in the front were blown out by the explosion, and the flames poured out the window holes and licked the sides of the old painted building.

They drove off down the main driveway and down the road.

As they turned onto the main road, they stopped a moment and looked back at the house. By now it was almost completely engulfed in flames, and the big bales of straw on the porch were burning like torches.

Albert stood looking at the mailbox by the road. He walked to it and picked up the little piece of wood that said TAYLOR and placed it back on the mailbox.

They drove the green machine down the main road and turned into the Browns' driveway. The tail lights from the Jeep could be seen as Juan brought the Jeep to a stop. The farmhouse could be seen burning in the distance, and the horizon glowed. As they drove back to the house, they honked the horn three times.

The girl appeared from the silos. "Saw you coming down the driveway and I didn't know who you were, so I hid." The tone of her voice showed obvious relief.

"Glad you made it back," she looked at Albert.

"We need to get some sleep," said Albert. "Someone needs to stand watch."

The boys jumped from the green machine, and Albert walked to the jeep to help Juan lift Jenny from the back seat.

Albert stepped over to Julie. "Julie," he said, "this is Jenny. She's had sort of a bad day, could you help her, please?"

"Sure," she said, and she helped Juan walk the girl into the house.

"Hey, Two," yelled Albert, "run over and turn that generator on, please. We need lights for a minute, and I need a shower."

The generator was quietly humming, and Two was walking back to the house. Albert and Three were on the porch. "Let's shut all the lights out but just a couple so no light can be seen from the road, okay?"

"Sure," said Three. "I'll shut the switches off at all the yard lights." Three walked out into the driveway and walked toward the barn.

"How long you want that generator on for?" asked Two.

"Probably an hour or so," said Albert. "I'm having Three shut off the outside lights, and we want to keep the drapes closed. Somebody needs to keep watch, I figure three shifts, you want the first one?"

"Might as well," said Two. "I don't think I could sleep." He picked up a rifle and walked toward the silo and walked up the stairs to the platform.

Julie walked out of the house and shut the door quietly behind her. "That girl' asleep now," she said, "and Juan's sitting with her. What happened over there? Juan wouldn't talk about it."

"About five guys raped her and killed her parents and her brother," said Albert.

"That's terrible," said Julie, "who are those people?"

"I guess they're Chinese," said Albert. "They came in on that big plane. Maybe there's a whole bunch of them, maybe they're taking over the country. I sure wish Dad was here."

"You've done a pretty good job," said Julie, as she laid a hand on his shoulder.

"Thanks, but I'm scared to death. I'm still a kid and I like it that way," he admitted. The strain of responsibility was taking a toll

"Remember the old saying, 'A boy becomes a man when a man is needed,' " Julie said. "What do we do now?"

"You can sleep in my bedroom tonight. There's clean sheets on the bed, and it's the first room on the left," he told her.

"What about you?" she asked

"We're going to take turns watching. I'll set the alarm for a couple of hours and sleep on the couch."

"There are towels in the bathroom, across the hallway. The lights will be on for another 30 minutes or so, so if you want to wash up you better hurry."

"I'm really tired," she said. "Call me if you need me."

"Good night."

"Good night."

She disappeared into the house; Three had finished turning all the outside lights out. Thankfully, there was a full moon and the yard was brightly lit, so bright, in fact, that the moon threw shadows across the deck.

Three stood beside Albert and spoke. "Full moon, poor fishing, poor hunting, time to stay home with Mama."

"Dad used to say that all the time," said Albert.

"Wish he were here," admitted Three.

"Me, too."

"Maybe he'd make some sense of all this. Hope they're all right."

"Don't worry about them. He'll take care of Mom."

"But who is going to take care of us?" The worry could be heard in Albert's voice.

"Why, you are, big brother," said Three. "I'm going to sleep now, wake me when it's my turn, Two said he wasn't tired, but I sure am. Seems like a hundred years ago that we caught those fish. Darn, I never cleaned those fish. Hope they stay alive in that big tank."

"Good night," said Albert. "Generator's off in 20 minutes."

"Night, bro," said Three. "Turn it off now for all I care."

Albert stood for a minute on the deck, listening to the night sounds. "Lord help us," he said out loud.

He walked back into the house and sat at the kitchen table until Julie sneaked between the bathroom and the bedroom. He caught a brief glimpse of bare legs and feet below a big red towel. Then he went into the bathroom and showered, and when he was done he walked outside and turned off the generator. He walked down the driveway far enough that he could see the front of the house and made sure that there were no lights in the house or that number Two was visible in the bright moonlight.

He was just too tired to think.

He laid a loaded gun beside the chair and set the

battery alarm clock by feel as he had done a hundred hunting trips before, reclined in a chair and was asleep in two breaths.

He awoke two minutes before the alarm went off. He pushed the button to keep it from going off and had to sit and think a minute to remember where he was. He picked up the gun and walked out to the silo to relieve number Two. The full moon had traveled across the sky, and everything was the same color of gray, and objects cast long black shadows. He climbed the steps to the landing; Two was sitting, leaned against the silo.

"How's it going?" he asked.

"Quiet as a tomb," said Two. "There was a herd of deer came past here going out to the field to eat. If anything came by, they'd be spooked."

"Go ahead on down," said Albert. "I'm awake now."

"I'm still not sleepy," said Two. "I'll try to sleep, but you know me. Sometimes I'll go days with just a nap or two."

"Relieve me in a couple of hours," said Albert, "or I'll wake Three."

"Don't wake him," said Two. "He needs sleep like I don't need it. If you wake him up, he'll be a bitch the rest of the day. I'd rather stand watch than hear his shit all day." He carried his gun down to the ground, and Albert watched him walk across the driveway to the house.

The sun began to rise in the east; it had been an unremarkable evening. Two must have been more tired than he thought. The moon had set two hours before, and that part of the night had been black. Albert stood up and stretched. Everything was covered in dew. He picked up his wet rifle and walked down the stairs, across the driveway, across the porch and into the house. He walked down the hallway to the room where Three was asleep and shook him gently. Three awoke with a start.

"It's morning," whispered Albert, "your watch."

Three jumped up, picked up his gun, and without saying a word walked quickly out the door toward the silo.

The living room had two large sliding glass doors that faced the east. Albert opened the blinds to both doors, and the sun streamed into the room. He walked to the refrigerator and took a bottle of Mountain Dew. He removed his shirt, hung it on the back of a chair and sat at the table sipping the pop. He was watching the sunrise when Juliette came into the room. She was wearing shorts and sandals and a white brassiere. She was carrying the blouse she had worn the day before, and it was soaking wet. She opened the door, shook the blouse out several times and hung it over the railing. She stepped back into the house and shut the door. She hadn't noticed Albert sitting there. She stretched and stood looking out the window.

"Good morning," he said.

She was startled. As she turned, she placed her hand to her throat.

"How long have you been there?" she asked.

"Couple of minutes," he said matter-of-factly. "Want a Dew?"

"Love one," she said. She stood frozen in the sunlight. She was blushing.

He stood up and went to the refrigerator and

brought her a Mountain Dew and opened it for her.

"Thank you," she said as she sipped the cold drink.

"Don't mention it," he said. "Turn around."

She had a questioning look on her face. "What for?" she asked.

"Just do it," he said.

She turned around; he walked up to her and moved her bra strap just a little.

"No tan lines," he said.

"No tan lines," she repeated.

He looked closer at her skin, "You have a most remarkable skin color," he said. "It's the perfect tan."

"Gets a little darker in the summer, lighter in the winter, comes from being 47 different races." She had always been proud of her multi-racial heritage.

He took a deep breath. "You sure do smell good, too," he said as he walked back to the table and sat down.

"Okay, it's my turn. Whose cowboy hat is that on the wall over there?"

"That's mine," he said.

"Put it on for me," she said.

He walked to the wall and put on the straw hat. "Now what?" he asked.

She stood back with one hand on her hip and the other at her chin. "That's it," she said. "I've had a recurring dream about a half-naked cowboy in boots, jeans, big belt buckle and a straw hat.

"Was it a good dream?" he asked.

"Always ends the same," she said.

"How's that?" he asked in a worried sort of way.

"I wake up," she said.

18

BILL, THE SHERIFF, sat in his office after the kids had left and thought about the highway patrol. Sergeant Henry, what a dick, he thought. No wonder people had such bad feelings for police. He was involved in law enforcement, and he hated that son-of-a-bitch. No, he really hated that son-of-a-bitch. He rose from his chair and opened a closet and removed an assault rifle and ammunition. From the back corner of the closet he took a small paper bag. As he walked out the front door, he said to the room at large, "I'm going to the airport. Call me if you need me."

It was a short trip to the edge of town. The dick would have used sirens, but he felt that it was unnecessary. He pulled into the armory since it was on his way to the airport, and there were four pickups in the parking lot. He drove right up to the front double doors and left his door open and the motor running. The lieutenant, a sergeant, and three enlisted men were arming themselves with helmets and rifles and flak jackets.

"Hey, Bill," said the Lieutenant.

"Hey, Bud," said the Sheriff, "did you get word to mobilize?"

"I was in old Mike's sporting goods just a minute ago, and Albert Brown was in there with the damndest story about a plane and an invasion, so I ran right over here. We haven't heard anything from the state level, but most of my guys are sick with something. Me and these guys were on that training exercise up in Minot till yesterday, and when we got back most of the other guys are really sick."

"I'm going to run on out to the airport and meet my guys out there. I'd say to come on out when you get ready. I've called the state for help, so you might get a call pretty quick. See ya," he said as he walked back out to his car and drove off.

"Load a couple of those shoulder rockets, Ted," said the Lieutenant. "A little extra firepower is a good thing. Sounds like we're pretty outnumbered." A few minutes later, the five men that comprised the entire Timberlake National Guard unit were driving in two trucks toward the airport.

The sheriff turned down the airport road. Another sheriff's car was parked in the middle of the road with its lights on, and a highway patrol car was in the ditch at the crest of the hill covered with bullet holes.

Sergeant Henry was hiding behind his car and looking at the airport, while the deputy sheriff stood beside his car and talked with three civilians. The sheriff parked in the ditch and walked toward the four men.

"What's the scoop?" he asked.

"Well, Chief," said the deputy, "looks like about a hundred bad old boys took over the airport. They might have killed everybody out there for all we know. We do know that they shot Wilkinson. His body is up over that ridge in the ditch beside his car. Henry, the wonder boy up there, came driving up like superman with his lights blazin', and about the time he got over that hill they opened up on him and he damn near got his ass shot off before he could get back. It sounded like a range war. Now his car's all shot up. There's a big old airplane down there; didn't think you could land something that big here. Anyway, that must be how they got here. Seems like they moved into that big building in the new industrial park. What was the name of that company that Joanie's kid works for?"

"The Syracuse Company." Bill's older sister, Joanie, had been so proud when her boy had landed that high-paying job with the new computer company in town. He would make nearly $9 an hour, no benefits, but who could afford benefits any more?

"Yeah, that's it. Syracuse. They all went over there, seems like they just went in the building, but they sure don't want to be bothered. Couple of guys over yonder shoot at anything that moves up here. What do you want to do now, Sheriff?" asked the deputy.

"Who are these men?" asked the Sheriff.

"They say they're contractors up from Dallas, supposed to work on the radios or radar or some shit at the airport. They had a flat tire."

The Sheriff looked them over, one old white guy, a young black guy and a white girl that looked like a guy; they were standing beside a white van with Texas plates. They all three wore white tennis shoes and white leisure suits with a patch on the front that looked like the NASA logo, but with the letters NATA. The girl was wearing old-fashioned, heavy-framed sunglasses.

"Sorry," said the Sheriff to the girl.

"What's that stand for?" Bill asked the girl, as he pointed to the logo on her chest.

"North American Telemetry and Avionics," said the man. "We're the guys that keep those planes flying straight."

"Can you people stay out of the way?" he asked them.

"That is part of our job description," said the older man.

Bill walked up the hill to the patrol car. His boots made a noise in the gravel, and Sergeant Henry turned and looked up from his crouching position.

"Get down, Bill," he said, "dirty bastards damn near killed me."

"Too bad," Bill said.

"What?" asked the Sergeant.

"Too bad the bastards missed," Bill said. He really hated this guy.

"I called the State and they're busy everywhere, what with this power outage and all, but they said they'd do what they could."

"Meaning what?" asked Bill. "Are they gonna send some help?"

"Don't know, think so, but I just don't know," said the patrolman.

"You sure don't," said Bill as he walked back to his deputy.

Bill spoke to the deputy, "That son-of-a-bitch is as dumb as a box of rocks, no, dumber. The National Guard, all five of them, should be coming up here pretty quick. I guess these old boys could just about do anything they want right now. Tell you what, Randy, keep an eye on them, don't try to do anything heroic. If it looks like they're coming this way, call me on the radio and then get the hell out of their way, I'll run back to town and try to get the Army down here. Oh, tell those civilians they're on their own, but that I recommend that they get the heck out of here, maybe go back to Dallas."

He jumped back in his car and drove as fast as he could back to his office. "Matilda?" he asked, "have you contacted the Governor's office?"

"Yes, sir, I have," she said, "and they told me they would get back to me."

"Please call the number and patch it through to my office," he said as he quickly sat behind his desk and laid his hand on the phone.

In a few moments the phone rang. He had it to his ear before it finished the first ring. "Who is this?" he asked in a serious tone of voice.

"This is Betty Ann Moseley, secretary to the Governor."

"This is Sheriff Bill Robinson. Please let me speak with the Governor. It is quite urgent."

"I'm sorry, sir, the Governor is ill today. Is there something I can help you with?"

"Let's see, dear, we have a slew of dead people down here, an invading army not two miles outside of town; the National Guard can only send five men. How can you help me?"

"Well, sir, as I told the lady earlier, we have had serious illness among the National Guard. Many of them have been called up to active duty for months now, the Army has all been shipped overseas, the Governor came down with some sort of flu, the power has been out all day, and the Lieutenant Governor is out of the office. For most of the morning the phones didn't work. I guess you're on your own."

"So you're telling me to call out the Boy Scouts?" The phone went dead.

He slammed the phone down on the receiver, then slammed the phone down again. Then he started to slam the phone down again and stopped and set the phone back in the receiver and stood up out of his chair and picked up a wooden chair, and by hitting it again and again on his desk broke it to pieces.

Matilda stepped into his office and spoke as if nothing had happened. "Mike Williams is here to see you."

"Send him in, Mary, and thank you."

He sat back down at his desk and looked up as the tall red-haired man came into the room. Mike ignored the wreckage of the chair. Bill had a history of violence directed toward furniture. Whatever floats your boat, he thought.

"Call out the militia, Mike," Bill said. "We've got about a hundred guys landed at the airport, they're just waiting for something. The Army's overseas, the National Guard is called up and overseas, the old men and children that are left in the guard are sick, the Governor's sick, the Lieutenant Governor's sick, we're screwed."

"That's what I'm here about," said the big man. "We were all bullshittin' on the ham radio this morning, and Tim Redmond down in Derby tells me that a truck carrying one of those containers tipped over, and inside the container is a bunch of dead Orientals. They had a kitchen and a bathroom and lights and food and a bunch of guns and shit. He said that truck had a bill of lading to deliver that container to the airport right here in River City."

320

"Who knows about this?" asked Bill.

"You and me and the half of the planet that listens to ham radio."

"So that's what they are waiting for," said Bill, as if a light had turned on in his brain.

"Who?" asked Mike.

"Those hundred guys at the airport," exclaimed Bill. "We wondered why they just swooped in and now they just sit."

"Let's see, if they find out that their supplies aren't coming, they will try to break out and do who knows how much damage."

"There's something else," said Mike. "This wasn't the only plane. We heard of ones in Dallas, Denver, L.A., Arkansas, Vegas I think, and some back East, Washington, Philadelphia, like that. Nobody has heard about it 'cause the power's out all over, and that caused quite a mess. Guess they've done some real damage. Hell, they may have taken over the country by now."

"Not this part of the country, not yet," said Bill in a commanding tone, "not yet at least."

"Guess we're on our own. At least they've given us a little time," said Bill. "Get every man, woman and child that can hold a gun, get 'em to the armory, send as many guns and as much ammo as you can get. Mary will give you a purchase order number. We've got a hundred guys we know about here and now."

"Send somebody over to see Able Garcia. Tell him to send all the Mexicans he can, legal or not. Tell them if they fight for this country, I'll fight to get them citizen status. Hell, tell the bastards I'll marry 'em myself."

"Did you hear that, Matilda?" Bill said as he ran out the door.

"I'm coming, too," she said. "I can shoot."

"Let's get the guns out of this office and all the ammo then."

Mike hurried out the door and drove down the street.

Bill and Mary loaded what guns they could in the back of the car.

"Run back in real quick and let those three guys out of the cells, Mary," he said. "They're only in on marijuana possession; they're harmless. Besides, Tim Whitmore is a pretty good shot."

They drove as fast as they could to the armory. The front door was open, and the Sergeant was sitting at the front desk.

"Hey, Roger," said Bill. "We've got a real problem. I called the Governor's office and he's sick, the Army's out of the country, the Guard is called up and out of the country; it's up to us to repel this threat."

"Sort of like a militia?" asked Roger.

"Just like a militia," answered Bill. "I sent Mike to get people and guns, and they're all supposed to meet here. These old boys think there's a couple of container trucks coming their way full of guns and stuff, but what they don't know is that they're on their own, just like us."

"They're a trained army though," said Roger.

"Okay, fine, let's just shoot ourselves in the head right now and get it over with, you go first."

"I'm not saying that," said Roger. "What I mean is that we need to take it easy."

"What kinds of weapons do you have hidden

around here that we laymen could use?"

"This stuff is all pretty simple," said the Sergeant. "Just point and shoot. Today's army can be pretty simple." It has to be, thought Bill, with the education system the way it is in this country.

The two men went into the armory, which was a big vault with a large metal-hinged door and a combination lock.

"This is a rifle company, which is that we have enough small arms for 200 men, and plenty of ammunition. It's all here in the vault."

"Let's set them out here in the hallway and put the ammunition right beside the rifles," Bill directed. He began to lay the rifles along the wall. Bill passed him the ammunition, and he placed it alongside the rifles.

Soon the people began to arrive, singly and in groups, men and women and teenagers. When about 80 people were in the auditorium, Bill stepped up on the bleachers and addressed them.

He turned and faced the wall with the giant American flag. "Repeat after me," he said loudly, "I pledge allegiance to the flag of the United States of America and to the Republic for which it stands, one Nation, under God, indivisible, with liberty and justice for all."

The crowd had recited the words along with him, word for word.

"Hello, neighbors," he said. "This morning a plane load of foreigners landed at the airport. They killed several people, and I have been told that this has happened all over the country. They may be responsible for the power failure. They may have taken over the government of this country. We are going to destroy these guys before they destroy us."

A wave of enthusiastic cheering broke out from the crowd.

"Silence!!" he screamed.

"This is not a pep rally. We are fighting for our homes here and our way of life. Look around among yourselves. Before this is over, probably half of you will be dead.

"I called the Governor for help and he is sick, the Army is out of the country, the National Guard is out of the country or sick, somebody's got to be in charge, and right now it's me."

"There are about a hundred well-trained and well-armed soldiers occupying the Syracuse building near the airport. We think the reason they haven't moved anywhere yet is because they are waiting for some containers full of men and supplies. Our guess is that they traveled light so the plane would have enough fuel to get all the way here without refueling. They need those supplies. They don't know, but we do, that those containers ain't gonna make it. When they find out, they are sure to come into town and try to link up with their buddies. Our job is to keep them bottled up down there."

"Anybody here have military training?" he asked.

A dozen hands were held up.

"Get to the front of the room with Sergeant Dance."

"How many people have Ph.D.s?"

Three hands went up.

"Stand by that wall," he said, and pointed to the left.

"How many people have master's degrees?"

Six hands went up. "Stand over by that wall," he

pointed straight away to the opposite wall. "Spread out so there is some distance between you."

"Everybody else line up along that wall," he pointed to the right-hand wall.

They lined up.

"I'm going to give you a number, you remember it."

He started at the left and walked past the people counting one through six.

When he was finished, the room had begun to buzz with people talking.

"Silence!" he screamed.

He went to the wall where the Master's Degrees were standing. He started at the left and stood before the first, a man in his late 30s. All the ones line up behind. What's your name?" he asked.

"Jim," the man said.

"Ones to Jim."

He walked to the next, a woman in her late 40s.

"Two's here."

And so it went until he had six small groups of people.

"You ex-military types, please join a group."

He turned to the Ph.D.s.

"You guys make sure these groups are sort of equal. Then I want them in order from weakest to strongest, left to right, take five minutes. People that came together should be in the same group, work that out. Make sure that any mechanics are put in the weak group. They have a special mission."

He walked back to confer with the Sergeant and to get a drink of water. The fountain didn't work. "Damn," he yelled.

It took 15 minutes for the groups to be rearranged, but finally they were standing in their groups.

"You doctors, if you have any suggestions, step in at any time."

He looked at the six groups of people. "We will change your numbers now," and he pointed to the left. "You are one, then the next, you are two, and so on until all groups are numbered."

"The way I see it," he began, "is that these guys are going to need transportation. Since they didn't bring trucks with them, they are going to expect to take ours. Group one, it will be your job to disable all transportation devices, SUVs, school buses, cars, trucks, anything these boys can use to join their friends. We want to slow them down and pick them off one at a time. Were there any mechanics?"

Two hands went up from group one.

"Good," he said with relief.

"These guys are trained soldiers, we're not. Don't be heroes, be as safe as you can, but let's keep them away from our homes. The worst mistake we could make is to back these guys into a corner where they only have a choice between fighting or dying. Whatever we do, we want to let these guys fly back where they came from. Whatever you do, don't hurt that big plane."

"Squad two, work your way around using the back roads and get along the hills north of the airport and watch that road."

"Three and four, team up with the cops on the south of the hill on the airport road."

"Five needs to set up on the west side of airport road on 86 Highway."

1 with no success. The men have eaten what
⅃s in the building. If the containers don't show
ɔn't see how we can maintain this position.
ɜ not drink the water, if our agents have been
ful, and we must assume that they have, for
ɔoisoning."

General walked away. This type of talk was
productive.

ve all the supplies brought to this building
ɜ plane?"

s, sir," said the Colonel.

denly, an explosion shook the building. The
n rushed to the door and pushed their way
ɜral soldiers to get a better look. A ball of fire
ng from the airport two blocks away, and the
uld be felt from there.

ɹat was that?" asked the General to no one in
ɑr.

vas our plane, sir," said one of the men. "A
ɔk pulled up to it and parked under a wing. A
t out and ran away, and a few moments later
k exploded."

General removed his pistol from its holster
•t the messenger in the head.

ɜ certainly won't be flying home now," said
ɪeral.

ɜ won't be eating that food either," thought the
I.

"And six set up on the east side of the airport road
on 86. The Sergeant here has walkie-talkies. Each
squad gets one; I'll be Papa Bear."

"You Army guys need to help pass out the guns to
the squads and then show them how to use them. Take
some extra guns along with you in case you run into
any other volunteers."

The training lasted two hours, and there was only
one minor mishap. Carly Bishop, the dental assistant,
shot a hole in the roof.

The volunteers took their guns and ammunition
and drove themselves to their appointed locations.

It was evening before squad two had gotten in
place, just in time to see the gray pickup pull off the
airport road.

The small radio on Bill's hip beeped. He raised it
to his ear and pushed the button. "Go ahead," he said.

"Papa Bear, this is squad two, we finally got into
position. There was a gray pickup truck pulling into
the airport from the north."

"Roger," said Bill.

19

THE GENERAL EXPLAINED to the driver the back roads to take to the airport. No doubt by now the authorities would have mobilized some sort of backwoods defense and would be waiting just beyond the horizon for permission to act from some higher authority. Americans had been made docile and had been disarmed. For years, the Chinese-made video games that American children had lived on contained subtle subliminal stimulation that weakened their wills. Even the most seemingly violent video games often resulted in the opposite effect.

He spent the remainder of the trip on the phone. The urban landings in Denver, Dallas and Los Angeles had gone well. The city people were especially vulnerable to this type of attack. Once the power went out, it was only a short time before the fear of starvation set in, and then came the panic. The water shortage speeded the panic; Americans did like to flush those toilets.

Louisiana and Missouri had been almost complete failures; the independent nature of the citizens of those states and their ability to defend their homes had overcome the threat. If a hillbilly couple gets a divorce, are they still brother and sister? He disappointed himself by remembering that old joke.

He arrived at the Syracuse l
back roads. One local sheriff's
the road but was expecting the th
not without and stood smiling l
the gray pickup slowed and the

What had once been a call
of cubicles and computers had b
ter of his invasion. Half of th
cleared of computers; the other
by the fourth squad to interru
vices remained after the power
zone was near a Syracuse buil
were linking the sites together.

He walked to the Senior Co
"Report, please, Colonel."
"Airport secured, sir. This b
pared for the containers. Secure
tion are now open to six of o
redundant phone services feedi
worked better than planned."

"The second squad has repor
resistance in the direction of to
out no skirmishers until you ret
for orders."

"Any word from any of the c
trying to keep the worry out of h
with no success to make conta
for this site. This could be a di
their weapons, their food and su
between the dock and the airpo
overwhelmed with visions of su
his pride was responsible for de

"Not a word, sir. We've trie

nicati
food v
up, I
We da
succes
fear o

Th
count

"H
from

"Y
Su
two m
past se
was ri
heat c

"V
particu

"It
fuel tr
man g
the tru

Th
and sh

"V
the Ge

"V
Colon

20

BOB FUQUA OWNED DVDs of most of the James Bond movies. He was never healthy enough to get into the military, so he went to airplane mechanics school to be near the action. He had spent the morning rebuilding a fuel pump for a Cessna 185 when the big plane touched down. He knew in an instant that it was trouble. It had come in low and fast and without warning. As it approached the terminal, he made the right decision; he climbed among the spare parts on the mezzanine and hid. When he heard the gunshots, he knew what was happening. He crawled into the clutter a little further. He heard them searching the hangar, but he stayed quiet. After they had left, he waited a long time and then sneaked down. He quietly sneaked into every room and peeked around every corner trying to see what they were up to. He found the bodies in the front office and in the tower. He felt bad for his friends, but why didn't they have sense enough to hide, too?

When he was in the tower, he looked out at the giant plane. The doors were open, and there was no guard. All the soldiers had gone over to the Syracuse building. An idea came to him; he could be of help without much risk. He would wait a while though; maybe someone would come and rescue him and he wouldn't need to be a hero. But maybe everybody in town was so busy with the power outage that no one even knew about the airport.

He thought and he thought, and he finally made up his mind that if no one came by soon, then he would take action. He took the keys for the tank truck from the front office. He made sure that the tank was full. He went to the recycle bin and collected an armload of old newspapers and quite literally filled the cab of the truck with crumpled up newspapers and rolled down the passenger side window.

Time went by, and no help had arrived. He quietly pushed open the hangar door enough for the tank truck to go out. He drove the truck to the big plane and parked it under the wing. He quickly jumped out of the truck and kept the keys. He took the hose from the rear of the tank truck and poured aviation gas all over the ground and the side of the truck. He left the nozzle open and dropped the nozzle in the passenger seat of the truck. He ran around the back of the truck again and opened a big valve that allowed fuel to spill out onto the runway. He went back to the driver's side of the truck and lit one edge of the papers.

When he was certain that they were burning, he ran as fast as he could back to the safety of the hangar. He had just entered the safety of the hangar when the explosion deafened him, and the searing heat spread through the opening in the door.

He had done it, he thought. Somebody would hear this. Somebody would know. He was a hero. He ran through the hangar and out the other side and kept running, and only after he had gotten to the end of the runway did he stop to look. He could feel the heat and could see that the big plane was fully engulfed in flames. He turned around and kept running.

21

GROUP ONE HAD enlisted the aid of several mechanics and several seniors from the high school. They took to their work with a vengeance, and by slashing tires and removing coil wires had successfully disabled most means of transportation. The other squads had reported that things were quiet and that there had been no further vehicle movements since the gray truck.

Bill was standing behind the highway patrol car and watching the lack of movement at the airport. He mobilized a group of volunteers to break into the grocery store and bring food to the people on watch. "I would sure like to know what they're thinking down there," he said to the deputy. "Let's send a couple of volunteers down there to get a closer look, see if you can find someone willing."

The deputy returned in 30 minutes with two junior high aged boys. "These kids live down the road. They say they know a big drainage pipe that comes real close to the Syracuse building. Figured we ought to give them a go."

"Okay," said Bill, "but you kids don't take any chances. He handed them a radio. Take this, but keep it off unless there's something we really need to know about."

"Okay, Bill," said one of the boys.

They took the radio and ran off down the road. "I guess they're old enough to be in the Army," said Bill. "Plenty old to fight and die for the old men, but too young to vote or drink. The leadership in this country sucks."

"There might not be any leadership left in this country," said the deputy.

Bill remained silent, liking his job.

They watched from the hillside as the boys worked their way behind the hill and into the culvert that brought the drained water from the airport. They had obviously done this many times before, as evidenced by the dexterity the boys showed in scampering along the large rock riprap.

Several minutes later, as Bill walked back to his patrol car that was parked in the middle of the road, the radio crackled and a young voice was speaking.

"Bill, Bill, this is Bobby Ray, you better look at this. We're getting the heck out of here."

Bill rose from the seat of his squad car and walked to the top of the hill just in time to see the driver ignite the gasoline truck.

"No!" he shouted, but to no use.

The tank truck erupted in flames, and soon the big plane was engulfed in flames.

They could see several soldiers run out of the Syracuse building and watch the plane burning.

The heat was so intense, even on the hill, that the paint on the side of the white van appeared to discolor.

"That tears it," said Bill, "now they've got no way to escape. Tell all the people to get ready to fight."

But nothing happened that day; the soldiers went back into the Syracuse building and slept.

22

ALBERT AND JULIETTE sat at the kitchen table sipping Mountain Dews and talking.

"What exactly happened over there last night?" She asked.

He gave her a brief rundown of the events of the previous evening, and he left out nothing.

"My Lord," she said. "That poor girl. Was she physically hurt otherwise?"

"I suppose we'll know this morning. Juan has been watching out for her all night."

They heard a shuffling noise in the hallway. As they both looked up, Two entered the room, carrying his rifle.

"Morning, Albert; morning, Julie," he said. "Is there any more Dew?"

"Plenty more in the fridge," said Albert. "Just don't keep the door open too long. The power is off again."

"Yes, Mother," said Two.

He set the gun on the counter, opened the refrigerator and opened the bottle of pop. He drank half the bottle in one drink.

"Anything going on?" he asked the room.

"Same as last night," said Albert.

"Is Three on the silo?" asked Two.

"Sent him out about an hour ago," said Albert.

The young man stared at Juliette for a moment and said, "Nice view this morning. Guess I'll check on the chickens and Three." Without another word he picked up the gun and walked out the door.

"Your brothers are nice," said Juliette.

"Yeah, nice pains in the butt," said Albert with a smile. The last two days had formed a bond that they all shared.

A moment later Juan and Jenny Taylor walked into the room.

Both Albert and Juliette looked up. "You feelin' okay? "asked Albert.

Juliette slapped him on the arm. "What an insensitive thing to say?" she said. "Of course, she isn't feeling okay."

He shook his head.

Juliette stood up and walked to the other girl.

"Hi," she said, "my name's Juliette. We met last night. Just call me Julie."

"Or any other five-letter word that comes to mind," said Albert.

Julie ignored him and continued, "I'm a nurse. Is there anything I can help with?"

"Yes, there is," said Jenny, and she took her hand and they walked back into the bedroom.

Juan took a seat next to Albert, and they both listened to the sounds of crying coming from the other room.

"Guess she needs to get that out of her system," said Juan. "She never cried, not once."

"We did," said Albert.

The two men sat in silence.

Perhaps an hour went by, and Juliette and Jenny

emerged from the bedroom. Jenny's eyes were red and tear-stained. As they walked by the table, Juliette picked up her drink. "Could Jenny have a pop?" asked Juliette.

"Sure, sure," said Albert, and hurried to the refrigerator. He returned with an opened bottle and gave it to Juliette. Both girls walked out to the deck and sat down on the swing.

"Let's go check out the boys," said Albert. As they walked to the back door, he picked up two rifles and handed one to Juan.

Two and Three met them halfway across the driveway.

"Nothing's going on," said Three. "The house is finished, but the hay bales must have been wet, see the smoke." He pointed to the south, and they all looked at the smoke on the horizon.

"We can't leave the girls here," said Albert. "Would one of you like to sneak into town and see what's up?"

"I'll go," the two boys said in unison.

"I need some sleep," said Juan. "I sat up all night and I'm beat."

"Go on into bed," said Albert. "I'll keep an eye on this place and wake you if there's a problem. Two and Three, why don't you both take the Gator in the back way and be real quiet. Those bastards might have taken over the planet by now. You'll have to cross the creek, but the water should be low enough. I'll be sitting on the front porch watching the road."

Two and Three ran to the barn and emerged a few minutes later in the green machine; they drove it past the barn and west through the pasture.

Juan and Albert walked back into the house. They stood for a moment looking at the girls who were swinging in the swing and talking. Jenny was holding Juliette's hand. "That's probably good for both of them," said Albert. "Get some rest, I'll make a lot of noise if someone shows up."

* * * * *

Several hours later the Gator returned.

The girls were still sitting on the porch. Albert walked back through the house and spoke with the boys.

"Looks like old Bill got the whole town mobilized," said Two. "Men, women, children, dogs, it's scary. I never seen so many guns in my life. I guess old Mike dug deep. They said he saved a bunch of World War II stuff that his dad collected, machine guns and shit. Bill said he had more stuff than the armory."

"Whoever those guys are, they're holed up in that big old Syracuse building out by the airport. Bill thinks they're waiting on some reinforcements or something. Anyway, Bill set up roadblocks on the airport road north and south of the airport."

"Where is all the National Guard, and the Army?" asked Albert.

"The Army's gone overseas, the Guard, most of them, are gone there, too. Guess a bunch of those that were left got sick somehow, and that leaves nobody to guard the fort."

"Did Bill tell you what we should do?" asked Albert.

"He said to stay put and try to guard the place in case they break out. He said to immobilize the cars and trucks and stuff so they can't escape. He wants to destroy them; guess they killed a bunch of people at the airport yesterday."

"Did you see that black smoke from the airport?" asked Three.

"No," said Albert, "I wasn't looking that way."

"Somebody drove a gasoline truck up to that big old plane and set fire to the truck and plane, dangdest fire you ever saw. We were right on that hill where they shot at us, saw the whole thing."

"Was Juliette's car still there?" asked Albert.

"We tried to bring it back, the keys were in it, but it wouldn't start," said Two. "We grabbed her bag though. It's in the Gator, I'll go get it." He ran out the door and brought in the bag.

"Now that you guys are back, we'll take turns on the silo. I'll go first." He picked up his rifle and went out the door."

"Let's get some food on the table," said Three. "I'm starved."

The evening was uneventful, with everyone taking turns standing guard duty.

In the late part of the afternoon, a white van pulled up the driveway. On the side of the van printed in large letters were the words NATA, the white paint on one side burned and peeling. Three people stepped out of the van, two men and a woman dressed in white coveralls. The younger man wore a pair of glasses with heavy frames and was looking from side to side. The younger man approached Two and Three, who were sitting on the rear deck cleaning their guns.

"Excuse Me," said the man, "but we work for the airport authority, and this power outage has caused difficulties with our radar. Your field there is exactly due east of the airport. Would it be all right if we sort of put a temporary beacon out there. There are some crazy people at the airport right now, but as soon as they leave we can finish."

"Knock yourself out," said Three. "Just stay out of the way."

"That we know how to do," said the man. "Could you please tell everyone that we'll be back tomorrow? I see you have guns there, and we wouldn't want anything to happen."

"No problem," said Three.

The three loaded into the van and drove back down the road.

The sun set and the evening passed with only the changing of the guard to break the silence. The girls slept.

The sun rose and everyone was still tired and slept in.

23

SUNRISE ON THE third day brought big changes for the invaders. The General had been unable to contact the container troops, and there was now serious doubt as to whether they would arrive. With the destruction of the plane, the water situation had become critical. The General and his officers had conferred and decided that they must break out and try to join with one of the other elements. The planes landing near the major cities had been the most successful. City dwellers were less independent, poorly armed, and more willing to bow to the invaders. Male city dwellers surrendered quickly and were exterminated. Female city dwellers were not considered to be a threat and were kept alive for other purposes.

The Chicago landing had been successful, the containers had arrived on time with the extra supplies, and the takeover was taking place ahead of schedule. The General decided to take his forces to the Chicago area and link up with them. They could then work their way back to this spot and complete their mission. The death squads had been active to the north for two days. He had been unable to contact them, but felt sure that they were creating havoc.

Twenty men were assigned to travel south toward the town and secure transportation, preferably SUVs with four-wheel drive, or cars or trucks or vans. They traveled on foot along the west edge of the runway and through the woods. The first farmhouse they encountered was the Jenkins farm. Seth Jenkins had inherited this land from his great-great-grandfather. His family had accumulated a little land at a time, and now they owned 1250 acres and farmed twice that. The power outage had cut short their yearly vacation to the Black Hills, and they had just returned home. As they unpacked their new blue Ford Explorer, they were attacked by a band of armed men who spoke a strange language. Seth, his wife Mary and the twin 14-year-old girls, Margaret and Milly, were all executed. The men dragged the personal possessions out of the SUV, and one man was chosen to drive it back to the Syracuse building.

A brand new 3/4-ton red Ford pickup was parked in the garage with the keys inside. Another man was chosen to drive this truck back. The soldiers continued toward the town on foot. The second house they encountered was nearer to town, and it had been deserted. The only vehicle at the farm was an older model Toyota, and even though the keys were in it, it would not start. The soldiers continued to the next house, and two cars parked in the driveway with the keys inside would not start either.

As the soldiers came closer and closer to town, the houses were built closer and closer together. There was no sign of people, and any cars or trucks they encountered would not start.

They came to a high school on the outskirts of town; behind it were parked perhaps 20 school buses. The keys were in the busses, but none of them would start. They began to become concerned that they would not complete their mission. When they left the school, they were crossing the football field, and suddenly from the bleachers came a devastating barrage of small arms fire that killed all but five of the soldiers. They returned fire with their automatic weapons and killed Mary Lou Tompkins, a veterinarian, and Billy Bob Grady, the owner of the Ace Hardware store. Leon Sanders, the only freshman on the debate team, had his left arm severed at the elbow. The five survivors ran back to the school busses and hid inside them. They were quickly surrounded by a curious array of armed citizens, soldiers and law enforcement personnel.

The ranking member of the survivors told the men that they must surrender, and he threw his guns out the door of the bus and came out with his hands in the air. Jim Tompkins, husband of Mary Lou and ex-Marine, had been issued a semi-automatic weapon. His arms and clothes were covered with the fresh blood from his dead wife. He waited calmly until the last of the soldiers had come out of the bus with their hands up. He opened fire, and the men fell dead from left to right. When he had emptied his clip, he dropped his gun to the ground and without a word walked back to the body of his wife.

Everyone else simply turned and walked away.

* * * * *

When the blue Ford Explorer came bouncing back over the runway, followed shortly by the new pickup, the General walked to the colonel and told him to attack the hill to the south. He presented him with a hand-drawn map with the location of the Taylor farm highlighted. When more vehicles came back, he was to load the men and meet him at the location on the map. While the colonel was attacking the southern hill, he would take the trucks filled with men and meet up with the death squads to the north. He directed an NCO4 to line the vehicles in front of the Syracuse building and fill them with armed men.

He walked into his makeshift office and put on his pack and picked up his rifle. He held his phone to his ear and tried to get a signal, but the battery was dead. "Those damned containers should have been here," he said, and threw the phone against the wall, and it broke in several pieces. As he left the building, he looked at the caravan, a gray pickup, a red pickup, a blue SUV and a late model Toyota Camry recently owned by the late airport secretary. When he returned to the trucks, they were all loaded and the passenger seat in the front pickup was empty. A soldier stood beside the opened door. As he passed the red pickup, he noticed the girl, Corporal Sholing, in the passenger seat. It was the first time he had seen her since they had landed. He had been so busy that he had forgotten to give her that little promotion she had earned by keeping her mouth shut. He'd tell her later. He walked to the front truck, turned and gave an order for the Colonel to commence the attack to the south, sat down in the seat and gave directions to the driver to go north on the country road as fast as possible.

Almost immediately, gunfire could be heard to the south. These civilians would be no match for a well-trained army. He expected the fighting to be over in less than 30 minutes.

The small caravan turned north on the country

road. The second squad had been awakened from their rest by the sounds of the attack to the south. They were all hiding behind trees and rocks as the cars and trucks drove past at a high rate of speed. The first two trucks drove past them with little damage, while the SUV and the Camry received the brunt of the fire. Two men in the SUV were seriously wounded, and the gas tank of the Camry ignited and the burning car swerved into the ditch. Three of the men survived the crash, but were covered with flames as they ran from the car. They were gunned down in the middle of the road. The two trucks and the SUV continued down the road at a high rate of speed.

* * * * *

When the big plane exploded, Bill knew that their situation had really changed. He called the doctors and the soldiers for a meeting.

"Look," he said, "they can't leave by plane now. That means we can attack them down there or wait for them to come to us. Surely they know by now that their friends in the containers aren't going to make it. That means they are going to try to make a break for it. They are going to need transportation; they have to come into town to get it. They will try to get to a car dealership or some busses or something. That means they either come up this road or go south along the runway and through the woods. If it was me, I'd come right up this road because if I was them I wouldn't expect any resistance. Agree?"

Everyone nodded.

"Okay then, we'll keep an eye on the runway, and if they sneak that way they have to end up coming past the high school. We'll get them there or we'll get ready for them right here."

He sent word to a backhoe company which began to dig big holes at the top of the hill behind the parked patrol cars. The backhoe piled the dirt in front of the holes so that when the soldiers came up the road well-entrenched riflemen would surprise them.

This work continued for the rest of the day and into the night. By the time the attack came, machine guns had been placed in front of the holes.

When the General gave the order to attack and the soldiers came running up the hill, the policemen pulled their cars out of the way to reveal well-entrenched machine gun nests. The attacking soldiers didn't stand a chance. They were attacking up a road with no cover. The machine gunners waited until the last minute, and the fight for Danner's Ridge was over in less than 10 minutes. The field was covered with dead and dying invaders.

Only a few escaped.

24

THE CARAVAN OF trucks sped down the road, raising a cloud of dust behind. As they passed the Brown ranch, the General turned to look down the road to the house and noticed a flash of light from high up on the silo. They drove on down the road and came to the intersection. When they had turned, the General noticed a thin plume of smoke rising from where the Taylor farm had been. He became concerned.

The killing squads had agreed to meet here at this farm after they had completed most of their killing. Their orders had been to kill the people and to spare the buildings. What was the cause of this smoke and where were his men?

The caravan stopped in front of the Taylor farm. All that was left of the building were several round bales of hay that were still smoldering on what was left of the front porch. The house and garage had been destroyed, but the barns and outbuildings were untouched. A riderless horse with a saddle grazed on the tall grass beside the big red barn.

The General stopped the caravan at the driveway. He stepped out of the truck and gazed at the smoldering ruins with dismay.

"Where are my soldiers?" he asked.

"Where is my home?" He turned to look at the

mailbox and read the word TAYLOR. He suddenly had trouble catching his breath.

He stepped back into the truck. "We must meet up with the others," he said. "Drive back down that road to the last house, and we will see what is going on. There was something unusual about that place."

25

THE MORNING OF the third day dawned.

Juan had been standing guard on the silo and came running into the house. "Wake up!" He yelled. There are a lot of gunshots from around the airport, something's happening."

Albert rose from the couch and went to the kitchen counter that had been piled high with every weapon in the house. "Let's get armed," he said to the rest. Everyone came into the kitchen and left fully armed.

"Go back up to the silo, Juan. Two and Three, go over to the generator house and shut it off. You girls run out to the barn and hide in the back. I'm sure if they come here it will be the same as it was the last time; they'll come to the house and blast us. Juan, make sure you have one of those 30-06's with a tight scope."

"Remember, everybody, if they come down the road, and there's way too many of them, run into the woods and get down the creek and into town. If we can't defend this place, it ain't worth dying over."

"Look," said Juliette, "we've talked about this all day. We are not going to sit idly by or hide in the corner. We can fight, and we will fight."

"Okay, fine," said Albert, "but when you see me making tracks for the woods, you best be following and you best be running."

They all took their places and waited.

Forty minutes later they heard the sound of trucks on the main road. Albert ran to the front window and looked out. Juan laid the rifle on the railing of the silo and looked toward the road. He watched through the scope as two pickups and an SUV drove at high speed down the road, past the house and turned toward the Taylor farm.

He saw the white van pull into the field behind the barn using the back way.

Juan moved to the other side of the silo and watched as the caravan stopped for a moment in the road in front of the burning house. When they turned around and came back in the other direction, he yelled at the top of his lungs.

"They're coming back! They're coming back!"

They all watched as the cars pulled up the driveway. They were all in place and ready for the attack that was going to be leveled at the house.

* * * * *

The caravan drove into the driveway and turned around one at a time and went back to the main road. They drove to the driveway and turned toward the house. The mailbox was a replica of a red barn, and on the side was painted the word "Brown."

Two trucks and an SUV drove down the driveway and toward the house. "When you get to the end of the driveway, go left," said the General. "Don't go to the house."

The caravan drove past the house and turned quickly toward the barn. The caravan pulled to a stop, and the General jumped out of the truck. "Out, out," he said, and ran into the barn. The trucks came to a stop and everyone jumped out and went into the barn.

26

WHEN THE CARS pulled into the driveway and toward the barn and the occupants all ran into the barn, Albert and the boys were all shocked.

"What are we going to do now?" Two asked Three. "The girls are in the barn, we can't shoot that way. Son-of-a-bitch, let's run to the house."

They ran toward the house and across the back porch and into the house.

"What do we do now?" asked Three. "The girls are in the barn right in the way. We can't shoot in that direction."

* * * * *

The general ran into the barn and stood back from the door. He had entered so quickly that the two girls were caught by surprise. When he leveled his gun at them, they dropped their guns. "Lay down," he commanded. They did as they were told. He watched out the door as the others ran into the building.

"Listen," he said there are six of us left. We'll take this place over, then get some gas and join the others. I saw a flash from that tall structure. Someone's up there with a rifle. Two of you get him. I saw two boys run into the house from that building. They may have been armed. Two of you get over to that building and shoot into the house. One of you stay with me. Looks like I have a little unfinished business to take care of."

Two of the men ran to the underside of the silo and began to climb the stairs. Two of the other men went to the generator building and began to fire into the house. The rifle fire into the house made it impossible for Albert or Two or Three to go into the road to get a shot at the men who were climbing the silo stairs. They began to shoot back at the men in the generator building with the machine guns they had taken from the invaders.

* * * * *

The large multi-colored truck pulling the big generator came to a stop along the side of the road. Mary and Alise and Ashlee and Mary Two were in the blue truck and pulling the SUV on the trailer.

"What's that popping noise?" Carl asked Tom.

"Somebody's shooting, down there by the barn," screamed Tom.

"Get out and tell the girls to drive down the road until we come and get them. I'll disconnect this generator," said Tom in a hurry.

Carl ran back to the truck that had stopped behind them, while Tom ran behind and disconnected the generator in the middle of the road.

Carl jumped back in to the cab of the truck. "Sounds like machine gun fire to me," he said.

"What the heck do you suppose is going on?" Tom said breathlessly. "Three days ago we left the house. We felt we were armed to the teeth, and we come home and there's a small war being waged at our own home."

They both checked their weapons to make sure they were loaded.

"Looks like a soldier ran into the generator house," said Tom. "They're shooting into the house. Let's get them at least."

He drove the big truck across the field at a high rate of speed and rammed it into the corner of the generator building. The two men that were in the building were taken by surprise and turned their guns on the big truck. Tom and Carl jumped from the truck, and each one of them got their man.

When Albert saw the big truck coming toward the generator building, he told Two and Three to increase their fire so the men would be distracted and not see the big truck coming. After the truck hit the generator building and the men were gone, Albert ran across the road and shot one of the men who was climbing the stairs. The other man had nearly reached the level that Juan was on.

Juan stepped around the corner and at point blank range shot the man.

* * * * *

The General approached the two girls lying on the floor in the barn. "This situation is under control," he said. "I recognize this one," he said, and kicked Jenny in the head, and she went unconscious. "I've had her already. You're a pretty little thing," he said to Juliette.

"Soldier," he called to the one remaining soldier, "Help me tie this girl up."

"I said help me tie this girl up," he said in a commanding tone, and turned to look at the soldier. He recognized the girl, Corporal Sholing, and she was pointing her gun at him.

"You pig," she said, "all I went through for you

and not even a damned promotion. That beating you gave me ruined me; I can never have children." She emptied the clip into the General and dropped the gun to the ground.

Juliette picked up her gun. She thought she saw a man with dark glasses looking in the window, but then he was gone. She ran to the door of the barn just in time to see the big pink truck hit the generator building.

She walked into the driveway and watched as Albert ran from the house and stopped and aimed and fired toward the silo. She heard the gunshot from Juan's rifle.

Suddenly everything was silent except for the lady soldier crying as she cradled the head of the dead General.

* * * * * *

Tom walked out into the middle of the road and called to Albert. "Is that all of them? And who are they?"

"That's it, Dad," Albert said.

Tom stepped out into plain sight and motioned for the truck to come up from the road.

* * * * * *

"Daddy," said Juliette, as she walked up to Carl.

"Boy, am I glad to see you, little girl," he said, and gave her a big hug. "Your mother will sure be happy to see you."

"Mother?" she asked. "She's in Hawaii."

"Not any more," he said, "her traveling days are

over. We've decided to get back together and stay right here," he said with a smile.

"That's really good news," said Juliette.

* * * * *

Juan ran into the barn to help Jenny who was just coming to. He helped her out the door, and Juliette came up and the two of them half-walked and half-carried Jenny to the porch.

* * * * * *

The blue truck and trailer came into the driveway, and Mary and Mary Two jumped out and gave Albert a hug. Two and Three came out of the house, and they hugged them as well.

Juliette had looked at the scar on Jenny's forehead and left her with Juan who was holding her. She ran to the truck and gave Alise a hug.

They both had to jump back when the white van drove past them and drove down the road.

"Who was that?" asked Tom as he drew his gun from the holster.

"Airport guys," said Two. "They were afraid of getting shot."

Ashlee persuaded Three to take her to the house to find a drink.

Several minutes later, Carl and Tom were standing near the car with their arms around their wives. Carl nodded in the direction of the porch. Tom looked and saw that Juliette and Albert were standing together, talking to Juan and Jenny. Jenny was apparently doing fine. Juliette and Albert were holding hands.

"What do you suppose we should make of that?" asked Tom.

"It'll make a real nice ending," laughed Carl. The ladies agreed.

THE END

Dear reader,

It is my most sincere hope that this writing has given you a little entertainment, a small break from the daily grind. When Brian read this book for the first time, one of his comments was that he wanted the sequel. This made me pause and think. Of course, I have left the country in one hell of a mess. Okay, fine, this should be a trilogy. There is a lot of cleaning up to do. Very well.

If you would like for me to sign this book for you, just tell me what you want me to say on the blank page provided. Send me the book, and I will sign it just for you and send it back. Please enclose a $5 bill to cover the brain damage at this end.

If you would like a signed copy of the second book, please tell me what you want me to say on the following blank page and enclose $13. When the second book is finished, I will send it to you or whomever.

Thank you.

Mike Seymour
P.O. Box 31
Council Grove, KS 66846

Send to: *(Your name and address here. Please print clearly.)*

_____

_____